Matthew stood behind Glory, positioning her halo.

Glory looked so much like an angelic bride as she stood there that Matthew couldn't help himself. He leaned closer and pressed his lips very lightly to the back of her neck. His kiss was more of a breath than an act.

"My hair's falling down." Glory tried to reach her arm up to her neck.

"You're fine."

"Yeah, men always say that, even when we have broccoli in our teeth."

"You don't have broccoli in your teeth."

Matthew knew they still had a half hour before the performance started, but he also knew that he'd better get Glory to her place before he gave in to the urge to kiss her again. Not even that growing stack of cookies on the counter would distract the church women if they happened to look over to see him kissing the Christmas angel.

JANET TRONSTAD

Janet Tronstad grew up on a small farm in central Montana. One of her favorite things to do was to visit her grandfather's bookshelves, where he had a large collection of Zane Grey novels. She's always loved a good story.

Today, Janet lives in Pasadena, California, where she works in the research department of a medical organization. In addition to writing novels, she researches and writes nonfiction magazine articles.

An Angel for Dry Creek
Janet Tronstad

Love Inspired®

Published by Steeple Hill Books™

STEEPLE HILL BOOKS

Steeple
Hill™

ISBN 0-373-87081-7

AN ANGEL FOR DRY CREEK

Printed in U.S.A.

Be not forgetful to entertain strangers; for thereby some have entertained angels unawares.

—Hebrews 13:2

This book is dedicated with love to my parents,
Richard and Fern Tronstad.
First they gave me roots and
then they gave me wings.
Who could ask for more?

Chapter One

Glory Beckett peered out her car window. She'd driven all day and now, with the coming of dusk, snowflakes were beginning to swirl around her Jeep. The highway beneath her was only a faint gray line pointing northeast across the flatlands of Montana. Other than the hills and a few isolated ranches, there had been little to see in miles. Even oncoming traffic was sparse. For the first time in three days she questioned her hasty decision to leave Seattle and drive across country.

She must be a sight. For ease, she'd given up on curls and simply pushed her flaming auburn hair under a beige wool cap her mother had knitted one Christmas long ago. Her lips were shiny with lip balm and she'd forgotten most of her makeup in Seattle. She considered herself lucky to have remembered her toothbrush. She hadn't had time even to pray about the trip before the decision was made and she was on the road. She'd let the captain scare her for nothing. He'd been a cop too long. Just because a stray bullet had whizzed by her last Wednesday, it was no reason to panic and leave town.

Ever since he'd married her mother last month his worrying had grown worse. She'd reminded him she'd picked up a lot of street savvy in the six years she'd been a sketch artist for his department, but it didn't help.

And maybe he was right. She could still feel the stress that hummed inside her, not letting up even when she prayed. The bullet was only part of it. It was the shooting she'd witnessed that was the worst of it. Even though she'd seen this crime with her own eyes instead of the eyes of others, it still rocked her more than it should. Crimes happened. She knew that. Sometimes she spent a long time in prayer, asking God why something happened. God had always given her peace before.

But prayer hadn't been able to calm her this time. Her nerves still shivered. She didn't feel God was distant. No, that wasn't it. He comforted her, but He didn't remove the unease. Not this time. Since Idaho she'd been thinking maybe stress wasn't all there was to it. Her nerves didn't just shudder, they itched. Something was pushing at her consciousness. Something that she should remember, but couldn't. Something to do with what she'd seen that afternoon at Benson's Market when the butcher, Mr. Kraeman, had been killed. *Dear God, what am I overlooking?* The kid who had shot Mr. Kraeman had been arrested and taken to the county jail. The investigation was closed, awaiting nothing more than the trial. The killer had been caught at the scene. She should relax.

Maybe this cross-country trip would help. She'd always wanted to just take off and drive across the top

of the United States. Idaho. Montana. North Dakota.
Minnesota. Right to the Great Lakes. And now that her
mother had married the captain, there was nothing
holding her back. It was odd, this feeling of rootless-
ness.

In a small town farther east on Interstate 94, the bare
branch of an oak tree rested lightly against an upstairs
window. Standing inside and looking out through the
window, a man could see the soft glow from the security light reflected on the snow in the crevices of the
old tree. The snow sparkled like silver dust on an angel's wing.

The midnight view out this second-story window
was appreciated by his young sons, but Matthew Curtis
didn't get past the glass. All he saw was a window
without curtains and his own guilt. If Susie were still
alive, she'd have curtains on all the windows. If only
Susie were alive, the Bible verses the twins memorized
for Sunday school would have some meaning in his
life. If only Susie were still alive, everything would be
different. If only... Matthew stopped himself. He
couldn't keep living in the past.

"Is so angels," Josh was saying as Matthew helped
him put his arm into the correct pajama opening. Tucking his five-year-old twin sons into bed was the best
part of the day for Matthew. "Miz Hargrove said so.
An' they got a big light all round 'em." Josh was fas-
cinated with lights.

Mrs. Hargrove, the twins' Sunday school teacher,
was the closest thing to a mother the two had these
days. She was one of the reasons Matthew had put aside
his own bitterness and rented the old parsonage next to
the church when they'd moved to Dry Creek, Montana,

six months ago. He wanted the twins to be able to go
to church even if he didn't. In Matthew's opinion, a
man who wasn't talking to God during the week had
no business pretending to shake His hand on Sunday
morning just to keep the neighbors quiet.

"I'm sure Mrs. Hargrove is thinking of the angel
Gabriel," Matthew said as he smoothed down Josh's
hair. Josh, the restless one, was in Power Rangers pajamas. Joey, the more thoughtful twin, was in Mickey
Mouse pajamas even though he didn't really like them
that much. Joey wasn't enthused about anything, and
Matthew worried about him. "And that angel definitely
exists."

"See," Josh said to no one in particular. "And my
angel can have ten wings if I want and a Power Ranger
gun to zap people."

"Angels don't carry guns," Matthew said as he
scooped the twins into bed and tucked the quilt securely
around them. The weatherman on the news had predicted a mid-December blizzard. "They bring peace."

"Peace," Josh said. "What's peace?"

"Quiet," Matthew said as he turned down the lamp
between the twins' beds. "Peace and quiet." And a
reminder. "No guns. Angels don't like guns."

Matthew kissed both twins and turned to leave.

"I want to see my angel," Joey whispered. The longing in his voice stopped Matthew. "When can I see
her?"

Matthew turned around and sat down on the edge of
one of the beds again. "Angels are in heaven. That's
a long way away. Most of the time it's too far—they
can't come down and see people. They just stay in
heaven."

"Like Mommy," Joey said.

"Something like that, I guess." Matthew swallowed.

"Miz Hargrove said that when God took our mommy, He gave us a guardian angel to watch over us," Josh explained.

"I'm here to watch over you." Matthew pulled the covers off his sons and gathered them both to him in a hug. He blinked away the tears in his eyes so his sons would not see them. "You've got me—you don't need an angel."

"We got one anyway," Josh said matter-of-factly, his voice muffled against Matthew's shoulder. "Miz Hargrove says."

The night road was sprinkled with square green exit signs marking rural communities. Glory had pulled off at a rest stop close to Rosebud and slept for a few solitary hours, curled up in the back seat of her Jeep. Finally, around four in the morning, she decided to keep driving. It was quiet at that time of night even when she came into Miles City, where over 8,000 souls lived. Once she left Miles City behind, the only lights Glory saw were her own, reflected in the light snow on the ground. If all of this darkness didn't cure her stress, nothing would.

Glory needed this time to think. The shooting at the grocery store, and the long minutes afterward when she waited for the paramedics to arrive, reminded her of the accident that had changed her own life six years ago. Gradually, sitting there in the grocery store, all of the old feelings had surfaced. The terror, the paralyzing grief and the long-lasting guilt. Her dreams had stopped the night of the car accident that took her father's life. That night Glory stopped being a carefree college graduate and became a tired adult. She'd awakened in the hospital bed knowing her life was forever changed. Her father was dead. Her mother was shattered. And the words inside Glory's head kept repeating the accusation that it was all her fault. She'd had the wheel. She should have seen the driver coming. It didn't matter that the other driver was drunk and had run a red light. She, Glory, should have known. Somehow she should have known.

There was nothing to do. Nothing to bring her father back.

She tried to put her own pain aside and comfort her mother. Her mother had always seemed like the fragile one in the family. Glory vowed she would take care of her mother. She would do it even if it meant giving up her own dream.

Glory didn't hesitate. Her dream of being a real artist wasn't as important as her mother's happiness. She took the job as a police sketch artist and packed away her oils. Right out of art school, Glory had wanted to see if she could make it in the art world, but the accident had changed all of that. Dreams didn't pay the bills. She'd be willing to live on sandwiches while she painted, but she couldn't ask her mother to do that with her.

But now, seeing her mother happy again, Glory could start to breathe. She no longer felt so responsible. The captain would take care of her mother. Maybe, Glory thought, she could even dream again. She'd always wanted to paint faces. All she needed to do was give her notice to the police department and take out her easel full-time. She had enough in savings to last awhile. When she put it that way, it sounded so simple.

The more miles that sped beneath the wheels of Glory's Jeep, the lighter her heart felt. Maybe God was

calling her to paint the faces of His people. Faces of
faith. Faces of despair. All of the faces that showed
man's struggle to know God. She needed to rekindle
her dream. For years she'd been—

"Dry…" Glory murmured out loud as she peered
into the snow at the small sign along the interstate.
Even with the powerful lights of her Jeep she could
barely read it. "Dry as in 'Dry Creek, Montana. Pop-
ulation 276. Five Miles to Food and Gas.' "

Glory turned her Jeep to the left. A throbbing headache was starting between her eyes, and her thermos of
coffee had run out an hour ago. It was five-thirty in the
morning and she wasn't going to count on there being
another town along this highway anytime soon. There
was bound to be a little café that served the ranchers
in the area. She didn't have much cash left, but her
MasterCard had given her a healthy advance back in
Spokane and it would no doubt be welcomed here, too.
She'd learned that roadside coffee was usually black
and strong—just the way she liked it.

Matthew woke with the dawn and went to check on
the twins. Ever since Susie had died, he'd been aware
of how easy it was for someone to simply stop living.
He couldn't bear to lose one of his sons. So he stood
in his slippers and just looked at them sleeping in their
beds. The security light from the outside of the old
frame house shone through the half-frosted window and
gave a muted glow to the upstairs bedroom. He pulled
the blankets back up on Joey. The electric heater he'd
put in the twins' bedroom kept the winter chill away.
But the rest of the house was heated with a big woodstove, and he needed to light it so the kitchen would
be warm when the twins came down for breakfast.

There were no windows in the hall and the dawn's light didn't come into the stairway that led down to the living room. He took one sleepy step down the stairway. Then another. He needed to add a light for the stairway. Just one more thing in the old house that needed fixing. Like the— Matthew stepped on the loose stair at the same time as he remembered it. The board's edge cracked and his foot slipped. All he could think of as he tumbled down the stairs was that the twins would have no one to fix their breakfast.

Matthew clenched his teeth and fought back the wave of black that threatened to engulf him. Thank God he was alive. "Josh, Joey," Matthew called in a loud whisper. The pain the words cost him suggested he'd broken a rib. That and maybe his leg. "Boys—"

He didn't need to call. They must have heard his fall, because almost immediately two blond heads were staring at him. "Go next door." Matthew said the words deliberately, although his tongue felt swollen. Pain continued to swim around his head. "Get help."

Glory left her Jeep lights on so she could see to make her way to the door of the house next to the church. She had stopped at the café long enough to see that the Closed sign had fly specks on it. It didn't look as if a meal had been served there in months. By then she needed some aspirin for her headache almost more than she needed her morning coffee. When she saw the lights on inside the house that must be the parsonage, she was relieved.

Matthew relaxed when he heard the knock at the door. The twins must have already gone for help. Maybe he'd blacked out. That must be it. Someone had turned the lights on.

Glory heard a rustling behind the door and then she saw it open slowly. She had to look down to see the small blond head, covered by the hood of a snowsuit, peek around the edge of the door. The boy must be going out to play before breakfast. "Is your father here?" she asked as she pulled off her cap. "Or your mother?"

"Who are you?" Another blond head joined the first one. This one had a scarf tied around his neck, even though his Mickey Mouse pajamas didn't look warm enough for outdoor playing.

"My name's Glory. But you don't know me." And then remembering all the warnings children received about strangers, she added, "Don't worry, though. And don't be afraid."

"Don't be afraid." The boy in the snowsuit echoed her words slowly. Glory watched his eyes grow big. "Where are you from?"

Glory decided they didn't get much company around here. They'd probably never heard of Seattle. She pointed west. "A long way away—over those mountains."

"Do you like guns?" the boy in the pajamas demanded.

"Guns? No, I don't approve of guns. Not at all."

"And she's got a big light behind her," the other boy said. "Just like Miz Hargrove said. A glory light."

"Those are my Jeep headlights. Special high beam," Glory explained. "They'll turn off in a minute. If I could just see your father. All I want is an aspirin and maybe a little peace and quiet…and then—"

"Peace and quiet." The twins breathed the words out together as their faces started to beam. "She came."

"Boys," Matthew called weakly. Who were they talking to? He couldn't make out the words, but surely it didn't take that long for someone to figure out he needed help.

"We need you," the twins said as they opened the door wide and each reached out a hand. Glory noticed they were both in slippers. "Our daddy's hurt."

Matthew decided he'd blacked out again, because a woman's face was staring at him. She had hair the color of copper, and it fanned out around her face like a halo. He'd never seen her before. Maybe he was hallucinating, especially because of that sprinkling of freckles that danced across her nose. No one could have freckles like that. So pretty. He tried to concentrate, but felt the darkness closing in on him. He wondered what the perfume was that she wore. It smelled like cinnamon. Cinnamon and something else. That reminded him he hadn't fixed breakfast for the twins. And his job at the hardware store—old Henry would be fretting mad if he called in from his vacation in Florida and no one answered the phone at the hardware store.

Glory looked down at the man in dismay. She could see he'd fallen down the stairs and his leg was at an awkward angle.

"Where's your phone? We've got to call 911," she said as she turned around to the twins. "We'll need an ambulance right away."

The boys just looked at her expectantly. The one had already taken off his scarf and the other was halfway out of his snowsuit. "Can't you just make daddy all better?" one of them finally asked.

"I'm not a doctor," she said quickly as her eyes scanned the living room. Old sofa, wooden rocker, plaid recliner, Christmas tree with lights but no orna-

ments—ah, there, on the coffee table, next to a magazine, was a phone. She dialed the numbers: 911. Nothing. Glory shook the phone. She must have dialed
wrong. She tried again: 911. Still nothing. What was
the matter? There was a dial tone. Surely—then it
dawned on her. There was no 911 here. Probably no
ambulance, either.

"Who's your nearest neighbor?" Glory put down the
phone and turned to the boys. She could already feel
her hair flying loose as a result of the static from taking
off her cap earlier.

"Mr. Gossett," the boy in the Power Rangers pajamas finally said, but then he leaned closer and confided,
"But you won't like him. He drinks bottles and bottles
of whiskey. I seen them. Miz Hargrove says he's gonna
go to hell someday."

"Well, just as long as he isn't planning to go today,"
Glory said as she pulled her knit cap over her head and
walked toward the door.

The next time Matthew woke up he was in the clinic
in Miles City. He'd recognize the antiseptic smell of a
clinic anywhere. And the gruff voice of Dr. Norris in
the background.

"My boys." Matthew croaked out the words. His
mouth felt as if it was filled with dry sand.

"Don't worry, your boys are fine," Dr. Norris said
as he turned around. "At least for the moment."

"What?"

"Your angel is unloading the vending machine
downstairs on their behalf," the doctor said with a
smile as he leaned over Matthew. He picked up a small
light. "Open wide. We need to check for concussions."
The doctor peered into Matthew's eyes.

"What angel?" Matthew asked, and then brightened. "Oh, you mean Mrs. Hargrove. I was hoping someone would think to call her."

"That's not Mrs. Hargrove," the doctor said as he frowned slightly. "At least, not the Mrs. Hargrove I know. I assumed Angel was a family nickname."

"For who?" Matthew asked, bewildered.

"I meant I assumed you called the woman Angel and that's why your sons..." The doctor's voice trailed off and then he added suspiciously, "It's not like a five-year-old to call a woman Angel."

"What are you suggesting?" Matthew started to rise. The room tilted, but he bit his lip and kept going. "And why you would let my boys just go off with a stranger—"

"Don't worry." The doctor put his arm around him and forced him to lie down again. "I'll have the nurse go bring them here. I'm sure it's just some simple misunderstanding. The woman certainly looked harmless enough."

Harmless isn't how Matthew would have described her a few minutes later. She was too pretty to be harmless. Her copper hair was still fanning around her face. This time he saw her gray eyes more clearly. They looked like a stormy afternoon in summer when the blues and grays swirled together without quite mixing. And his sons were looking at her as if they were starstruck. "What are you doing with my boys?"

"What am I doing?" Glory said, dumbfounded. Whatever happened to thank you? Thank you for getting that grumpy Mr. Gossett up in the early-morning hours so he could get help from Mr. Daniel, who ran the volunteer fire department's medical transportation unit. Thank you for writing a fifty-dollar check so the volunteer department would respond to your request, since you were new in town and not on the "paid" list. Thank you for following along in the Jeep the forty miles into Miles City just so the twins could be with you.

"What am I doing?" she repeated, trying to keep her voice calm. "You mean when I'm not emptying my last quarters into the machine out there so that Josh can get a package with only yellow M&M's in it?"

"They don't make them with only yellows," Matthew said. She reminded him of fire. The way her hair shone in the fluorescent light.

"I know," the woman said wearily.

"You asked me what I wanted," Josh said simply. "I thought it'd be easy for you, since you're—"

Glory held up her hand to stop him.

Matthew watched as Josh closed his mouth. The woman had more powers than he did, Matthew thought to himself ruefully. He could never get Josh to close his mouth when he wanted to speak.

"That might be the wrong way to say it," Matthew said, easing back to the bed. He needed to clear his mind. "I'm grateful for all you've done, of course."

"You're welcome," Glory said politely. She needed to remember the man was disoriented. Disoriented and not nearly so naked now that the doctor had wrapped a wide white bandage around his rib cage. She wondered if he remembered that she'd been the one to gently run her fingertips over his chest to check for broken ribs before she put a blanket over him and they waited for the fire department to come. His chest was the kind that would inspire her if she were a sculptor.

"It's just—" Matthew bit his lips. "I don't know

who you are. And with all the strange people around lately…''

''She's not strange people,'' Josh protested. ''She's—''

''I'm Glory.'' Glory interrupted the boy and gave him a stern look. ''Glory Beckett.''

''She's an angel,'' Joey said, his eyes sparkling with excitement.

''And she's got a glory light,'' Josh added. The boy literally glowed with pleasure.

Glory bowed her head. She'd been through this explanation already. Four times. And that was before the requested M&M's miracle. ''I've got special beams on my Jeep. That's all it is. No angel magic.'' She turned to look at the man in the bed. Now he'd really be worried. ''I'm sorry, this isn't my idea.''

''I know.'' Matthew smiled, and then he started to chuckle until he felt the pain in his ribs. ''But you haven't tried to argue with the logic of our Mrs.—''

''Your Mrs.?'' Glory interrupted stiffly. She should have known there would be a Mrs. somewhere in this picture. ''If I'd known you were married, I'd have tried to locate your wife. But the twins didn't mention—''

''Married? Me? No, I meant our Mrs. Hargrove,'' Matthew echoed, his smile curling around inside himself. He liked the way her lips tightened up when she talked about him being married. ''Mrs. Hargrove isn't married. I mean—'' he fumbled ''—of course, Mrs. Hargrove *is* married, but not to me. I'm not, that is. Married.''

''I see,'' Glory said, and drew in her breath. ''Well, that explains the boys. A single father and all.''

''Oh,'' Matthew said ruefully. The woman hadn't been thinking of his being married at all. At least, not in those terms. "Is there something wrong with the boys?"

"Of course not," Glory protested. "They're wonderful boys." She'd already grown to like them. "They're bright—and warmhearted." She stopped. Sometimes, looking at children, she'd feel the pain again from the accident that had robbed her of the chance to be a mother. She was determined to fight that pain. She refused to be one of those sentimental women who either wept or gushed over every child they saw. She cooled her enthusiasm. "And they have good bone structure."

Glory patted the twins on the head. She was safe with bone structure.

Josh scowled a minute, before Joey poked him with his elbow.

"Is that something angels have?" Joey asked hopefully. "That good bone stuff?"

"No, I'm afraid not," Glory said as she knelt so that she was at eye level with the boys. "Angels aren't worried about bone structure. I don't even know if God created them with bones. Although I suppose with those big wings and all they'd have to have something like bones...."

"See, I told you," Josh began. "She knows—"

Glory held up her hand. "The only thing I know about angels is what I've read in the Bible. I wouldn't know an angel if I met one on the street."

"You wouldn't?" Joey asked sadly.

"Not a chance," Glory assured him. She started to reach out to ruffle his hair again, but then pulled back. Maybe little boys didn't like that any more than she'd liked it as a little girl. "But you don't need an angel. You've got a father—" She eyed Matthew a little skep-

tically and then continued determinedly, "A good father—and you've got Mrs. Hargrove, and each other."

"We don't have a dog," Josh said plaintively.

"Well, maybe someday you can get a dog," Glory
said. She was handling this pretty well, she thought.
"Wouldn't you rather have a puppy than an angel?"

Glory didn't look at Matthew. She knew she had no
right to even suggest he get the boys a puppy. But it
seemed like a small thing. And they really were very
nice little boys. Josh was already starting to beam.

"Can it be a yellow dog?" Josh asked, looking at
Glory as if she had a dozen in her purse. "I'd like a
yellow dog."

"Well, I don't know if today is the day," Glory
stalled.

"I don't want a puppy." Joey shook his head and
looked at Josh. "A puppy hasn't been in heaven. He
can't tell us what our mommy looks like."

Joey looked expectantly at his father. "Mommy used
to sing to us and make us cookies."

"Oatmeal with extra raisins," Matthew assured him.
The trust in his son's eyes made him forget all about
his cracked rib and his sprained knee. If he had been
wearing more than this flimsy hospital robe, he would
have walked over to them and hugged them no matter
how his ribs felt. "And she loved you both very
much."

"I don't even care about the cookies," Joey said
bravely. "I just want to know what she looked like."

"Well, surely you have pictures." Glory turned to
look at Matthew.

"There was a fire," Matthew said. The fire had
burned down the first house they'd lived in after they
moved away from Havre. At the time, it felt as if the

fire was just finishing the job fate had already begun. He hadn't known the twins would miss a few pictures this much.

"Well, your father can tell you what she looked like," Glory offered softly. For the first time, she wished she was an angel. She'd give those little boys a puppy and a cookie-baking mother, too.

"But I can't *see* her," Joey said. "Telling isn't seeing."

"I can help you," Glory said without thinking.

"What?" Matthew and Dr. Norris both asked at the same time and in the same disapproving tone.

"I can help them see their mother," Glory said, turning to Matthew. She would do it, she thought excitedly.

"Look, I guess it's fair play after all they've put you through," Matthew said indignantly. "But I won't have you making fun of their make-believe."

"I wouldn't do that," Glory protested. How could such a distrustful man raise two such trusting sons? "And I can help. I've drawn hundreds of pictures from descriptions I've been given."

"You could?" Matthew asked, and then blinked suspiciously fast. "You really could draw a picture of the boys' mother—of Susie?"

"Yes," Glory said. Why was it that the same dreamy quality in the boys' eyes irritated her when it was mirrored in the eyes of their father, the man who had been married to the woman she was going to paint? She squared her shoulders. She didn't have time to worry about a man. She was an artist now. She was going to paint a masterpiece. The face of one of God's creations. "It'll be my pleasure."

"Hallelujah," Dr. Norris said as he bent down and swabbed Matthew's arm. Then, as he stuck a needle in

Matthew's arm, he added. "Sounds like maybe she's an angel after all."

Matthew grunted.

Glory swallowed her protest. She was the only one who saw the self-satisfied nod the twins exchanged.

The Bullet kept his eyes averted. He wore his cap pulled low over his forehead even though the musty darkness shadowed his face. The inside of the parked limo was damp and the rain slid silently over the windshield. A streetlight overhead cast a feeble glow inside the car, outlining the man next to him.

"You're sure she's a new hit?"

"Not technically," the man finally admitted. His words were low and clipped. "But she's as good as…the other try was nothing…a gang shooting—slid by easy."

"I charge extra for repeats," the Bullet said, his lips drawing together. He didn't like it when clients tried to get gang kids to do their dirty work. "Extra for cops, too."

"She's no cop," the man said impatiently. "Draws pictures. That's all."

"Still, they look out for their own," the Bullet pressed further. "She got any cop training? Guns, anything?"

"Naw. She's easy."

The Bullet grimaced. "I'll settle for fifteen," the Bullet said. "Half up front."

The client nodded and held out a paper bag full of cash. "Here's seventy-five hundred, Mr. Forrest Brown."

The Bullet froze. Nobody knew him by name. He was the Bullet to all of Seattle. *If he knows who I am, he knows where I live. My God, he knows about my Millie!*

Chapter Two

"You best behave yourself," Mrs. Hargrove whispered to Matthew as she leaned on the counter of the hardware store. Matthew was sitting on a folding chair behind the counter with his leg propped up on a trash can. He wasn't feeling too well, and Mrs. Hargrove's powdered violet perfume didn't help.

"I assure you..." Matthew started, but he didn't have a full head of steam going and it was almost impossible to stop the older woman without one. Besides, truth to tell, he didn't really mind her scolding him. Listening to her gave him time to watch Glory set up an easel with the twins' help in the front of the store.

"Humph," Mrs. Hargrove said, turning to follow the aim of his eyes before continuing, "You may be a man of the cloth—"

"What?" Matthew jerked himself back to the conversation. That was his secret. No one here was supposed to know. "What do you mean?"

Sweat broke out on Matthew's forehead. He had hoped no one here would ever find out. How could he

explain that his faith was tied in knots? He used to love
the ministry, knowing he was helping people find
God's mercy. He'd known he needed to leave the ministry when he no longer believed in that mercy, when
he couldn't even pray in public anymore. That last
morning, he'd just stood in the pulpit, unable to speak.
Finally the choir director figured out something was
wrong and had the choir start a hymn. But the hymn
didn't help. He was still mute. All he could remember
were the words of the prayers he'd prayed for Susie
and the confidence he'd had. The words of those
prayers rose like bile in his throat. His prayers had
turned to dust when she died. How could a man with
no faith be a minister? "I'm not a minister. Not anymore…"

"But a man's a man in my book," Mrs. Hargrove
continued, and pointed her finger at him. "And that
woman over there is a sight more tempting than a real
angel would ever be. And don't think other people
haven't noticed."

"What other people?" Matthew looked around. The
only two other people in the store were Elmer and Jacob, two semi-retired ranchers who stopped by the
hardware store every morning for their cup of coffee.
They were arguing across the checkerboard Henry kept
by the woodstove. When Matthew looked at them, Elmer lifted his bearded face, gave him a slow knowing
wink, stood up and then started walking toward the
counter.

When Elmer reached the front of the counter, he
looked squarely at Matthew. "Heard you got yourself
an angel."

"She's not an angel," Matthew protested automatically.

Elmer nodded solemnly. "Looks like an angel to me. You lucky dog. Got an inside track with her, since she's staying at your place."

"Staying at my place—" Matthew echoed in panic. He hadn't given any thought to where Glory would stay. The only hotel around was back in Miles City. That would be too far. But where would she stay at his place? He supposed she'd have to stay in his room. The old house had only two bedrooms, and the sofa was too lumpy for a guest. No, he'd have to take the sofa. Which was fine, but he worried about her up in his room. He couldn't remember if he'd put his socks away last night or not. Last night, nothing—try the past week. Socks everywhere.

"She can't stay at my place. I'm single," Matthew said, relieved to remember the fact. Glory would never see his dirty socks. Or the calendar on his wall that was stuck back in September even though it was December 19. "It wouldn't be proper, would it, Mrs. Hargrove?"

Matthew smiled confidently. Being single did have certain advantages.

"I would ask her to stay with me. She seems like a very nice lady," Mrs. Hargrove said earnestly, and then shrugged her shoulders. "But I can't."

The smile that was forming on Matthew's lips faded. "Why not?"

"The twins love the Christmas story," Mrs. Hargrove explained. "They'd be very disappointed if they couldn't keep the angel in their house. Besides, the doctor says there's no way you can get up those stairs, so it's perfectly proper."

As though that settled the matter, Mrs. Hargrove ran her finger over the plastic jug of wrenches standing on the counter. "Doesn't that Henry ever dust anything in here? Decent folks wouldn't shop here even if they had any extra money.''

"Henry doesn't notice the dust,'' Matthew said. He wondered if Glory had noticed how dusty it was in the hardware store. Of course she'd noticed, he thought. He could see her frowning at the window beside her. It could use a good washing. He'd started to clean up Henry's store now that the man was gone to his daughter's in Florida for a long winter vacation, but Matthew had started in the back, in the stockroom.

"Excuse me, Mrs. Hargrove,'' Matthew said as he reached for his crutches. "I think I best get my bottle of window cleaner and—'' Matthew nodded in the general direction of Glory.

But before Matthew could stand, Glory came over to the counter.

"I'd like to buy a brush,'' Glory said. The hardware store looked as if it could use some business, and she assumed they had a fine-tip brush that could serve her uses. "Make that a dozen and a can of turpentine.''

"Brushes are over there,'' Matthew said, and started to rise. "Most of them are for real painting—I mean, not for artists, but there might be one or two small enough.''

"You just sit back down,'' Mrs. Hargrove said as Matthew fitted the crutches under his arms. "You aren't in any shape to be fetching brushes.'' Mrs. Hargrove walked toward the shelf and returned with a dozen paintbrushes. Glory put her platinum plastic card on the counter. "I assume you take credit cards.''

"Some days that's all we take,'' Matthew said as he pulled out the credit card duplicator and picked up the phone for verification.

Matthew punched in the numbers of Glory's credit

card. He didn't want to admit it, but hers was the first platinum card he'd ever processed. Most people in Dry Creek thought they were rich if they qualified for the gold card. "Is there something different about a platinum card?"

"Different?"

"Your numbers aren't taking," Matthew said as he punched another number to speak to an operator. "Maybe I'm doing something wrong."

"Oh." Matthew's frown had grown deeper as the operator on the other end spoke.

Matthew hung up the phone. "Your card's been canceled."

"Canceled? How could it be canceled?"

"It seems you're, ah, dead."

"Dead! But that's ridiculous. I mean—how?"

"They didn't say how it happened," Matthew offered. He didn't want to think of the implications of Glory trying to run a fraudulent card through his system.

"There's no 'how' to it," Glory snapped. "It hasn't happened. I'm perfectly healthy, as anyone can see."

"Perfectly," Matthew agreed. She did look healthy, especially with the indignant flush on her cheeks. Maybe she'd simply missed a payment or two and that was the reason they were canceling her card.

"Can I use your phone?" Glory finally said. She'd call the captain. He'd said he'd take in her mail while she was gone. He could solve the mystery. "Collect, of course."

Matthew handed her the phone, and Glory turned her back slightly to make the call.

"Thank God you called," the captain said when he heard her voice. "I was worried."

"I just called two days ago," Glory protested. "I'm fine, except for my credit card."

"Ah, yes. I canceled your card. Not as easy as you'd think. I had to claim official business and tell them you'd died."

"You *what?*" Glory protested and then, remembering her audience, turned to give a reassuring smile to Matthew and Mrs. Hargrove. She didn't want them to think she was broke, let alone dead. She turned her back to them.

"Someone jimmied your mailbox yesterday," the captain said. "Took your credit card bill."

"The bill—they can have it."

"With the bill, someone can trace you," the captain pointed out patiently. "Find out what hotels you're staying at. Where you're buying gas. It's not that hard. Someone real sophisticated will find a way to get your charges the same day you make them. By now, they probably know what state you're in. Remember that shot. First the shooting at the grocery store and then that shot coming the next day so close to you. I don't like it. Not with someone taking your credit card bill."

"Surely you don't think—" Glory sputtered. "Thank goodness I haven't used the card since Spokane. But I can't believe— It was probably just some kids breaking in."

"They didn't break in to the other mailboxes in your building."

"Maybe they got tired. Thought of something better to do."

The captain was silent. "Maybe. Then I keep wondering if something wasn't fishy about that shooting at Benson's. Could be more was happening than you've remembered."

"Just the butcher standing by the meat counter. Had a package of steaks in one hand and the time card of one of his assistants in the other."

"We checked the name on the time card. The clerk didn't have a dispute."

"Least, not one they're talking about," Glory added.

"No extra keys on him, either," the captain continued. "If it was a robbery, there was no reason to shoot the man. He wasn't holding anything back."

"But if it was a robbery, why wait to make the hit when the armored transport had just made the pickup to go to the bank?"

"Ignorance?"

"Yeah, and anyone that ignorant wouldn't think to trace a credit card." Glory pushed back the prickles that were teasing the base of her spine. The captain was paranoid. He had to be. She hadn't been the only one at Benson's. She'd already told the police everything she knew. Besides, the bullet that had gone whizzing by a day later was gang related. The department was sure of that.

"Yeah, you're probably right. I'll go ahead and call the credit card company."

"Good." Glory took a deep breath. "When can I use the card?"

"Ten days. Takes them that long to verify," the captain said hesitantly. "I'll wire you some money. Your mom and I are heading off for that trip we told you about, but we'll drop it on our way. Tell me where you are."

"Dry Creek, Montana," Glory said. She looked over her shoulder. Matthew and Mrs. Hargrove were trying to look inconspicuous, a sure sign they'd overheard everything.

"Trouble?" Matthew said sympathetically as Glory hung up the phone and turned around. He could see she was embarrassed. "Don't worry about the brushes. Henry runs tabs for people all the time. You can pay when you can."

"No problem. I'm expecting a money order to come here to the post office, maybe even tomorrow," she said brightly.

Matthew looked at Mrs. Hargrove. Mrs. Hargrove looked at Matthew.

"We don't have a post office," the older woman finally said.

"No post office?" Glory said as her stomach started to sink. "Can I borrow the phone again?"

The captain's phone rang seven times before the secretary came on the line to say he'd just walked out the door to leave for his vacation.

"Can you leave a message just in case he calls before he leaves?" Glory asked. She wished she'd brought the captain's new unlisted home phone number with her. She hadn't bothered, because her mother and the captain were going to be on their trip.

After she left the message, Glory turned around. She was stuck. Stuck in Dry Creek. Unless. "I'd be happy to work in exchange for the brushes. The store looks like it could use some more help."

Matthew hesitated.

"I'm willing to work for minimum wage."

"I wish I could," Matthew said apologetically. "But we've already got a dozen job applications in the drawer. There aren't many jobs in Dry Creek this time of year. There'd be an uprising if I gave a job to an outsider when so many people here want one," Matthew finished lamely. Maybe he should chance the anger of the townspeople.

"I didn't know it was that bad." Glory said.

"We get by." Mrs. Hargrove lifted her chin. "In fact, there's talk of starting a dude ranch over on the Big Sheep Mountain place."

"That's just talk," Elmer said sharply. "The Big Sheep's been a cattle ranch for more than a hundred years. Started out as the XIT Ranch and then became the Big Sheep. We've got history. Pride. We don't need a bunch of city folks messing things up with their Jeeps and fancy boots. You know as good as me, they won't stay inside the fences. They'll scare the elk away. Not to mention the eagles. Before you know it, the Big Sheep Mountains will be empty—no animals at all, not even the cows."

"Better that than empty of people," Mrs. Hargrove replied as she tightened her lips. "It's old fools like you that can't make way for progress."

"Old fool? Me?" Elmer protested. "Why, I rode in the Jaycee Bucking Horse Sale last May. On Black Demon. Nothing old about me." He sighed. "Ah, what's the use. You're just worried about your son's family."

Mrs. Hargrove nodded slowly. "He said they'd have to move come spring if something doesn't open up. He's worked for the Big Sheep Mountain Cattle Company for ten years, but this rustling has them in a bind. They're losing too many cattle and they're going to start laying off hands." Mrs. Hargrove refocused on Glory as though just remembering she was there. The older woman settled her face into a polite smile. "I don't mean to go on about our troubles. We get by just fine. God is good to us."

"Of course," Glory said carefully. She knew a wall

of pride when she bumped into it, and Mrs. Hargrove had it in abundance. Matthew did, too. She hadn't given any thought to how Matthew managed on his salary, but now she remembered the frayed collars on the twins' shirts and the mended pocket on Joey's jacket. She'd have to send him some money when she got home. In fact—

"How about a check? I can pay for the brushes with a check," Glory offered in relief. She wasn't totally stranded, after all.

"A check is fine," Matthew said heartily. He'd remember to pull it out and replace it with cash from his own pocket before he took the checks to the bank. He had no doubt her check would bounce as high as her credit card had and he didn't want to embarrass her further. "It's $12.64 for the brushes and turpentine."

"Good." Glory started to write the check. "And I'll add a little extra for you—"

"You don't need to tip someone who works in a hardware store," Matthew said stiffly. A red flush settled around his neck. "The service is free."

"Of course," Glory said quickly. There she'd gone and offended him. She finished the check. "Twelve sixty-four exactly."

Glory counted the checks in her checkbook. She had ten left. That was enough to pay for meals and a hotel for a few nights.

"Where's the hotel from here?" she asked. She couldn't remember seeing one, but there must be one. Every town had a hotel.

"There's no hotel here," Mrs. Hargrove said as she nudged Matthew.

"Oh. Maybe a bed-and-breakfast place?"

There was a long pause as Mrs. Hargrove nudged Matthew again.

Matthew finally said, "I'm sure there's someone in town with an extra room who would let you—"

"Well, aren't you in luck, then," Mrs. Hargrove said with a determined enthusiasm. "Since Matthew hurt his knee, his room will be empty. The doctor says he can't climb the stairs with his sprain, so I'm sure no one will think anything of it. Besides, the twins are good chaperones."

Matthew felt trapped and then guilty. The least he could do was provide her lodging. "We'd be honored to have you stay with us for a few days."

"There's no one who does this more like a business?" Glory asked. The thought of staying in this man's room made her feel uneasy. She'd smell his aftershave on the pillows and see his shirts in the closet. "I can pay." Surely one of those families that wanted a job would take in a boarder for a few nights. "I'll even throw in a turkey for Christmas dinner."

"I'm afraid there's only Matthew and his boys," Mrs. Hargrove said.

Glory bent her head to start writing her check. "How does one hundred dollars a night sound?"

"One hundred!" Matthew protested. No wonder she had financial troubles. "We're not the Hilton. Besides, you'd be our guest."

Glory had finished the check by the time he finished. No wonder he had financial troubles. "I can be your guest and still pay a fair price."

"No, there's no need," Matthew said.

"I insist," Glory said as she ripped off the check and presented it to him.

Matthew raised his eyebrows at the amount of the

check. He supposed it didn't matter what amount she wrote the check for when it was going to bounce anyway, but three hundred dollars was a lot to pay for several nights' food and lodging.

"Consider it a Christmas present," Glory said grandly. "For the twins."

"They'll appreciate it," Matthew said dryly.

Glory flipped her wallet to the plastic section. "You'll want to see my driver's license."

"Henry doesn't bother. He knows the folks here who write checks," Matthew said as he took a sidelong look at the driver's license anyway. He was pleased to see she was Glory Beckett. She might be a bad risk from the credit company's viewpoint, but she wasn't a thief. That is, unless she was so polished she had gotten a fake driver's license to go with her story.

"He doesn't know me," Glory said as she moved her driver's license so it came into Matthew's full view. "You'll want to write down the number."

"All right," Matthew said as he noted her driver's license number.

"Good," Glory said as she put her checkbook back in her purse and turned to walk back to her easel.

"You're not going to cash those checks, Matthew Curtis," Mrs. Hargrove demanded in a hushed whisper as they watched Glory sit down to her easel across the store in front of the display window.

"Of course not," Matthew agreed as he slipped the checks out of the drawer.

Carl Wall, the deputy sheriff, was running for re-election and his campaign slogan was No Crime's Too Small To Do Some Time. He'd happily jail an out-of-towner for writing a bad check and brag about it to voters later.

Ten minutes later, Glory repositioned the easel. Then she arranged her brushes twice and turned her stool to get more light. She was stalling and she knew it. She suddenly realized she'd never painted a portrait as agonizingly important as this one. The sketches she'd done of criminals, while very important, were meant only for identification and not as a symbol of love.

"Do you want your mother to be sitting or standing?" Glory asked the twins. The two identical heads were studying the bottom of a large display window. They each had a cleaning rag and were making circles in the lower portion of the window while Matthew reached for the high corners, standing awkwardly with one crutch.

"I don't know." Josh stopped rubbing the window and gave it a squirt of window cleaner. "Maybe she could be riding a dragon. I've always wanted a picture of a dragon."

"Mommie's don't ride dragons," Joey scolded his brother. "They ride brooms."

Matthew winced. Susie had been adamantly opposed to celebrating Halloween and, consequently, the twins had only a sketchy idea of the spooks that inspired other children's nightmares.

"No, sweetie, it's witches who ride brooms." Mrs. Hargrove corrected the boy with a smile as she picked up a cleaning rag and joined Matthew on the high corners. "Maybe you could have a picture painted of your mother praying."

"No," Matthew said a little more loudly than he intended. His memories of Susie praying tormented him. He knew she would be heartbroken that her death had brought a wedge between him and God, but his feelings were there anyway. If he lived to be a hundred, he'd never understand how God could have answered his prayers for so long on the small things like good crops and passing tests but when it came to the one big thing—Susie's recovery—God had let him down flat. No sense of comfort. No nothing. He'd expected his faith to carry them through always.

Matthew didn't feel like explaining himself. His arms were sore from the crutches and he hobbled over to a stool that was beside Glory. "I want the twins to remember their mother laughing. She was a happy woman."

"Well, that'd make a good picture, too," Mrs. Hargrove said, and then looked at the twins. The twins had stopped wiping their circles and were listening thoughtfully. "You'd like that, wouldn't you?"

The twins nodded.

"Okay, smiling it is," Glory said. This Susie woman sounded like a saint, always smiling and praying and baking cookies, and Glory had no reason to resent her. None whatsoever, she thought to herself. "I assume she had all her teeth."

"What?" Matthew seemed a little startled with the question.

"Her teeth," Glory repeated. "If I'm going to paint her smiling, I need to know about her teeth. Were there any missing?"

"Of course not."

"Were any of them crooked?" Glory continued. "Or chipped? Did she have a space between the front ones?"

"They were just teeth," Matthew said defensively. Why did he suddenly feel guilty because he couldn't remember what kind of teeth Susie had? He knew her image was burned onto his heart. He just couldn't pull up the details. "Her eyes were blue—a blue so deep they'd turn to black in the shadows."

"Eyes. Blue. Deep," Glory said as she wrote a note on the butcher paper she'd stretched over her easel. "And her nose, was it like this? Or like this?" Glory sketched a couple of common nose styles. "Or more like this?"

"It was sort of like that, but more scrunched at the beginning," Matthew said, pointing to one of the noses and feeling suddenly helpless. He hadn't realized until now that the picture Glory was going to paint was the picture that was inside his head. He'd spent a lot of time trying to get Susie's face out of his mind so he could keep himself going forward. What if he'd done too good a job? What if he couldn't remember her face as well as he should?

"Pugged nose," Glory muttered as she added the words to the list on the side of the paper. "Any marks? Moles? Freckles? Warts?"

"Of course not. She was a classic beauty," Matthew protested.

"I see," Glory said. She tried to remind herself that she was doing a job and shouldn't take Matthew's words personally. "I have freckles."

Glory winced. She hadn't meant to say that.

"I noticed them right off." Matthew nodded. "That's how I knew you couldn't be an angel."

"I see," Glory said icily. Couldn't be an angel, indeed. Just because Susie didn't have freckles. She'd show him who couldn't be an angel. "Any other identifying facial marks?"

"I liked the way your hair curled," Matthew offered thoughtfully as he remembered lying on his back after his fall and looking up at Glory. "It just spread all out

like a sunflower—except it was brass instead of gold.''
He had a sudden piercing thought of what it would be
like to kiss a woman with hair like that. Her hair would
fall around him with the softness of the sun.

"I meant Susie. Did she have any other identifying
facial marks?" Glory repeated.

"Oh," Matthew said, closing his eyes in concentra-
tion. Could Susie have had freckles after all? Even a
few? No, she'd made this big production about never
going out in the sun because her skin was so fair—like
an English maiden, she used to say. What else did Susie
always say? Oh, yes. "Peaches and cream. Her skin
was a peaches-and-cream complexion."

"Well, that's a nice poetic notion," Glory said as
she added the words to her list.

"What do you mean by that?" Matthew opened his
eyes indignantly. Glory had gone all bristly on him, and
he was trying his best to remember all the details just
as she wanted.

"It's just that peaches have fuzz—and cream even-
tually clots. The whole phrase is a cliché. It doesn't
describe anything. No one's skin looks like that. Not
really."

"Well, no," Matthew admitted. "It's just hard to
remember everything."

"True enough." Glory softened. She had gotten descriptions from hundreds of people in her career. She
should know not to push someone. Often a victim
would have a hard time recalling the features of their
assailant. She imagined the same thing might be true
when grief rather than fear was the problem. "Don't
worry about it. We'll do it one step at a time. We'll be
done by Friday."

"But Friday's not the pageant. You've got to stay

until the pageant," Josh said solemnly. "They've never had a real angel before in the pageant."

"I'm not an—" Glory protested automatically as she turned to the twins. They both looked so wistful. "I'm sorry, but I can't stay. Even though I'd love to see my two favorite shepherds in their bathrobes."

"How'd you know we're wearing bathrobes?" Josh demanded.

"She's an angel, that's how," Joey said proudly. "She's just an undercover angel, so she can't tell anyone. Like a spy."

"Do you know everyone's secrets?" Josh asked in awe.

"I don't know anyone's secrets," Glory said, and then smiled teasingly. "Unless, of course, you do something naughty."

"Wow, just like Santa Claus," Josh breathed excitedly. "Can you get me a *Star Trek* laser light gun for Christmas?"

"I thought we talked about that, Josh," Matthew interjected. "You know Santa is just a story."

"I know," Josh said in a rush. His eyes were bright with confidence. "But she's an angel and she can tell God. That's even better than Santa Claus. God must have lots of toys."

"We'll talk about this later," Matthew said. He'd have to sit down with Josh and explain how the universe worked. Whether he asked God or Santa Claus for a present, it didn't matter. Neither one of them could buy Josh a gift unless it could be found in Miles City for twenty dollars or less.

"Can you tell God?" Josh ignored his father and whispered to Glory. "I've been a good boy, except for—well, you know—the bug thing."

Glory didn't think she wanted to know about the bug thing. "I'm sure you have been a good boy," she said as she knelt to look squarely at the boy. "I'll tell you what, why don't you draw a picture of this laser gun and color it. That way, if you want to send God a picture, He'll know what it looks like."

"Me, too," Joey asked. "Can I make a picture, too?"

"Why not?" Glory said, and included him in her smile. Even if her credit card wouldn't live again by Christmas she could send a check to one of her girlfriends. Her friend Sylvia ran a neighborhood youth center and would be visiting that huge toy store in Seattle anyway. Even though most of the kids Sylvia worked with were more likely to own a real pistol than a water pistol, Sylvia insisted on treating them as though they were ordinary children at the holidays. The kids loved her for it.

"But..." Matthew tried to catch Glory's eye.

"Daddy needs one, too," Joey said. The twins both looked at her with solemn eyes. It had taken her several hours to figure out how to tell them apart. Joey's eyes were always quieter. "But Daddy's old."

"No one's too old for Christmas wishes," Glory said.

"Really?" Joey smiled.

It was dusk by the time Glory finished her sketch of Susie and they all went home for dinner. Glory offered to cook, but Matthew declared she had already done her work for the day. Glory was too tired to resist. Sketching Susie had been difficult. Matthew had never wanted to look at the full face of the sketch, and so she'd pieced it together an eyebrow at a time. Even when she'd finished, he'd pleaded fatigue and asked to look at the sketch on the next day.

Matthew went to the kitchen to cook dinner, leaving Glory on the sofa with a *Good Housekeeping* magazine.

"I've learned to be a good cook," Matthew said a little bleakly as he sat down a little later and leaned his crutches against the dining-room wall. The smell of burned potatoes still hung in the air even though all the windows were now open. "Dinner doesn't usually float in milk."

"Cereal is all right," Glory assured him. She'd realized when the smoke drifted into the living room that dinner would be delayed.

"I like the pink ones," Joey said as he poured his bowl full of Froot Loops.

"I always keep cornflakes for me," Matthew said as he handed the box to Glory. "I'm afraid we don't have a wide selection."

"Cornflakes are fine," Glory said. "I often eat light."

Matthew chided himself. He should have realized. She lived on the road, likely by her wits. Of course she ate light. He should have made sure she had a decent meal.

"We'll eat better tomorrow, I promise. Something with meat in it. And if you need anything, just ask."

"I will," Glory assured him, and smiled.

Her smile kicked Matthew in the stomach. The sun shone about her when she smiled. No wonder his sons thought she was an angel.

"Daddy?" Joey was looking at Matthew.

Matthew pulled himself together. It was time for grace.

"Hands," Matthew said and offered his hand to Joey

on the one side. He didn't realize until his hand was already extended that Glory was on his other side.

"I'll say grace," Josh offered as he put one hand out to Joey and the other to Glory. He looked shyly at Glory. "I washed. I'm not jammy."

"I know." Glory smiled softly as she reached easily for his hand. His small hand snuggled trustingly in her palm. She held her other hand out to Matthew. His hand didn't snuggle. Instead, it enveloped her. She swore her pulse moved from her wrist to the center of her palm. She wondered if he could feel the quickening beat in her. What was wrong with her? He'd think she'd never held a man's hand before. Not that she was holding his hand now. It was prayer hand-holding. That's all. Just because his thumb happened to caress the inside of her finger.

"Okay, Daddy?" Josh asked again, looking at his father. "It's my turn to say grace."

Matthew nodded his permission. What was wrong with him? Even Josh was looking at him funny. Matthew was beginning to think he'd never held a woman's hand before. Glory's skin was softer than fine leather. She must use some kind of lotions on her hands because of her work in paints. That must be it. Just lotions. He cleared his throat. "Sure. Go ahead."

Josh bowed his head and carefully screwed his eyes closed. "Thank you, God, for this day and for this food and for our comp—" Josh stumbled "—comp-any. Amen."

"Thank you, Josh," Glory said when he looked up again. "I'm honored to be your company."

"If there's anything you need…" Matthew offered again.

The only thing she needed, she thought later that

evening, was some more paint. The twins had been put to bed and she was sitting on the sofa reading her magazine and talking with Matthew as he sewed a button on Josh's winter coat. The light from the two lamps made round circles on the ceiling and bathed Matthew in a yellow glow. She hated to tell the twins, but it was their father who looked like the angel. His chestnut hair waved and curled all over his head and down to his collar. Forceful cheekbones sloped down to a square chin. He was the most manly-looking man she'd seen in a long time. Not that, of course, she assured herself, there was anything personal in her admiration.

"I best get the fire banked for the night," Matthew said.

"Let me do it," Glory said as she set aside the magazine. "Rest your leg. Just tell me how and it won't take a minute."

Matthew pulled himself up by holding on to the bookshelf and then put one crutch under his arm. "No need, I can do it."

"But I'd like to help," Glory protested as she rose. "You're in no condition to be banking a fire."

"I'm fine," Matthew said. "It takes more than a sprained knee to stop me."

Glory looked at him. A thin sheen of sweat was showing on his forehead and it was definitely not hot in the room. "You've got more pride than sense."

"Pride?" Matthew said as he hobbled over to the woodstove. "It's not pride. It's learning to take care of yourself. I've learned not to rely on others. I can do whatever I need to do to take care of me and my boys."

"Without help from anyone," Glory said dryly. Relying on others was the key to trust. Trust in others. Trust in God.

"We don't need any help," Matthew said as he lifted the grate on the stove. "It's best not to count on anyone else. I can do what needs doing."

"Can you?" Glory said softly as she watched Matthew reach down and pick up several pieces of wood. The fire wrapped golden shadows around his face. His frown burrowed itself farther into his forehead. She had no doubt Matthew could do everything that needed to be done in raising his sons—everything, that is, except teach them how to have faith. For how can you have faith in God if you can't trust anyone, not even Him? No wonder the boys clung to the belief she was an angel. It would take an angel to bring healing to their little family.

The Bullet folded his socks and put them in an old duffel bag that was carefully nondescript. No logos. No fancy stripes. Just brown.

"My uncle…" the Bullet said as he added a sweater. "He's sick. Spokane."

Millie nodded. She'd just come back from her job at Ruby's Coffee Shop and sat on the edge of the bed with her back straight and her eyes carefully not looking at the socks. She always looked so fragile with her wispy blond hair and slender body.

"I—ah—I'll be back soon," the Bullet continued. *She knows where I'm going. Oh, not the location. But she knows the why.* "A week or so is all."

Millie nodded again and stood up. "Better take another sweater. It's cold in Spokane." She walked to the closet.

"No, let me." The Bullet intercepted her. He didn't want Millie to be part of any of this, not even the packing.

"Don't go. You don't have to go." Millie turned to him and spoke fiercely.

"I already told my uncle I was coming," the Bullet said slowly. It was too late to change his mind.

Chapter Three

Matthew stared at the glass coffeepot in his hand. He'd come to the hardware store at eight o'clock just like any other regular working day. But never before had the coffeepot been so sparkling clean and never before had a can of gourmet hazelnut coffee stood beside it. Old Henry was fussy about his coffee, and he always made it plain and strong. "Nothing fancy," he'd often say. "My customers are ranchers, not ballet dancers."

Glory and Matthew had shared a ride to the store after dropping the twins off at the church's nursery. "I think your customers might like some of these coffee flavors," Glory said.

"Coffee flavors?" Matthew hadn't slept well last night and he wanted his coffee thick and black with no frills. It wasn't the sofa that had kept him awake or even the pain in his knee. No matter how many times he turned over on the old sofa, his mind kept wandering back to dreams of Glory. Now he needed a good kick of coffee to keep him awake.

"You know, orange, raspberry, chocolate," Glory replied as she pulled the three bottles out of her purse. She hadn't slept well last night. She assured herself it was the creaking of the old house that had kept her awake and not the picture that stayed in her mind of Matthew adding more wood to the fire last night. She had gotten up this morning determined to make good progress on her painting today. That meant coffee.

"That's nice," Matthew said as he tried to hide as much of the white doily under the sugar bowl as he could. He'd have to tell Elmer and Jacob that the doily was a Christmas decoration. He expected they'd tolerate the concept of a few holiday decorations more kindly than the idea that their domain was being citified. Citified wasn't popular here. As it was, the two old men spent half their time here arguing about the dude ranch over on the Big Sheep Mountain Ranch. Anything that smacked of change and city people was suspect. And coffee flavors. The next thing you knew she'd want a...

"Cappuccino machine—that's what we need," Elmer said a half hour later. He was sipping his orange-flavored coffee most politely and beaming at Glory as she set up her easel. "I've always had a hankering to have one of those coffees."

"I don't even know if they have a cappuccino machine in Miles City. We'd have to send to Billings to buy one," Matthew protested.

What was wrong with Elmer? Once he'd complained because Henry put a different kind of toilet paper in the bathroom. And yet, here he was, wearing a new white shirt, the kind he only wore to funerals. "And no one's complained before. You've always liked the usual."

"But sometimes it's good to have a change," Glory said from her place by the window.

"Yeah, don't be such an old stick-in-the mud," Jacob said as he peered into his coffee cup suspiciously. Apparently Jacob didn't find anything too alarming in his cup, because he took a hot, scalding gulp. "Ahh, none of us are too old to try something new."

"I thought I'd set Susie's sketch up in the display window, too," Glory said. It had occurred to her last night that most gas stations wouldn't take checks. She could use some cash. "I might get another order for a portrait."

Matthew swallowed. He'd prefer to rearrange these receipts and dust the merchandise all morning. Anything to put off looking at the picture of Susie.

"I've got the sketch ready," Glory said. She'd placed the drawing of Susie on her easel. She'd drawn Susie smiling and holding a plate of oatmeal cookies almost level with her chin.

"I see that," Matthew said as he stood and hobbled over to the sketch. He took a deep breath. He felt the rubber band squeeze his heart. He'd been unable to cry at Susie's funeral. He'd just sat there with that rubber band squeezing the life out of him. This time he'd take a quick look and be done with it. He felt as if he'd been called upon to identify someone in the morgue. It wasn't a duty he wanted to prolong.

"That's her," Matthew said in surprise. He'd expected an identification picture of Susie, something that looked like a passport photo where you see the resemblance but not the person. But Glory was good. It was Susie's eyes that smiled at him from the paper.

"I wasn't sure about the cheekbones," Glory fretted.

She didn't like the stillness that surrounded Matthew. "I think they might be a little too high."

"No, it's perfect. That's Susie."

Matthew braced himself for the inevitable second wave of pain. Susie had trusted him to save her life, trusted his faith to make her well. He'd never forgiven himself for letting her down. Somehow he hadn't prayed hard enough or loud enough to make any difference.

"Did she have a pink dress?" Glory interrupted his thoughts. Matthew's face had gone white and she didn't know what else to offer but chatter. "I thought I'd paint her in a pink dress with a little lace collar of white."

"Pink is good," Matthew said as he turned to walk away on his crutches. The sweat cooled on his brow. He'd made it past the hard part. He'd seen Susie again. Seen the look of trust on her face. He'd promised he'd take care of her and he had failed. He had told her God would come through for them. But he'd been wrong. In the end, Matthew had bargained bitterly with God to let him die. But God had not granted him even that small mercy. Matthew kept his face turned away from everyone. He'd fight his own demons alone.

"You like pink, do you?" Elmer said as he walked over to Glory.

"Who, me? No, I'm more of a beige-and-gray type of person," Glory said. She didn't like the closed look on Matthew's face or the ramrod straightness of his back when he'd turned around. But he'd made it clear he didn't want to talk.

"Beige—gray—that's good," Elmer murmured as he leaned closer to Glory.

Matthew hobbled stiffly back to the counter and sat back down on his chair. The air cooled the remaining

sweat off his face as he watched Elmer make his
moves. The old fox. Matthew took a deep breath. Today he'd rather watch the nonsense with Elmer than
hold on to his own pain. He wanted to live in today
and not yesterday. It made him feel better to know he
wasn't the only one being charmed by Glory. No wonder the old man drank his orange coffee as if he enjoyed
it. "No checker game this morning, Elmer?"

"Checkers—ah, n-no." Elmer stammered a little. "I
thought I'd sit and talk a bit with the ang—with Miss
Glory." Elmer gave a curt nod in Glory's direction.
"Get acquainted, so to speak."

"That's very friendly of you," Glory said. She'd
watched Matthew make his way to the counter and had
relaxed when he turned to face them. When he started
watching them, she turned her attention to Elmer. The
old man was safer. She didn't mind company while she
painted and almost welcomed it while she set out her
brushes as she did now. Since Matthew had approved
the sketch, she'd move on to the first stages of the oil
painting.

"My pleasure," Elmer said, and then took another
dainty sip of his orange coffee. "It isn't often we have
a young woman visiting—at least, not one your age."

"Hmm," Glory murmured pleasantly. She'd need to
mix some blue with that mauve to get the eye color
right.

"Your age," Elmer repeated. "And what might that
be?"

"Twenty-eight."

"Ah," Elmer said.

Matthew watched as the older man marked down a
figure in a little notepad he pulled out of his pocket.

"And your birthday?"

"March 15."

"Good month," Elmer said as he nodded and marked another figure in his notepad. "That means you were born in oh three, fifteen, ah, 19...ah...?"

"Say, what are you doing?" Matthew demanded in surprise as he hobbled over to Elmer and stared at the older man.

"What?" Elmer bristled as he slid the notepad into his jacket pocket. "Just making conversation."

"You're planning to buy a lottery ticket from your daughter in L.A., aren't you?" Matthew said in amazement. "And you're getting some lucky numbers."

"It's all right." Glory looked up at the two of them and smiled. "At least that way, he'll have to call her."

"Yeah," Elmer said smugly as he patted the notebook in his pocket. "It'll be our family time. Nothing better than talking to your family."

Matthew grunted. "You've got better things to talk about than numbers and lottery tickets. Besides, her numbers aren't magic. She's not an angel."

"And how do you know that?" Elmer lifted his chin. "She could be. The Bible says we sometimes entertain angels unaware. Right in Hebrews 13:2. I looked it up."

"But the angels aren't unaware." Glory didn't like the direction this discussion was going. She was as earthbound as anyone. "And an angel? I assure you, I'm not one." She was just finishing up the right eyebrow on Susie's picture. Eyebrows were important character pieces. They could make a face look innocent, bewildered, sad. Glory had settled on innocent for Susie.

"You could be," Elmer stubbornly insisted. "You just might not want us to know."

Matthew snorted. "An angel wouldn't lie." He didn't know why he cared, but it gave him a funny feeling to have people talk about Glory as though she was an angel.

Not that the people of Dry Creek didn't need an angel. Fact is, they needed a whole troupe of angels and a basket of miracles, too. He didn't begrudge them their hope. It's just that he, of all people, knew the disappointment that came when expected miracles didn't happen.

The bell over the door rang as the door swung open and a half dozen little children in snowsuits walked in. A huge gust of wind and Mrs. Hargrove came in behind them.

"Josh! Joey!" Matthew recognized his sons, or, at least, he recognized their snowsuits. There was much flapping about before the hoods were down and the young faces looked around the hardware store.

"There she is!" Josh shouted to his friends, and pointed at Glory.

Matthew tensed.

"Hi, there." Glory looked up at the children and smiled. Their bright snowsuits made a lovely study in color. Blue. Red. Pink. Even a purple one. "I should paint you all sometime. Just like this."

"I see you do have everything set up," Mrs. Hargrove said in satisfaction as she stepped out in front of her charges. "I was hoping you did. The children have never seen a real artist at work. If you don't mind them watching. I thought it'd be educational."

Matthew relaxed. That's why they were here.

"And she's an angel, too," Joey boasted quietly.

Matthew bit back his tongue. If Josh had done the boasting, he'd have corrected him in an instant. But it had been so long since he'd seen Joey care enough to speak up about anything, he didn't have the heart to correct him.

"Well, maybe not quite an angel," Matthew did offer softly. "Sometimes a good person can seem like an angel to others without really being one."

"Josh said she'd take our pictures to God," said another little boy, Greg, glancing sideways at Glory. "For Christmas."

Glory put down her brushes and turned to face the expectant faces looking at her. She noticed that most of the pockets had a piece of paper peeking out of them.

"I'd be happy to take your pictures," Glory said as she stepped forward. It had been a long time since she'd done this much Christmas shopping, but it'd be fun. Sylvia, she knew, would enjoy being her go-between and Glory had enough in her checking account to cover it. "Just be sure you put your full names on the pictures—first and last."

"Last, too?" one of the boys asked, his forehead puckering in a quick frown. "I can't write my last."

"Maybe Mrs. Hargrove can help you," Glory said. "But I do need first name and last name so the right present gets to the right child."

"I thought God knew our names," a little girl in a pink snowsuit said suspiciously as she stepped out of the leg of her suit. "If you're his angel you should know, too."

"I'm not an angel," Glory said.

"Then why do you want our pictures?" the little girl demanded.

"She'll give your pictures to your parents." Mrs. Hargrove stepped in front of the children. "It's your

parents that—'' She stumbled. Glory could see why.
Those shining little faces looked up with such trust.

''My parents already said I won't get no Betsy Tall
doll,'' the girl said. ''They said it's too ex—cen—
sive.''

''Expensive, dear.'' Mrs. Hargrove corrected the pro-
nunciation automatically. ''Too expensive. And I'm
sure there are other dolls.''

The hope was beginning to fade on the young faces.

''I'd be happy to take your pictures,'' Glory said
again softly. She held out her hands and the children
quickly stuffed their pictures into them.

''Mrs. Hargrove will help me figure out who's
who,'' Glory assured the children.

Glory was watching the children and didn't hear
Matthew coming up next to her.

''I'll help with the pictures,'' Matthew whispered in
her ear.

Glory jumped. Matthew startled her. He was
so…well, just so close. He unnerved her. She pulled
away slightly. ''I don't need help. I'm fine. I can take
care of it.''

''How? You're not an angel.''

''Just because I'm not an angel doesn't mean I can't
buy a few gifts.''

''For children you don't even know?''

''I know them now.'' Glory shrugged. What was it
with this man? Didn't he believe anyone could do
something for someone else just because?

The bell over the door rang again, and this time a
teenage girl slipped inside. She had a tiny gold ring in
her nose and a streak of red dye going through her hair.
Fashion, it appeared, hadn't neglected southeastern
Montana.

"Linda." Matthew greeted the girl carefully. "What can we help you with?"

"What do you think, big guy?" Linda cooed softly. The girl lifted her eyes to Matthew. She was holding a five-dollar bill in her hand and she waved it around.

Glory winced. The girl was playing at something she obviously didn't even understand. And she was looking at Matthew as if she was starving and he was a super-sized hamburger. Which was ridiculous, Glory thought. Sure, he was good-looking in a rugged kind of a way. And sure he smelled like the outdoors and sure he had biceps that would get second looks at the beach and— Glory stopped herself. Okay, so the girl wasn't so far wrong. He was worth staring at. But that didn't mean the girl had any right to do it.

"Hey, Linda," called the little boy, Greg. "Come meet the angel. She's gonna get us presents."

Linda flicked an annoyed glance down that then softened at the enthusiasm on Greg's face. "That's nice. But I need to talk to the angel myself."

"I'm not—" Glory began.

"I need some advice," Linda interrupted impatiently. The teenager looked assessingly at Glory and held out the five-dollar bill. "Some love advice."

"From me?" Glory squeaked.

"I need to know if I should marry the Jazz Man."

"The Jazz Man?" Matthew asked as he leaned his crutches against a wall and sat down on a chair. "You don't mean Arnold's boy, Duane?"

"Yeah." Linda looked at him and snapped her gum. "He's forming a band. Calling himself the Jazz Man." She stood a little straighter. "Wants me to be his lead singer."

"And he's proposed?" Glory asked in studied surprise. She might not know a lot about love, but she did know about business.

"Yeah, why?" Linda looked at her cautiously.

"Mixing business and pleasure." Glory shook her head in what she hoped was a convincingly somber fashion. "He won't have to pay you if he marries you."

"Yeah, I never thought of that," Linda said slowly, and put the five dollars on Glory's easel. "Thanks."

"What's the money for—" Glory began, but was interrupted by the bell ringing over the door again.

This time the ringing was incessant and loud. A stocky man in a tan sheriff's uniform stepped into the store and looked around quickly. His eyes fastened on Glory.

"There you are," he said as he walked toward Glory and put his hand on the end of the gun that stuck out of his holster. "You're under arrest for impersonating an angel. You have the right to—"

"You can't arrest her." The protest erupted from all across the store.

"Oh, yes, I can," the deputy said as he clicked the handcuffs from behind his back and picked up the five dollars Linda had left on her easel. "I won't have no con woman plucking my pigeons. Not in my town she won't."

Plucking his pigeons, Glory thought in dismay. *Dear Lord, what have I done now?*

The Bullet leaned against the cold glass of the phone booth. The credit card company records showed the woman had stopped at a gas station in Spokane and then at a bank for a cash advance. He'd followed the usual procedure to find her. He knew loners in a new town found a bar.

"You'll never find her that way," the voice on the other end of the phone snorted.

"Why not? She's a cop."

"A Christian cop," the voice clarified. "Religious as they come. Doesn't drink. Try looking in the churches."

The Bullet swallowed hard. "Churches? Me?"

Chapter Four

"Easy now," Deputy Sheriff Carl Wall warned Glory when she stood up. He'd forbidden the others to follow them when he escorted her up the church steps and into a small office off the church's kitchen. She'd been sitting on the edge of the desk for ten minutes now while he argued on the phone. The cuffs he'd put on her hands hung open at her wrists. The key to unlock them was in his patrol car and so he did not lock them shut. They were more for show than because he thought the woman would bolt.

"Well, there's got to be a law against it, Bert," Carl was saying for the second time into the phone. He twisted the cord around his chubby ginger. "We just can't have folks going around claiming to be angels and things."

"I never claimed to be an angel," Glory said, even though she doubted he heard her. He hadn't paid any attention to her the past two times she'd said it. It wasn't because he hadn't heard her, she figured; it was because he wasn't listening. In her experience, hearing and listening were two different things.

"But an angel's different from Santa Claus," Carl argued into the phone's mouthpiece, ignoring Glory. He'd already twisted part of the cord around his finger, so now he looped another section around his hand. "Everyone knows Santa Claus isn't real, but folks and angels, well, that's a different story. She's more like a fortune-teller. Gotta be laws against that."

Glory looked around at the office. There was a boxy window at the end of the room. Everything else was long and skinny. The whole thing wasn't much wider than the desk. She guessed the room had been a pantry at one time, running as it did side by side the whole width of the kitchen. A bookcase lined one long wall and a chair stood to the side of the desk. A filing cabinet was tucked behind the door.

"Of course she hasn't got wings on," Carl sputtered in exasperation as he eyed Glory suspiciously. He untwisted the cord around his hand and rubbed the red mark he'd created. Glory pulled a book off the shelf and tried to ignore him. "But a person doesn't need a costume to con people. Crooks don't wear signs, for Pete's sake."

Glory opened the book she held. She loved the smell of old books. They were like old friends. Just holding the book steadied her. If she had to, she could call the police station in Seattle and have them vouch for her honesty. She doubted there were any laws against claiming to be an angel anyway, not even if she sprouted wings and flew off the Empire State Building.

"Well, I can't just let her go," Carl Wall whined into the phone. Then he looked at Glory again and turned his back to her as though that would muffle his voice. ''I've already taken her in. I'll look bad saying there's no law against it now. I'm going to write her up for impersonating even if the judge says no later.''

A movement through the window caught her eye. Something was happening in the street. Glory looked at the deputy sheriff's back and slid closer to the window. She saw Matthew, standing in the middle of the dirt street and waving a crutch around. The people from the hardware store were gathered around him and Matthew wasn't the only one waving something. Mrs. Hargrove had a broom. Elmer had a yardstick. It looked as if Matthew was giving a speech, but she couldn't hear it through the closed window. She braced her fingers against the frame of the windowpanes and pushed up. A puff of cold air came inside, a puff of dirty cold air, Glory decided as the dust beneath the window blew onto her coat. But she could finally hear the voices outside.

''He'll listen to voters. That's all he wants,'' Matthew was saying. A trail of white breath rose from Matthew's mouth. It was cold. Matthew wore a wool jacket over his shirt. It wasn't nearly enough to keep him warm, in Glory's opinion. ''There's no need to threaten him with any more than that.''

''But he's got our angel,'' Elmer protested.

''We don't know she's an angel,'' Matthew said. Glory noticed he had only a slipper on his injured foot. He needed to be inside. She was pretty sure the doctor had told him to stay inside.

''But we don't know she's not, either,'' Elmer persisted as he dipped his yardstick for emphasis. ''The Bible talks about angels. It could be. We don't know. And who wants to take a chance! Do you?'' Elmer took a breath. "Do you want to be responsible for turning an angel out of Dry Creek?"

The question hung in the air like brittle frost.

Glory pushed the window higher. This was getting interesting.

"Shut that window," Carl yelled. He was putting down the telephone and had finally noticed where she was. "You aren't going to get far, jumping out that window and evading arrest."

"I wasn't going to jump," Glory said in astonishment. "I was just listening to the people in the street out front. I think they're campaigning against you."

Carl Wall scowled at her. "Mighty lippy for an angel, aren't you?"

Glory grinned. "I'm not an angel."

"Oh, I know that, but do they know it?" Carl pointed out the window to the people on the street. Glory looked at them. They were gesturing as they talked, and periodically someone would wave a broom. They looked like a mob of janitors. Carl cleared his throat and continued. "These people are my responsibility. As I said, I won't have anyone plucking my flock—not while I'm on duty."

"I've not asked for a dime from anyone," Glory protested indignantly. "Linda put that five-dollar bill on my easel. I didn't ask for it. I would have given it back if you hadn't stepped in. I don't want anyone's money."

"Maybe not yet. But you'll want it sooner or later, won't you?" Carl said as a sly smile slid over his face. "What else can you do? You don't have a job—"

"I have a job," Glory interrupted firmly. "Not here, of course, but I do have a job with the Seattle Police Department."

Carl snorted. "Expect me to believe that. You—a police officer. Where's your badge?"

"Well, I don't have a badge...."

"I didn't think so," Carl said with satisfaction.

"I work for them as a sketch artist. You know, drawing pictures of criminals from the descriptions given by the witnesses."

"Hmph." The deputy appeared to consider her words and then shook his head. "Naw, I don't think so. What I think is you're a slick customer trying to make a buck off the poor folks of Dry Creek. Taking advantage of their good holiday spirits. And I aim to catch you at it. The minute you ask for a dime, you're mine."

"It looks like I'm yours anyway," Glory said dryly. She wondered why she wasn't fighting harder to leave this little town. But she felt as if she'd begun a story, and she wanted to stay around a couple of days to see what the characters did next. "Sounds like you're all set to make a false arrest."

Carl scowled. "Don't be telling me how to do my job."

Glory didn't answer, because there was a loud knock at the door. Well, it wasn't so much of a knock as it was a pounding. A very loud pounding. The sort of sound a crutch would make in the swinging arm of an impatient man.

"Open up!" The command came with the crutch pounding.

Carl Wall walked back to the door and swung it open.

There he stood. Her avenging angel. Glory swallowed. It must be a trick of light. Maybe the reflection of the snow outside. She'd read in her Bible about angels last night and her imagination was being overactive. But Matthew sure looked like Daniel's vision, even down to the halo of golden light surrounding his head. She mouthed the words silently. *"There stood a certain man—his face like the appearance of lightning, his eyes like torches of fire."*

Glory swallowed again. Definitely torches of fire.

"Your game's over," Matthew said, and stepped inside the room.

Glory started to breathe again. The halo of light didn't follow Matthew. It stayed just where it was and, when her eyes followed the beam downward, she saw the flashlight in Josh's mittened hands. The boy loved lights even in the day. She smiled. She wasn't crazy. It was artificial light. That's all. She was perfectly able to tell the difference between an angel of God and an ordinary man.

"You can't arrest her," Matthew said as he looked squarely at Carl Well. "She hasn't done anything illegal."

"Loitering," the deputy said smoothly. "There's always loitering."

"She wasn't loitering." Matthew took a deep breath.

"Then what was she doing in the hardware store?" the deputy pressed.

"Painting." Matthew paused.

"For pay?"

"No, not for pay, but—"

"Then it's loitering," the deputy said in satisfaction. "Next thing to panhandling. Street artists. If she's got no job, she's loitering."

"Well, if she needs a job, she's got a job," Matthew said in exasperation. "She's working for me."

Carl looked from Matthew to Glory and then back

to Matthew. The satisfied look on the deputy's face grew. "Told me she worked for the Seattle Police Department."

"Well, she doesn't. She's working for me," Matthew said forcefully, as though he could convince the deputy of his statement by the sheer pressure of his words. "As of today."

"But I—" Glory started to protest. Why was it these people were so willing to believe she was an angel and so reluctant to believe she worked for a police department? Which was more likely? Then she saw the look on Matthew's face. Pain was drawing his skin tight. He shouldn't be on his feet. She looked back at the deputy. "What difference does it make where I work—if you're going to arrest me, do it. If not, let me go."

"Arrest you? He can't arrest you!" Mrs. Hargrove pushed her way into the room and stood there looking solid and indignant.

"Don't be telling me how to do my job."

"I'm a voter and I can jolly well tell you how to do your job!" Mrs. Hargrove jabbed her finger in the deputy's face. "Besides, I've known you since you were in diapers. That ought to count for something."

Glory watched the muscles slowly coil in the deputy's face.

"Hmph!" Mrs. Hargrove crossed her arms and said smugly, "Can't lock her up anyway. We don't even have a jail."

"Well, I won't have to lock her up. I'll settle for a ticket if I can find an upstanding citizen to take responsibility for watching her—maybe see she does some community service." The deputy looked pleased with himself. "Yes, an upstanding citizen is just what I need. Maybe someone like a minister."

"But we don't have a minister, Carl Wall, and you know it," Mrs. Hargrove said indignantly.

"We would have if you'd given the nod to my cousin Fred," the deputy said smoothly.

"Your Fred isn't trained to be a pastor." Mrs. Hargrove put her hands on her hips. "Besides, he isn't even a believer."

"Well, he needs a job. He sent in his résumé. You didn't have any other applicants. In my book, that makes the job his."

"Being a pastor isn't just a job. It's a calling. Besides, it's a good thing for you we don't have a minister around." She drew in her breath sharply and looked at Matthew.

"If there's no minister, that leaves jail. I can always send her to the jail in Miles City."

"But that's an awful place," Mrs. Hargrove protested. "They're talking about closing it down. It's not even heated, just a big old cement block. You can't put someone in there in winter!"

"Well, it's not my first choice. But since you're too good to have the likes of Fred as a minister, I guess I don't have any other options now, do I?"

"The voters won't like this."

The deputy shrugged. "I tried to be reasonable. I'm sure Fred mentioned he was willing to read the Bible and get an idea of what the thing was all about. On-the-job training, so to speak. But no, you need to have someone who believes the whole thing. It's not too late. Fred's probably at home right now. We can call him and make the deal," he added smugly. "Remember, no minister means the angel goes to jail."

"But..." Mrs. Hargrove struggled to speak. "This is outrageous!"

"No minister means the angel goes to jail," the deputy repeated stubbornly.

"I'm a minister," Matthew said softly. It was freezing outside and still a thin sheen of sweat covered his forehead. "At least, according to the state. Marrying, burying—I can do all those. I expect I can keep my eye on an angel."

"You're a what?" The deputy looked skeptical.

"A minister." Matthew had a sinking feeling. He shouldn't have said anything. But he couldn't stand the thought of Glory spending time in that jail.

"You had a church?"

"Yes, in Havre."

"Well, why aren't you preaching here? We could use a minister at the church," the deputy persisted. "Even Fred would give way to a real preacher."

"I don't preach anymore," Matthew said evenly. His breath was shallow, but he was plowing his way through. He couldn't let his annoyance flare. Not if he wanted the deputy to cooperate.

"What? You retired from it?"

"In a way."

"Mighty young to be retired."

"Most people change jobs over a lifetime."

"But ministers?" the deputy asked, puzzled. "I've never known a minister to just quit his job before."

"Well, now you do," Matthew snapped. "Just let me know what I need to do to supervise the ang—I mean, Glory, and I'll do it."

"See, we do have a minister," Mrs. Hargrove said triumphantly. "God provides."

"Well, God isn't providing much," the deputy said as he nodded toward Matthew. "But I suppose it'll be all right." The deputy admitted defeat grudgingly. "I'll just write that ticket and you can set her up with some worthwhile community service. She works off the fine. If she messes up, she pays the fine. Simple. I'll check in later this week.''

"Community service?" Matthew asked in surprise. "Doing what? All our roads are snowpacked. We don't have a jail. Or a library. Not even a post office. We don't need anything done."

"Except," Mrs. Hargrove interrupted hesitantly, "we do need an angel for the Christmas pageant."

"Ah, yes, the pageant." Matthew sighed. Odd how this pageant had grown so big in the minds of everyone this year. Several of the churches in Miles City had decided to send a few visitors to Dry Creek for the annual Christmas Eve pageant. It all sounded very friendly. But Matthew knew enough about churches to know what was happening. A few do-gooders in Miles City had asked a handful of single people, likely mostly widows, to visit Dry Creek on Christmas Eve and they'd accepted, feeling righteous. No doubt it was a gracious way for the churches to deliver food baskets to some of the poorer families in Dry Creek. But even after they hosted their pageant, Matthew doubted the people of Dry Creek would accept charity. The people of Dry Creek were proud and they'd get by on their own or not at all. Food baskets from outsiders would not be welcome.

"We've got the costume—wings, robe, everything," Mrs. Hargrove continued, "All we need is the angel."

"That's settled, then," the deputy said as he pulled out his ticket book.

It wasn't settled at all in Glory's mind, but she decided to take the hastily scrawled ticket so the deputy would leave. There'd be no fine. She knew any judge would dismiss the charges when he saw the ticket. She'd save her objections for later.

The only reason Glory let Mrs. Hargrove talk her into looking at the costumes was so Matthew would sit down. He was being gallant and standing with his shoulder leaning on his crutch. At least if they moved to the costumes, he'd take a seat.

The costumes were stored in a small room on the other side of the church kitchen. Mrs. Hargrove pointed it out and then left with the children. The room had one small square window, high on the wall, and a single light bulb hanging from the ceiling. Glory stood on a small stool to pull down the angel wings. Matthew sat on a hard-backed chair in the corner of the room.

"Watch the dust," Matthew warned as Glory pulled the wings off the high shelf. Waves of dust floated down over her.

Glory sneezed. "Too late."

Yes, it is too late, Matthew thought to himself glumly. He'd vowed to keep his secret, and now it would be all over Dry Creek in minutes. And the irony was it wasn't true anymore. He was no more a minister than Glory was an angel. Less, in fact, because when she stood with her head in front of that single bulb, she at least looked like an angel. Flying copper hair with flecks of gold. Milky skin. A voice that melted over him like warm honey. He found himself wishing he were still a minister, that his life had been uncomplicated by searing grief and confused pain. He already knew Glory well enough to know she'd never settle for less than a godly man. A man of faith. A man he, Matthew, couldn't be anymore.

"I expect the halo's up there, too," Matthew added as Glory dusted off the white cardboard wings. He could see the strand of gold Christmas garland hanging over the top shelf.

"You know, I'd be happy to do something else for community service," Glory said as she pulled the old garland off the shelf. It had lost most of its glitter and all of its fluff. "I could give painting lessons or something."

Matthew didn't voice his protest. He'd developed a longing almost as intense as his sons to see Glory dressed up in an angel costume. "I think Henry has some gold garland at the store. You could use that if you want."

"I don't know." Glory sat down on the stool. A faint cloud of dust still fell down around her. "I just don't feel like an angel this year."

"Oh." Matthew didn't want to press. He hoped the one word was enough.

"Well, look at me," Glory said. "Here I am—broke, in a strange town, almost arrested, uncertain what to do next with my life."

"Yeah, I suppose angels never wonder what to do," Matthew agreed. For a minute he thought Glory was reading his mind and heart. Then he saw the confusion on her face. He shifted on his chair so he could see her better. "They just get their marching orders and they march. Piece of cake. But none of the excitement of being human."

"I guess the grass is always greener. We look at them. They look at us," Glory agreed quietly and then asked, "Do you believe angels are really jealous of us?"

"I'm not a minister anymore." Matthew began his standard disclaimer. He was no longer qualified to give spiritual advice. "I mean, I'm licensed still. But that's all. Just for the state."

"I figured that out," Glory said. When she'd heard Matthew admit to being a minister, she'd felt the pieces click in her heart. Matthew as a minister made sense. "But that's not why I'm asking. I just want to know what you think."

Matthew leaned back. He tried to separate what he believed from what he'd trained himself to believe. When he was a minister, he'd chased away any question, any doubt. He believed in confidence. Now he was just Matthew.

"Yes," Matthew finally said. "Yes, I think they must envy us. We can have babies."

Glory smiled. "I never thought of that."

Matthew caught his breath. He was grateful for the shadows that hid him in the small room. She was beautiful when she smiled. Like a Botticelli goddess.

"What's it like?" Glory asked quietly, and startled Matthew. For a second he thought she was reading his mind; then he realized she was talking about babies. "When you had the twins," she continued. "What was it like?"

"Like winning the World Series."

"I thought it might be something like that," she said. "I envy you."

"Someday you'll know what I mean," Matthew said. The picture of Glory with a baby glowed warm inside of him. He bet the little thing would have milk-white skin and red hair. "It's like no other feeling. I can't even describe it. You'll just have to wait and see for yourself."

"I guess so," Glory agreed. She didn't want to tell him that there was no point in waiting—she knew she'd never have a baby. The accident had snatched that dream away from her. It wasn't that she didn't think he'd understand. He'd obviously known pain in his life. Maybe he'd understand too well. She just didn't want to see pity fill his eyes when he looked at her. And what else could he feel but pity? That's one of the reasons she'd avoided becoming close to men. She didn't want to see that look in the eyes of someone she loved.

"Will you have more babies?" Glory asked, and then hurried on at the surprised look on Matthew face. "I mean, if you remarried, would you want to have more children?"

"Children are the trump card in life. I'd have as many as I could."

Glory nodded. That was good. It was as it should be. He was a good father. His sons were good. It was all very good. It just didn't include anyone like her. "I'd like to go look for that garland now."

Matthew watched the light leave Glory's face. She put the cardboard wings under her arm and headed for the door. He had no choice but to follow.

The cold air hit Glory in the face and pinched the color out of her cheeks. It was only a hundred feet between the door to the hardware store and the door to the church, but it felt as if the few steps iced her to the soul. She needed to stop thinking about babies that would never be born. Her guilt was over. Her mother had forgiven her. God had forgiven her. Some days she'd even managed to forgive herself. It was over. She needed to stop grieving.

The smell of coffee greeted her when she stepped back into the warmth of the hardware store. Elmer and Jacob were still arguing.

"Heard them federal boys are going to close in on the rustlers now that they figured it isn't just happening here," Jacob insisted.

Elmer waved the words away. "They aren't even close. They don't know how. Why or when. What've they got? Nothing."

"They'll find them at the inspection plants, now that they're requiring papers before they grade the meat," Jacob said almost fiercely. "They'll find them. They've got to."

Elmer opened his mouth and then saw Glory. His mouth hung open for a full minute before it formed into an excited oval. He turned to Jacob and gummed his mouth several times before he got the words out. "Blazes, why didn't we think of it before?"

"Huh?"

"Look at her." Elmer pointed to Glory.

Glory's heard sank. She had a feeling she was falling deeper.

"She's a government agent," Elmer said triumphantly. "I heard rumors they were hiring a civilian to look into the cattle problem. She's a spy."

Glory shook her head. First angels and then spies. "You boys need to get out more."

"Don't worry, we understand," Elmer said with a wink. "You don't want to blow your cover."

"I don't have a cover," Glory said patiently as she heard the door open behind her. A gust of wind blew against her back and then stopped as the door closed.

"Why would you need a cover?" Matthew said as he used his crutch to hobble over to the counter. The dreams of Glory in his bed had stayed with him all day. "Didn't the twins get you an extra blanket last night?"

Glory blushed. "It's not that kind of cover." Glory

pulled herself together. Maybe she'd sleep on the floor tonight. It didn't seem quite right to sleep in Matthew's bed. "They mean cover like spy cover. They think I'm a spy for the government. Looking into some cattle business."

Matthew leaned his crutch against the counter. So that was it. Maybe it was business that brought a woman like her to a small town on the backside of Montana.

"You never did say why you were driving through," he said, keeping his voice light and casual. She'd be a good spy. That innocent look of hers hid a quick mind. He wondered if she worked for the FBI or the Department of Agriculture. "Or where you were headed."

"I wasn't headed anywhere. I was just driving," Glory said.

"It's winter. Most folks don't go driving through Montana for pleasure this time of year," Matthew countered. The passes were slippery over the Rockies and even the flatlands had their share of ice and snow. No, Montana wasn't a pleasant drive in the winter.

Glory shrugged. "I'm not most folks."

She had him there, Matthew thought. There was nothing ordinary or plain about her. She was the exotic orchid of the flower kingdom. The red-hot pepper of the spice family. The flaming gold of the color spectrum. He had a fleeting desire to tell her so. But then a thought came from left field and slugged him in the stomach. If she was undercover, she was someone else in another life. She could be someone's mother. She could be someone's daughter. Worse yet, she could be someone's wife.

"I could talk to the deputy if you've got somewhere else to be on Christmas," Matthew said. His stomach muscles tensed. She'd want to be with her husband on Christmas if she had one. "He can't hold you here."

"I'd thought about spending Christmas with my mother."

Matthew's stomach knotted. The mother could be a husband as easily as he stood here. "In Seattle?"

Glory nodded.

"You won't have a white Christmas there," Matthew offered. It was none of his business if she had another life that had nothing to do with Dry Creek, but he couldn't stop himself. "The twins would love to have you stay."

Glory stopped her head from nodding. She'd love to spend Christmas with the twins as much as they wanted her to spend it with them. But she had more wisdom than the twins. She knew that sometimes a day's happiness came with a price tag attached. If she stayed for Christmas, she'd regret it later when she had to leave. And leave she would. Because as much as she might dream about a life with someone like Matthew, she wasn't the woman for him.

No one could accuse the churches in Spokane of being quiet. It was prayer meeting night, and the Bullet sat first on the outside steps of one church and then another. He heard it all. John 3:16. "Amazing Grace." The Lord's Prayer. He'd felt a little self-conscious just sitting outside, but he did anyway. He wasn't fit to go inside, and he knew it. Besides, he needed to be at the door before anyone came out so he could be sure to see the woman if she left.

His plan earned him a few curious looks, but he congratulated himself on doing fine until he reached a church on the east side.

"Give me a hand," the old man asked as he started to climb the stairs.

The Bullet looked around, but everyone else was already inside the church. There was no one to help the man but him.

Chapter Five

Matthew was true to his word, Glory thought. Dinner her second night not only didn't float in milk, it didn't come from a cardboard box, either. He made a salmon loaf, baked potatoes and green beans. There were fresh chives for the baked potatoes and mushrooms in the green beans. Betty Crocker couldn't have done better.

"I could help," Glory said for the tenth time since Matthew had shooed her out of the kitchen. She listened to pans rattle as she sat on the sofa and Matthew did dishes. Glory tried to remember if she'd ever had a man make her dinner before—and then insist on doing the dishes even though he was on crutches. Not that Matthew had made the dinner especially for her, she reminded herself. The twins had needed dinner, too.

"Please, let me help. I'm not used to being waited on." She started to get up from the sofa.

Matthew grunted from the kitchen. "Stay put. Do you good to take it easy."

Two pairs of twin arms reached up to pull her back to the sofa.

"Don't angels have daddies to cook for them?" Joey asked quietly as she settled back down. He pressed so close to her she could feel his worry. "I told my daddy he needed to make angel food cake. Maybe then you'd stay."

Glory smoothed back the hair on Joey's forehead. "You don't need to feed me angel cake."

"We had to give our fish some fish food. That's all they ate," Josh added solemnly as though she hadn't spoken. He was on her other side. "They ate and ate, but they died anyway."

"Do fish go to heaven when they die?" Joey looked up at her quizzically.

"No, silly," Josh answered for her. "There's no water in heaven. Only clouds. Isn't that right?" He looked to Glory for reinforcement and then added scornfully, "Besides, fish can't be angels. They can't fly."

"You know, we should learn about angels," Glory said decisively. She remembered her father always took this tactic when she was a child. Everything led to a lesson. Once the twins learned about real angels, maybe they'd let her be human. The truth did set people free, even if those people were only five years old. "Let me go get a Bible."

"We got one." Josh ran to a shelf and pulled down an old black Bible. The gold lettering on the front said "Family Bible," and the back of the leather cover looked as if it had been scorched. Josh carried the Bible to her as if it was a basket of precious jewels. Glory put her fingers to the burned mark around the edge just to be sure. So, she thought, smiling, something had been snatched from that fire after all. There was hope for Matthew yet.

"Are you going to tell us about an angel?" Joey asked, his voice low and excited.

Glory flipped through the Bible. She knew just the angel for the boys. "Not only an angel, but some big cats, too."

Glory saw their eyes grow big.

"The king made a rule…" Glory said, beginning to paraphrase chapter six of Daniel. She knew the story well. She didn't need to read it from the Bible that lay on her lap.

The twins listened to the king's dilemma and the story of his evil advisors.

"Finally the king had no choice. He'd been tricked. He needed to put Daniel in a den with big cats called lions."

"Mrs. Hargrove told us about the lions," Joey whispered as he moved closer to Glory. "They eat people."

Josh shivered and snuggled closer to her other side. "I want a dog. No cats."

"These are special cats." Glory put an arm around each boy. They both shifted closer. "Not like the cats you know. Much, much bigger than the cats around here."

"A trillion times bigger?" Josh asked. He was clearly relishing the story.

"Almost. And there's no need to be afraid. There aren't any lions around here."

The twins looked momentarily disappointed and then Josh said. "But there's cats. Mr. Gossett next door has cats. They'll get you."

"Cats might scratch you, but they won't eat you."

"But they're *Mr. Gossett's* cats," Josh said as though that explained everything. "He doesn't eat. He drinks his meals. Mrs. Hargrove says."

"Maybe his cats don't eat, either." Joey took up the thought excitedly. "Maybe they lick you instead. Like an ice cream cone. Maybe that's how they eat. Lick, lick, lick—then you're gone. I've seen them lick people." He shivered. "I don't want them to lick me."

"You can't get licked away." Glory had forgotten how much young boys liked to flirt with danger. "Or get drunk away. Or bitten away. You're completely safe with cats."

Glory showed the twins the picture in the Bible. The reds and blues of the scene had faded, but the lions looked scary. And the angel still looked majestic with his flowing white robes and golden hair.

"That's an angel," Joey said in awe as he traced the picture. "With real wings."

Glory felt a pair of little hands reach up and lightly touch her shoulder blades as though checking.

"No wings," she assured them.

Matthew turned the light off in the kitchen and leaned against the doorway leading to the living room. He'd built a fire earlier, and the light made Glory and his sons look golden. Their heads were bent together over a book, two little blond heads with a bronze one in the middle. He had heard the excited whispers as he washed the dishes in the kitchen. He felt a swell of contentment fill him. He'd do more than wash a few dishes to give his sons time with a woman like Glory.

Then the shadows shifted, and Matthew saw what the three were reading. He tensed. The Bible. He'd bought that Bible when the twins were born. Susie had used it to record the twins' births—their weight, height and first gestures. They'd planned to be a family around that Bible. He and Susie had read from it for family devotions when the twins were in their strollers. They'd planned to record their anniversaries in the book and the births of more babies.

"It's time for bed," Matthew said abruptly. He supposed he shouldn't be surprised the twins had found the Bible. It wasn't hidden. He just hadn't expected to deal with their claim on it so soon.

"Aah," Josh groaned. "We were just at the good part."

"We can finish it tomorrow night," Glory said as she hugged each of the boys and then took her arm away so they could scoot off the sofa.

"Can we get a den?" Josh turned to Matthew. "Ricky's family has a den."

"Different kind of den." Glory tried to pluck the thought from him before he got going in that direction. "This kind of den is a cave. It's made from rock. All dark inside."

"Oh." Josh seemed to be thinking.

Matthew smiled. He didn't tell Glory, but he already knew a den would be made from blankets tomorrow. Josh loved acting. "Get washed up and I'll tuck you in." The boys ran out of the room.

"You can't!" Alarms went off in Glory's stomach. All thoughts of cats and dens vanished. *Tuck them in! Tucking in meant Matthew upstairs in the twins' room!* Matthew wasn't supposed to be able to climb stairs. She wasn't sure she wanted him to see the cocoon she'd built in his bed last night. She'd wrapped blankets around herself snugly, but she'd lined up one of his pillows to lie beside her in the night. She'd told the twins the pillow was her teddy bear, but a grown man would...well, he might see it differently.

"Figure of speech," Matthew said as he watched

Glory's face. The gold from the fire and the blush fanning out over her face made her look like rare porcelain. "I meant I'd give them a kiss good-night. Down here, of course."

"Of course." Glory smoothed down her skirt. "I should go up, too."

"It's only seven-thirty," Matthew protested as he lowered himself onto the sofa and propped his crutches against the wall. His shoulders ached and the palms of his hands burned where he leaned on the crossbar of the crutch. He should be thinking of sleep himself, but he was wide-awake. It occurred to him that his twins weren't the only ones who missed having some quiet time with a woman. "Sit with me for a while and talk."

Glory hesitated. The sofa that had seemed so large when she and the twins were sitting on it seemed to have shrunk now that Matthew was on the other end. She didn't want to be skittish and scoot over to the edge of the sofa, but she wasn't sure it felt safe to be within reaching distance of Matthew. Not that she expected him to reach for her, she told herself. Be reasonable. He only wants some light conversation after a day's work.

Matthew watched the reluctance streak across her face, and he remembered Elmer's words about her being an undercover agent. He wondered if she was remembering a husband or boyfriend who laid claim to her real life. He sure wished he knew if she was undercover.

"We don't usually have salmon, not even canned—not this close to the Big Sheep Mountains," he began. His mouth was dry. He wasn't used to entrapping a federal agent. "These mountains are cattle country through and through. Folks here pride themselves on beefsteaks, even now with all the..." He deliberately let his voice trail off to see if she'd pick up the scent like a federal agent would.

"Yes, the rustling." Glory latched on to the topic with relief. Nothing could be more impersonal than beefsteaks, she thought to herself with satisfaction. "How long has that been going on? Tell me everything you know."

Matthew's heart sank. She'd taken the bait with gusto. Maybe she was an agent, after all. Why else would a woman from out of town care about the rustling? "Cattle have been missing for the past year, I suppose. Probably started last winter. They free range most of the cattle around here in the winter, and so they don't do a complete count until the snow thaws and it comes close to calving time."

"Surely they don't leave those cows out all winter?" Glory asked in alarm.

Matthew smiled. That narrowed the field some. Unless she was a very good actress, she didn't work for the Department of Agriculture. "They have windbreaks set up, sometimes sheds, and the cows grow a thick coat. If it's real cold they can always wander down to the fences and someone will let them into the barn area. And they drop bales of hay to them, by pickup mostly. In bad winters they've dropped hay from small planes or helicopters."

"Well, maybe there's no rustling at all," Glory offered. She was having a hard time concentrating now that Matthew had started rubbing his shoulder. The crutches must be giving him trouble. His hands were what were giving her trouble. They were large and muscled, lightly haired and lightly tanned. "Maybe the cows are still out there."

"That's why it's so hard to know for sure when it all started," Matthew admitted. His hands found the knot in his shoulder and he sighed as he rubbed it. "A few cows here and there—who knows? Maybe they're holed up in a gully somewhere. But the Big Sheep Mountain Ranch has had their hands riding all over the range—covered it with a fine-tooth comb and didn't find the cattle or any carcasses. There needs to be one or the other. Even the buzzards can't carry off a whole cow."

"Sounds just like the Old West," Glory said. She'd never given too much thought to the life of a cow. Or a buzzard. Or a cowboy. "Is it the Big Sheep Mountain Ranch that's thinking of becoming a dude ranch?"

Matthew winced. His fingers had hit a nerve on his shoulder. "They don't call it dude ranch around here. I think the politically correct term is guest ranch. Doesn't offend the 'guests' as much. And, yes, it is the Big Sheep. If they follow through. They've had some tourism consultant down from Helena. It appears the scenery around the Big Sheep Mountains is as valuable as the cows. Maybe more so when you throw in the fact that we've got the Tongue River and the Yellowstone River close by and we're not far from Medicine Rock State Park. Some say we're the not-so-bad part of the Badlands, too."

"Well, at least the town will survive, then." Glory bit her lip. She shouldn't say anything, but Matthew was going to be even more sore after he finished trying to massage his one shoulder. His angle was all wrong.

"There's survival and there's survival. Some folks think the dudes will change the town so much we might as well lie down and die in the first place. Go with dignity. Elmer keeps going on about how he doesn't want to have to look the part of a rancher when he's face-to-face with some fancy lawyer who's only coming here for two weeks to pretend he does something real with his life. Says the old ghosts of all those cowhands that used to ride for the XIT Ranch in its glory will rise up and protest if we sell out like that."

"What do the women think?" Glory shifted on the sofa. Now Matthew was both massaging at the wrong angle and twisting his shoulder the wrong way, too. He'd throw his back out if he wasn't careful.

Matthew chuckled. "Mrs. Hargrove is all set to evangelize the dudes."

Glory couldn't stand it any longer. "Here. Let me massage that for you. You're going to end up back in the clinic."

Glory stood behind the sofa and put her hands on Matthew's shoulder. She'd kneaded the shoulders of a fair number of tired cops in her day down at the station. This shouldn't be any different. It shouldn't matter that firelight instead of fluorescent light streamed into the room or that her heart beat a little too fast when she touched one particular man's shoulders.

Matthew sighed. Maybe Glory was an angel, after all. Her touch certainly put him in mind of heaven.

"Well, Mrs. Hargrove might do some good that way." Glory refocused on the conversation. She needed to concentrate. "With her evangelistic zeal."

"I don't know about that. You know as well as I do they'll only see her as 'local scenery.' A person has a right to be taken more seriously than that. I'd rather folks openly disagreed with her rather than see her as scenery."

"What was it Paul said? 'I am all things to all men

whereby I might win some.'" Glory located the knot on Matthew's neck and rubbed it gently.

"He didn't mention anything about being scenery."

Glory felt the knot on Matthew's neck tighten beneath her fingers. He was even more tense now than when she'd started.

Glory had a flash of insight. "Was that what it was like for you?"

"Huh?" Matthew looked up at her too quickly.

"Being a minister," Glory said softly, and stopped massaging him. "Was that what it seemed like when you were a minister?"

Matthew took a deep breath and exhaled. How did she know? "Only at the end."

"After Susie died?"

Matthew nodded. "I was standing up there in front of the congregation and I felt so empty inside. Like I was only the picture of a minister standing in a pulpit. Like none of it was real."

"Grief will do that to you."

Matthew shook his head. He'd thought about this every day since he'd made the decision to walk away from that pulpit. "A real minister would have been able to cope. Oh, maybe not easily, but somehow. If I'm not able to be a minister in the bad times, what kind of a minister am I in the good times?"

"A human minister," Glory reassured him emphatically. She saw the defeat on his face. And the sorrow.

The sound of little feet padding swiftly down the steps distracted them both.

"I'm first," claimed Josh as he flung himself into his father's arms.

There goes one good massage wasted, Glory thought wryly. Pain didn't stop Matthew. He opened his arms wide enough to gather both boys to him. No matter what Matthew thought about his role as a minister, it was clear that his role as a father came naturally to him. Love between Matthew and his sons was a given. It was the bedrock of the twins' lives.

"Kiss?" Josh had left his father's arms and now stood before Glory.

Glory smiled. "Of course." She leaned down and hugged Josh. Then she gave him an exaggerated kiss, the kind she'd loved as a child. She "smacked" Josh so hard on the cheek that he started to giggle. Then she offered her own cheek. "Now me."

Josh puckered up and put his lips on her cheek for a big smack.

"Now Joey." Glory saw Joey was hanging back shyly. When she opened her arms to him he smiled and ran up to her. She repeated the ritual with him.

Then both twins went to the edge of the sofa and knelt down as if it was the expected thing to do. This was obviously their habit.

"God bless…" Josh ran down his list first and then Joey followed. They both blessed classmates, Mrs. Hargrove, their father, the angel and even Mr. Gossett's cats.

Glory had to admit she was surprised. The night before she'd been upstairs putting clean sheets on her bed when the twins had made their trip down for a kiss. She'd had no idea Matthew prayed with them. Correction, she thought to herself, Matthew didn't pray with them, he watched over them while they prayed. Rather fiercely at that, as though challenging God to refuse their simple requests.

"Susie would have my hide if I didn't raise them to pray," Matthew said when the twins had gone upstairs.

"But don't they wonder why you don't pray?"

"We haven't really come to that bridge yet." Matthew picked up the family Bible, intending to stand up and put it back on the shelf. But then he realized he couldn't stand, not holding the crutches and the Bible. So he set the Bible back down on the coffee table. "So far they just assume I pray beside my bed when it's my bedtime. Since I have a later bedtime, they don't see me."

"Before too long, they're going to realize—"

"I know. I'm a coward. I keep hoping that maybe by the time they're old enough to ask the question they'll be old enough to understand." Matthew shifted his shoulder. He wished Glory would massage his neck again.

"I hope you're right." Glory watched fatigue and pain sketch lines on Matthew's face as he sat there. "Your shoulder still hurt?"

"Yes."

Glory stood up and walked behind the sofa. She reached down and began to knead Matthew's neck muscles again. This time she felt him relax. He leaned his head back and closed his eyes. The light from the fireplace gave a golden cast to his face. She had a swift urge to lift her hands from his neck and trace the line of his jaw. The suddenness and the strength of the feeling surprised her. Abruptly she pulled her hands away from him. "You need your sleep. I should be going upstairs."

Matthew's eyes opened. "You're really good at giving neck massages."

"Experienced, anyway," Glory said. She was glad she was standing behind him and he couldn't see that her face was flushed. "I give them all the time to the men in the department."

"The police department?" Matthew asked warily. He remembered that's where she said she worked. He supposed it was possible. The FBI might borrow someone like her to do a little preliminary research on cattle rustling. She would find out things a regular agent wouldn't. Just look how the folks in Dry Creek had already taken to her. She inspired confidences. He certainly found it easy to talk to her. Too easy.

Glory nodded. "The captain taught me. He used to give them, too. Said it was one thing a policeman always needed." Glory was chattering and she knew it. But it helped her collect her composure. She'd never had these feelings while giving a neck massage to anyone else. "From all the time in the patrol cars. And then the stress."

Matthew listened. Okay, so the police department angle was true. He didn't think Glory would lie. Not even if she was undercover.

Glory didn't stop. "Some of the worst stress. The captain used to say being on patrol was like being squeezed into a little box for hours and then stepping out for a few seconds to get shot at."

Shot at! Matthew stiffened. "You don't work where you get shot at, do you?" The thought of anyone shooting anywhere near Glory made him want to lock her in the house and never let her out. He hadn't thought about the undercover job in that regard. Surely no one would shoot at Glory.

"Well, not often—"

"*Not often!* What's not often?"

"Well...usually not really," Glory said, stumbling.

Matthew relaxed. "That's good. But just for my

peace of mind, tell me, when was the last time someone shot at you?''

"Last Wednesday."

"Last Wednesday!" Matthew turned around and looked at her. She was already making her way to the stairs. "That's not often? *Last Wednesday!*"

"But it was nothing. Just some gang kids."

"Nothing! I don't care if it was kids, their bullets are just as real!''

Matthew stood up. He forgot he needed the crutch. He didn't even feel the pain in his knee. He knew he didn't have the right to order Glory to quit her job. But last Wednesday! She made it sound as if getting shot at was an everyday thing.

"Well, their bullets are not as straight as some," Glory said softly. She had one foot on the first stair and she smiled. She could tell Matthew that last Wednesday was the only time a bullet had come anywhere near her, that her job was as safe as being a plumber—but she found she liked the fierce look of protection that covered his face. In the firelight, with his chestnut hair mussed from the massage, he looked like a Highland warrior.

Matthew stopped himself from demanding that she quit her job. It was not his place. He knew that. But surely someone should stop her. "What does your mother think about that?"

"My mother thinks I'm a grown woman," Glory said. It was true. Her mother had been shocked that a bullet had hit the building close to where Glory was standing. But she hadn't worried about Glory's ability to take care of herself. Only the captain ever worried about her.

"Well, there's no doubt about you being grown."

Matthew ran his hand over his hair. He was beginning to feel the pain in his knee, and he sank back down to the sofa. "It's just, well, bullets. That's not good."

"I'll be fine," Glory said softly. She was touched he would worry about her. "I really don't get shot at often."

Matthew snorted and shook his head. "Not often. Last Wednesday."

"Not often," Glory repeated firmly as her feet climbed the second stair. She felt a smile curling around inside her. He cared about her. Matthew cared. Well, she thought as she tried to rein in her happiness, he cared that someone didn't shoot at her. It might not be so much after all. Even a stranger might care that she not be shot and killed. Or run over by a truck. Or fall off a building.

"Say, who fixed the step?" Thinking of tragic accidents reminded her of the loose board that had tripped Matthew the day before. Only it wasn't loose any longer. She saw the bright heads of the new nails that held the board firmly in place.

"I did."

"But you can't get up these stairs?" Glory measured the distance. The loose board had been near the top of the stairs. She looked down at Matthew sitting on the sofa in the firelight.

"I can if I do a kind of backward crawl—push, sit, push." Matthew looked up at her and grinned. "Mrs. Hargrove didn't think about crawling."

"No, I guess she didn't."

Mrs. Hargrove might not have thought about it, but Glory couldn't think of anything else. She thought about it when she brushed her teeth and slipped on her pajamas. She thought about it when she turned down the sheets on Matthew's bed. She even thought about it as she lay slipping into dreamland. And every time she thought about it she smiled. Matthew's virtue, not his knee, kept him downstairs. That was as it should be. She didn't want to start getting attached to a man she couldn't trust— What? The thought pulled her away from sleep and made her sit up straight in bed. Attached? Was she getting attached to Matthew? She knew she was a little attracted to him. Okay, a lot attracted to him. But attached and attracted were two different things. She couldn't afford to be attached. They had no future together. No future at all. And she'd best remember that. She couldn't afford to get attached. No, there must be no attachment. Absolutely none.

The Bullet carefully cut into his piece of lemon meringue pie.

His plans hadn't worked out. He hadn't counted on the floor inside the church being wet from all the rain. But when they reached the doorway, the Bullet saw the slickness. The old man didn't walk very well and the Bullet worried he might slip. *I can see him to his pew. Then I'll leave. Just a quick dive in and then I'll be gone.*

But the hymn started before he got the old man settled, and a woman pressed a hymnal into his hands.

After the service the old man, Douglas was his name, insisted on buying him a piece of pie. The Bullet gave up. What would it hurt to sit with the man a bit and have a piece of pie?

Chapter Six

The hoofbeats in Glory's dream turned to pounding. She woke uncertain if the pounding was real or in her head. It took a minute to remember where she was, but in the half-light of morning the room was beginning to look familiar. Matthew's room. She was safe in Matthew's room. But something had startled her, she decided. There, she heard it again. A pounding from downstairs.

Matthew was in the kitchen starting the fire when he heard the first pound on the door. He hadn't brought his crutches with him, but had hobbled from sofa to wall to doorway to chair so that he wouldn't need to prop them up when he lit the stove. It was a good plan, but it didn't get him to the front door any too soon.

"What's wrong?" Matthew yelled when he finally pulled the door open.

There stood Duane Edison, a slender teenager with dark hair that needed cutting and a scowl on his lean face that needed tending. The boy paused for a moment before demanding. "I need to talk to the angel."

Matthew didn't open the door any farther. "Can't it wait for morning?"

"It is morning," Duane said in surprise. "It's past six. The sun's even coming up."

"Not everyone lives on Montana farm time. She doesn't get up at five."

"I'm up." Glory could hear them as she walked down the stairs. She'd thrown a woolly robe on over her pajamas and put a pair of heavy socks on her feet. Her hair wasn't combed and her teeth weren't brushed, but she was up. "What's wrong?"

"You the angel?" Duane asked as he peered past Matthew's shoulder.

"Around here I guess I am." Glory sat down on the sofa. She was too tired to debate the fact before she'd even had any coffee. "What do you need?"

"You the one that got Linda all funny on me?" Duane entered the house.

"Aah, you're the Music man." Glory remembered.

"Jazz Man," Duane said, tight-lipped. The cold had pinched his face and left it colorless. He wore a black leather jacket and had his hands jammed far down into his pockets. "I'm the Jazz Man."

"Of course, I remember." Glory pulled her robe closer. It was cold in the house. "You're her boyfriend."

"Was her boyfriend," he corrected her sourly as he joined her on the other end of the sofa. He took his hands out of his pockets and rubbed them together. He looked up at Matthew. "Want me to start a fire for you?"

"Just got one started. It takes a few minutes to warm up. But thanks for the offer."

"Heard about your leg," Duane mumbled. "Need any help, let me know."

"Thanks. I appreciate that."

"It's not like I have lots to do now, anyway." The boy looked sideways at Glory. "Not since Linda gave me her ultimatum."

"Well, it's not like it needs to be forever. You kids are awfully young to get married." Glory stuck by her decision. Neither one of them looked a day over sixteen. It might not even be legal for them to marry without parental consent. "Way too young."

"Oh, we're still getting married." Duane looked up at her in determination. "It's just that now she wants a prenuptial agreement, says she won't even—" He stopped himself and looked at Matthew. "Well, you know, she won't—unless I sign an agreement." He looked at Matthew again, measuring him. "Is it true you're a preacher?"

"Was a preacher." Matthew nodded. Dry Creek didn't need a newspaper to get the news around. "Not anymore."

"Still, you probably don't…" Duane hesitated and then he hurried on. "I mean, you don't know what it's like."

Matthew squelched his chuckle. "I was a minister. I wasn't a eunuch. I know about sex and the trouble it can cause."

"It can get you into trouble, all right," Duane agreed with a sigh.

Glory decided the room was definitely getting warmer, even without the fire. "What kind of trouble are you and Linda in?"

"Oh, not that kind." Duane blushed. "We're careful."

"You wouldn't need to be careful if you didn't—" Glory stopped herself. If she knew anything about teenagers it was that one didn't inspire confidences by scolding them for the obvious. "What trouble is it, then?"

"It's money."

"Money?" Glory was surprised.

"Yeah, we need money if we're going to get married. Five thousand dollars."

"Why five thousand?"

"If we had five thousand we could put a down payment on the old Morgan place, not John's place, but his father's old place. It's not much, but it's good dry land and it's got a small house. Needs a new roof, but I could fix that. Already talked to the bank in Billings. They said we'd need five thousand at least. But neither of our folks have that to spare—couldn't ask them, anyway. So that's why I thought of music. I play a fair guitar and Linda sings real good. My friend Bob is good on the drums. Thought maybe we'd pick up some money at small county fairs and rodeos. Nothing big." Duane's face glowed proudly while he talked about their dream. "We'd have done it, too, except, well, you talked to Linda and..."

Glory's heart sank. "I didn't mean she should never marry you. Why, you both must still be in high school."

"Graduated last fall. Both of us."

"That'd make you how old?" Glory wasn't feeling any better. Giving love advice wasn't her calling in life. She should have sent the girl back to her mother.

"I'm nineteen. Linda's eighteen. We hadn't planned on going to college, so I've been helping my folks and Linda's working at a doughnut place in Miles City.

We've both been saving our money, but so far all we
have is twelve hundred dollars. That's why I thought
of forming the band. Thought we'd maybe even get
some Christmas gigs.''

"I know some retirement homes up near Havre that
might be willing to pay for a music program," Matthew
said. His minister friends would be so happy to hear
from him they'd probably pay the kids twice the usual
rate. "That's if you know any church music."

"We grew up in Sunday school," Duane said indignantly. "We know them all from 'The Old Rugged
Cross' to 'This Little Light of Mine.'"

"Well, that sounds like a good plan," Glory said.
"Tell Linda to invite me to the wedding."

"Oh, she'll have to be the one inviting, all right,"
Duane said with a bitter edge to his voice. "After the
prenuptial agreement, she'll make all the decisions."

"What?"

"The prenuptial," he repeated as though she must
know. "She said you told her not to let me take advantage of her talent, so the prenup puts her in charge
of everything. She's the lead singer. The money person.
First on the deed to the Morgan place when we sign
the paper. First in everything." Duane slumped down
on the sofa. "She's even the one calling the shots
about, well, you know…. Even kissing," he wailed indignantly. "Everything. She's in charge."

"Oh, dear," Glory murmured as her eyes met Matthew's over the slumped figure of Duane. Matthew's
eyes had a sympathetic twinkle in them.

Matthew leaned over and whispered to Glory, "Not
as easy as a person would think to be an angel. Lot
like being a preacher. Everyone expects you to always
know everything and always be right."

"Well, they picked the wrong person for always being right."

"No one's ever always right."

"How do I fix things now?"

Matthew straightened. "Duane, why don't you bring Linda here for supper tonight? Glory and I will talk to her."

"I hope you'll set her straight," Duane muttered as he stood. "A man can't have his wife wearing the pants in the family."

"There's nothing wrong with a woman making decisions," Glory began indignantly. "Most women have good heads on their shoulders."

"She going to be talking to Linda?" Duane looked at Matthew skeptically and cocked his thumb at Glory.

"You don't have a clue, do you, son?" Matthew put his arm around Duane's slender shoulders. "Being married isn't about one person making all the decisions. Being married is about teamwork. And a good team takes the best from both parties."

"Yes, sir," Duane agreed glumly as he walked toward the door.

"See you and Linda tonight at five-thirty," Matthew said as he opened the door for the young man. "And remember, think teamwork."

"Yes, sir."

Matthew waited for the door to completely close before he grinned and announced, "How about we start out with you talking to Duane? Then we switch."

"Sort of like good cop, bad cop?"

"Just giving them two perspectives."

"I don't think Duane wants two perspectives."

"That's why he needs them," Matthew said as he hobbled back to the kitchen door, whistling all the way.

Glory studied his face. It wasn't just the whistling. He was excited. "You like this, don't you? This people stuff. Giving advice. Solving problems. Helping out."

Matthew turned around as he reached the kitchen. "Yeah, I guess I do."

Glory fretted about Linda and Duane until she turned the key in the hardware-store door. Matthew was late taking the twins to school, so he'd asked her to open up for him so that Elmer and Jacob could get their coffee.

"Brrr." Glory watched her breath turn white. The hardware store was as cold inside as it was outside. "It'll take more than coffee to take the edge off this morning."

"It's a cold snap, all right," Elmer agreed. "Almost didn't get the pickup started to come down."

Yesterday Glory had set up her easel close to the front window of the hardware store. The night cold had frosted over the edges of the large window, but the middle was clear. She could look out and see the whole main street of Dry Creek.

Coffee could wait a minute, she decided. The view from this window was postcard perfect.

The Big Sheep Mountains stood solid and round in the distance, their low peaks wearing blankets of fresh velvety snow. About halfway down, the thick snow changed to thin gray patches mingled with muddy-green shrubs. On the frozen ground right outside in Dry Creek, old snow lined the asphalt street and bunched up against the buildings.

"How long has this town been here?" Glory asked as she turned to Elmer and Jacob. The two men were putting wood in the fire.

"Since the days of the Enlarged Homestead Act of 1909," Elmer said as he put a match to the kindling. "Folks—a lot of them from Scandinavia—came here. Trainloads of them—a body could lay claim to 320 acres of Montana and all they had to do was live on it for three years. Sounded like a dream come true."

Elmer paused to put his hands out to the warming fire. "Course, they couldn't predict the drought. And the hard times. Wasn't long before people all over these parts were leaving. They couldn't scrape together enough to plant crops, to eat, to live. But old man Gossett—father to the Gossett who lives next to the parsonage—owned the land here and he told folks we'd make it if we worked together. That's when they founded the town—called it Dry Creek after a little creek that used to flow into the Yellowstone. Folks thought the creek would come back after the drought ended and we could change the name of the town. The creek didn't return, but we kept the name. Kinda liked it after a while. Reminded us things have been worse. Gave us hope. We've always scraped by in Dry Creek before and we'll do it again."

"Hmph," Jacob added as he shut the door to the old woodstove.

Glory didn't know if he was agreeing or disagreeing "What do the young people do?" She was still thinking of Duane and Linda. "Do they stay or move away?"

"Most leave," Elmer said with a touch of scorn as he reached behind him for the electric coffeemaker. "There's not much work here and what work there is is hard work. Kids nowadays want it easy."

"Can't blame the kids for wanting to eat." Jacob defended them as he measured coffee into the filter.

"Maybe you need to start some kind of business here," Glory offered as she walked closer to the fire and rubbed her hands "I've read about Midwestern towns that brought in businesses so there'd be jobs for people. Maybe you could try that."

Elmer gave a bitter chuckle. "You see the window there. Look out it. Do you see anything that would make a big corporation move here?"

"I didn't say it needed to be a big corporation," Glory persisted as she spread her hands out to catch the heat that was already coming from the small cast-iron stove. "All you need is a few small businesses. Maybe an outfit that makes something."

"The women at the church made up a batch of jams one year that were good—I always thought they could sell them," Jacob said thoughtfully as he put his wooden chair in front of the fire.

"Well, that would be a start," Glory said as the bell over the door rang. A gust of cold air followed Matthew into the store. "Maybe they could hook up with a catalog. Do special orders. It'd definitely be a start."

The crutches kept Matthew from swiveling to close the door quickly, so another gust of cold came in before he got the door shut. "Sorry." Matthew wiped some fresh snowflakes off his wool coat. "Start of what?"

"Glory was thinking of new business ideas for Dry Creek," Elmer informed him as the coffee started to perk.

"What kind of businesses?" Matthew asked as he took off his jacket and hung it on a nail behind the counter.

Glory tried not to look, but the snowflakes made Matthew's hair shine. He had flakes on his eyelashes and eyebrows. The cold drew the skin tight against his cheeks and forehead. Lean a pair of skis against his shoulder and he could be an advertisement for sweaters or skis or some resort. He could be a model.

"Any kind of business." Glory shrugged. "Jams. Woodworking. Modeling."

"Modeling? You mean sitting for a painting?" Matthew asked thoughtfully. "Would anyone pay for that?"

"I've heard they do if you're nude." Jacob poured himself a cup of coffee.

"I wasn't thinking of nude modeling." Glory blushed.

"Kind of artistic for the folks around here," Elmer said as he joined Jacob at the coffeepot. "But I suppose folks would do it to make a buck." He looked at Glory. His face was suspiciously deadpan. "What do you art people pay for nude modeling, anyway?"

"I've never paid anything," Glory protested.

"Well, you can't expect someone to do it for free," Jacob chided her, and then paused. "Well, maybe they would for you. What do you think, Reverend, would you model for free for the little angel here?"

Matthew choked on his laughter. He didn't know if it was possible for Glory's face to turn pinker. He kind of liked it that way. "Maybe if she did one of those abstract paintings so no one would recognize me. I wouldn't want to embarrass the boys."

"I don't paint nude pictures. I wasn't even thinking of nude pictures. I meant modeling for catalogs and things."

Elmer nodded wisely. "Ah, underwear."

"No, not underwear." Glory forced her voice to stay calm. "I meant sweaters. Jackets. Clothes. That kind of thing. But that's only one idea. The jam idea is better. Why doesn't one of you mention that to the women?''

"Guess we could," Jacob conceded.

"There could be a big market for it if the dude ranch—I mean, the guest ranch goes into operation."

"Don't remind me," Elmer said.

But reminding him was exactly what Glory intended to do. It allowed her to sit back while the two older men lamented what the dudes would do to Dry Creek. She felt like fanning her face, but she knew the men would notice her behavior and remark on it, since it was still chilly inside the store. So she resolutely began to mix some oils on her palate. Blue and green. She'd use blue and green for something. She never should have thought about modeling—any kind of modeling. Even sweaters made her think of broad shoulders. And hats made her think of masculine chin lines. And belts of trim waists. No, she should wipe out any thoughts of modeling from her mind. She'd focus on the blue and green. She had the colors mixed before she realized she'd mixed the exact color of Matthew's eyes.

Matthew watched Glory bristle and pretend to ignore the older men. He wondered if he should remind her that she'd neglected to put on the smock that she'd worn yesterday when she was working with oils. It'd be a shame if she got paint on the sweater she was wearing, a light pink that emphasized the color in her cheeks. He rather liked that pink sweater—it made her look cuddly. Maybe instead of saying something he should just take her smock over to her.

It was hard to be gallant on crutches, Matthew thought, grimacing as he held out the smock to Glory. His hand had pressed wrinkles in it where he'd clutched it close to the bar of his crutch handle.

"Thank you."

* * *

The day passed slowly for Matthew. Glory spelled him at the counter so he could go home and bake the cupcakes he'd forgotten to make. The church day-care staff was having a bake sale to help pay for the set design for the Christmas pageant.

"They need any bales of hay?" Elmer asked when Matthew got back. "Tell them I can donate all they need."

"And if the manger needs fixing, I can see to it," Jacob offered.

"I don't know if hay and a manger is going to be enough this year," Matthew said as he hobbled behind the counter and sat down on his stool. "Everyone's got it in their head that this year the pageant needs to be special."

"I could spray-paint the manger gold," Jacob suggested. "Maybe put some bells on it or something. Tack on some holly, even."

"I'll pass the word along to Mrs. Hargrove." Matthew chuckled. "Don't know how else to jazz things up."

"Jazz," Glory muttered as her brush slipped. She'd been so engrossed in painting she'd completely forgotten about the Jazz Man and Linda.

"Saltshaker's on the stove." Matthew called directions to Glory from his place by the sink. Tonight he was letting everyone help with the dinner. The twins were in the living room making sure the magazines were set straight. Glory had an apron on and was boiling water for pasta. They were having chicken parmigiana.

"So you're going to go with the 'just a team' theme?" Glory asked as she bent down to locate a strainer to drain the pasta once it cooked. "Horses in harness, that sort of thing?"

"Well, I suppose."

"So what do you want me to say?"

"Whatever you want," Matthew said as he grinned over at her. "You're half of the team. You decide."

"Well, this half of the team isn't so good at giving advice." Glory found the strainer. "Look at what my advice has already done."

"Now, that wasn't your fault." Matthew defended her staunchly. "Linda came to you and asked for your opinion. Besides, all couples have this discussion—best to do it before the wedding."

"Let's just hope there'll still be a wedding after I'm through with them."

Matthew laughed.

"More garlic bread?" Glory offered the plate to Duane. He was wearing a suit and tie and Linda was wearing a long gray dress. The couple were obviously nervous and on their best behavior. Even the twins were sitting at the table politely eating.

Duane nodded and took a piece.

"You'll have to give me your recipe," Linda said, smiling slightly at Glory.

"Not my recipe. Matthew made the garlic bread."

"Oh, really?" Linda appeared interested and gave Duane a meaningful look. "So Matthew helped with the meal."

Glory choked on the sip of water she'd taken. "No, *I* helped. Matthew cooked the dinner—garlic bread to chicken parmigiana. I helped by boiling water for the pasta.''

''He did it all!'' Linda's face lost its politeness. She was delighted. She nudged Duane. ''He cooked the dinner!''

Duane groaned and looked at Matthew in disgust. ''Now see what you've done.''

Matthew nodded. ''I'd guess the guys tell you cooking is women's work?''

Duane nodded.

''Ever think how helpless that makes you?'' Matthew helped himself to another piece of garlic bread.

''Helpless?'' Duane growled. ''What do you mean?''

''Well, look at me,'' Matthew said. ''I've had to learn how to cook the hard way. Every man needs to know how to cook and clean. The chores should be split.''

''But I thought you said being married was teamwork,'' Duane protested. ''I do half, she does half. Nothing that says my half needs to be meals. Besides, getting married better be about more than who's going to do the cooking!''

Matthew laughed. ''It is. But I've got to warn you. Being married has its surprises!''

''Like what?''

Matthew sobered. He didn't want his failures to dampen the enthusiasm of the young couple before him. ''I never knew what it would feel like to be so responsible for someone. I'd sworn to take care of that other person with all of my heart and all of my might. To do anything to keep her safe.''

Matthew stopped himself. When the dull pain of loss at Susie's death had begun to ease, the guilt had started. He hadn't kept Susie safe. His faith had not been enough. But that was his failure. It was between him and God. No one else needed to suffer it with him. He should have sidestepped that question.

"Anyway, back to cooking." Matthew forced himself to smile. "The twins have paid the price of my learning to cook."

Duane cleared his throat. "Guess I could learn to cook some things. Maybe breakfast. Or spaghetti. Or something."

"My daddy can even cook angel cake," Josh boasted.

Glory groaned. "I'm not an angel."

"Not even a little?" Linda asked hesitantly.

Glory shook her head. Something was going on here. She didn't like the guilty look on the girl's face.

"Well, Debra Guthert asked me about you. I think she's writing you up as an angel for the paper in Billings."

Matthew had a sinking sensation. Debra Guthert lived in Miles City and wrote the "Southeastern" column for the *Billings Gazette.* Her column covered the ranches and small towns along the Yellowstone River, northeast of Billings past Terry and Glendive to the North Dakota border and the area south of Interstate 94 from Hardin to the Chalk Buttes. Except for a few colorful announcements from the Crow Indian Reservation, it was usually mundane things like family reunions and rattlesnake sightings. "Why didn't someone stop her?"

Matthew didn't need an answer to the question. An angel would make the Dry Creek Christmas pageant the social event of the winter. Which would mean— suddenly Matthew felt much better.

"You have to stay now." Matthew turned to Glory.

Even Glory couldn't refuse the power of the press. "It's in print."

Glory looked around her. Five pairs of hopeful eyes. She groaned. How could she leave Dry Creek now?

Matthew stared into the embers of the fire. He'd wrapped so many blankets around himself he felt like a mummy. He was warm enough. The sofa was soft enough. The house was quiet enough. But he couldn't sleep. The frozen pain he'd lived in for the past four years was shifting. He could hear the cracking inside him as surely as he could hear the cracking of the Yellowstone River when the spring thaw came. And that cracking scared him. If his pain left him, he knew he'd want to love again. And how could he love again? He couldn't take another chance on love. He'd failed one woman. He didn't need to fail another one, especially not Glory.

"Go ahead and call her," Douglas urged the Bullet. The sadness in the old man's eyes was steady. "You don't know what I'd give for one last phone call with my Emily."

Douglas was standing in the guest bedroom of his house with the receiver of a black phone stretched out to the Bullet.

What have I gotten myself into? The Bullet didn't know what to do. He was sailing in uncharted water. He knew how to act around other hit men. He knew how to act around clients. But a friend? A new friend? He didn't know the rules.

Chapter Seven

Glory wished she had a pair of sunglasses to hide behind. Two people had already stopped by the hardware store to ask her to sign their copy of the "Southeastern" column in this morning's *Billings Gazette*. Linda had not exaggerated. The column talked in glowing terms of the two little boys who believed an angel had come to Dry Creek for Christmas.

Mrs. Hargrove predicted that attendance at the Christmas pageant would soar now that everyone from Billings knew about the angel. In fact, it appeared that attendance might be too high. No one knew what to do with all the people they were expecting.

"We could open the windows to the church and people could stand outside and watch the pageant through them," Jacob said. Earlier he'd noted that the "Southeastern" column might have spread farther than Billings. "They might not hear the shepherds singing, but they could at least see them come down the aisle."

Jacob, Elmer and Mrs. Hargrove were gathered around the potbellied stove, drinking coffee and plan-

ning the Christmas pageant. Mrs. Hargrove had called
a substitute to take over for her in the day-care program
so that she could devote herself to planning for the
pageant now that it looked as if it would be such a big
affair. It was already December 22. They didn't have
much time to plan for all the extra people coming.
Glory decided that if you didn't listen too closely to
the words, you would almost think the three were planning a war. Or at least a Southern ball.

"We'll need a place for coats." Mrs. Hargrove had
a clipboard on her lap and a pencil in her hand.

"It'll be too cold. People won't give up their coats,"
Matthew said from his stool behind the counter.

Matthew was, Glory would almost swear to it, sorting nuts and bolts. What else could he be doing? He
had a long piece of twine and he kept attaching first
one nut and then a bolt to it. She was the only one who
was sane this morning, she assured herself as she added
the Madonna look to her sketch. She'd found out that
Lori, the little girl who wanted the Betsy Tall doll, was
going to be Mary in the pageant. Glory had decided to
do a rough ink sketch of the girl from memory. It might
come in useful for a program for the pageant. Now that
she'd decided to stay for the event, she found herself
getting excited.

"There's not going to be enough room." Mrs. Hargrove repeated her worry as she wrote a number on her
notepad. "The church won't hold more than a hundred
people. And that's if we put folding chairs in the aisles,
open the doors to the kitchen and move the tract rack
into the office."

"The young'uns are smaller, they'll squeeze in, sit
on a parent's lap—maybe even on the floor," Elmer
suggested. He rested his elbows on the table that usu-

ally held a checkerboard. Today the game board was missing and a pot of coffee stood in its place.

"Maybe we could get in a hundred and fifty." Mrs. Hargrove frowned as she added some numbers on her notepad.

"Wonder if we should charge?" Jacob asked from the sidelines. He'd stood up to get a new mug and was walking back toward the stove.

"Charge!" Mrs. Hargrove puffed up indignantly. "Why, we can't charge! It's a holy moment. Christ coming to earth. Shouldn't be any money changing hands."

"I just thought it'd make things easier for Christmas." Jacob spread his hands and sat back down on a straight-backed chair. "Raise a little money for the children and all."

"Well." The puff went out of Mrs. Hargrove, and she glanced sideways at Glory. "It would help. Don't suppose God would mind if it was for the children. Maybe we could just ask for a donation. We could get some of the things they wished for. Awful hard to see children go without at Christmas."

Glory stopped her sketching. She'd spent some time last night sorting the pictures she'd received from the children of Dry Creek. "I'm going to place the order. I've already called my friend Sylvia. She's going to help me. I'm just waiting to find out if there are other children who want to bring me a Christmas wish. Josh and Joey said they'd spread the word."

Matthew looked up from the ornament he was making, but kept silent. Josh had told him Glory had asked them to invite all of the children of Dry Creek to bring her a drawing. He knew Glory couldn't possibly be buying presents for all of the children in Dry Creek.

Why, there must be forty children under twelve in the area. And there'd be another fifteen or so who hoped they were young enough for an angel present. And if all the children were like his two, that'd mean the presents were at least twenty dollars apiece. It'd add up to a thousand dollars minimum.

Matthew knew he should speak out. But he couldn't. If it was anyone but Glory making such ridiculous claims, he'd have no trouble. But this was Glory. He wanted to believe in her as much as the children of Dry Creek did.

"Well, we need to have faith this Christmas," Mrs. Hargrove said. "We might not have all of the money in the world. Fact is, we may not have much of it. But money isn't everything with God. The Lord fed the five thousand with a few loaves and fishes." Mrs. Hargrove had a determined look on her face that said if He could do it, they could do it. "We should be able to get the children something. Christmas isn't about big gifts, anyway."

Glory gave up. It was clear the adults in Dry Creek did not believe her. But she knew the children did, and that's what counted. "If you want, you could give out sacks of peanuts and candy."

"Jacob and I could make popcorn balls," Elmer said, his eyes lighting up in anticipation.

"And the angel could give out sacks of candy," Jacob suggested.

"The children would love that." Mrs. Hargrove spoke authoritatively as though that settled the matter. "And it would make a good picture for the *Gazette* if they send a photographer."

Glory looked around the hardware store. The shelves had been recently dusted, but it was obvious the merchandise took a long time to sell. There were some hammers. An assortment of screwdrivers. A row of small household goods like toasters and irons. Even a row of doorknobs and plumbing fixtures. The people inside the store were so convinced she was penniless that she didn't know how to convince them otherwise. All they knew of her was what they'd seen in this store and Matthew's house. She had money in neither of those places. Therefore, in the eyes of the adults of Dry Creek, her resources were limited. They liked reading in the newspaper that she might be an angel, but they didn't believe she had the power to buy even a few gifts.

Matthew watched the thoughts chase themselves through Glory's mind. He wondered if she knew how expressive her face was. When she was happy, she glowed. When she was mad, she steamed. When she was embarrassed, she blushed. Right now she was feeling frustrated. Her face was a clear road map. He liked that.

"If we're going to do candy for the children, I can also get the Ladies' Fellowship to make cookies and coffee for the adults," Mrs. Hargrove offered. "Doris June can make her lemon bars."

"You might even set up a table and sell some of that jam I hear about," Glory suggested. She wondered what was making Matthew frown like that. She'd been watching him out of the corner of her eye all morning.

"The ladies would love that." Mrs. Hargrove beamed. "We could raise money for the church. Maybe we'll raise enough to get a substitute pastor for a few services next year. I do so miss having a preacher on Sunday mornings."

Matthew kept his eyes on his ornament. He was step-

ping close to quicksand. First Susie and now this.
"Sounds like you do pretty good, though. I hear hymn
singing every Sunday morning."

"We take turns reading from the Bible, too," Mrs.
Hargrove agreed, and then sighed. "But it's not the
same. And I've been thinking for the pageant it'd be
nice to have a real preacher to at least give a small
devotional. Especially with all the people coming.
They'll expect—"

The bell above the door rang, announcing the entrance of Tavis, the son of the Big Sheep Mountain
Ranch owner.

Matthew breathed more easily. He was saved by the
bell. He didn't like the direction Mrs. Hargrove's
thoughts were taking. He would rather wear angel
wings than preach.

The cowboy was a distraction. In his early twenties,
Tavis was lean and wiry. Since it was December, he
wore his winter Stetson, the one with wool flaps that
could be pulled down over his ears if needed.

"Hi." Tavis nodded to Matthew and then to the
group around the stove. His gaze slid over to Glory,
and he tipped his hat. "Ma'am."

Glory looked up from her sketch. She supposed the
man in the hat was another autograph seeker. He certainly was walking toward her as if he had a mission
in mind. He didn't get more than two strides toward
her before Matthew spoke up.

"Can I help you?" It didn't take Matthew more than
a minute to remember that Tavis was single and the
reputed ladies' man of the Big Sheep Mountain Ranch.
Matthew had not dated anyone in Dry Creek, so he
assumed the few other single men in the area didn't
even count him as competition when someone like

Glory landed in town. He supposed word of the angel had gotten to the bunkhouse at the Big Sheep just as soon as this morning's *Gazette* was delivered, and Tavis had come to investigate.

"Ah, just picking up some nails." Tavis turned to Matthew with a wink.

Matthew grunted. It was the angel, all right. The Big Sheep Mountain Ranch bought their nails by the double case a couple of times a year. Henry had the boxes shipped directly to the ranch from his supplier in Chicago. They'd just processed an order last month. "Ran out, did you?"

"Ah, no—just wanted a handful of those little ones." Tavis twisted his hat. He stood in the middle of the floor, not moving closer to Glory, but obviously not retreating, either. "Thought I'd, you know, hang a few pictures in the bunkhouse."

"Oh." Elmer busied himself with his coffee cup. "Since when do you hang pictures in the bunkhouse?"

"Aunt Francis has been trying to get us cultured, and now that the *Gazette* said there's an artist in town—well, we thought we should get a picture for the wall."

Glory measured the cowboy with her eyes. He'd gained a few points with her by calling her an artist instead of an angel, but she hadn't worked with the guys in the police department for nothing. She knew a man on the prowl when she saw one. And this one was not just on the prowl. He was out to prove a point. She'd wager Tavis was duded up for her benefit. His Stetson was midnight black with no smudges or unplanned dents. His jeans were so new they still had the package crease down the leg. His face was freshly shaven and his hair neatly trimmed. She wondered if he'd be nearly as interested in her artwork if she hadn't been written up in the newspaper or recommended by his aunt.

"I could paint you a scene around the Big Sheep Mountains," Glory offered. The snowcapped mountains took her breath away each morning. The sky was pale blue today and the sun shone off the snow as if it was freshly polished silver. "But I won't have time until the pageant is all taken care of."

"The Christmas pageant? I haven't been to that for years."

"It's going to be special this year," Mrs. Hargrove said, determination giving an edge to the words. "Tell everyone at the Big Sheep—this year will be special."

"If you need any help, let us know. The boys and I are always glad to help." Tavis managed to face Mrs. Hargrove and smile at Glory at the same time. "Lifting things—that kind of thing."

Tavis held up his arm and flexed his muscle. "Comes from lifting hay bales."

"We might need to have you hoist some of the visitors up on your shoulder," Matthew suggested from the counter. He supposed Tavis was harmless. Glory didn't seem to be taking the bait. The cowboy kept flashing his smiles in Glory's direction, but she didn't beam back at him. She was polite, but that was it. "Trying to figure out how to get everyone inside the church to see it. Now that it's been mentioned in the *Gazette*, more people will be coming."

"Well, who says you need to have it in the church?"

Matthew almost chuckled at the look of horror that spread across Mrs. Hargrove's face as she spoke. "Not have it in the church? Where else would we have it? We can't have it here. The café's closed, the school's too small and we can't have it in the street!"

Tavis twirled his black hat around in his hands. He'd gone full circle. "You could use our storage barn."

"Your barn!"

Matthew was the first to see the possibilities. "Why not? The Big Sheep barn is huge. We could build some bleachers. There's lots of space for parking. It's right on the edge of town. Everyone knows where it is."

"But a barn?" Mrs. Hargrove wailed.

"Jesus was born in a stable," Glory reminded them all. She liked the idea. "That's about as close to a barn as you can get."

"But a barn? I think you still have cows there. What'll you do with them?"

"We can move them out," Tavis said.

"Or not," Matthew said. "A few cows around might add atmosphere."

"Cows in the pageant!" Mrs. Hargrove was horrified. "What will people think of us?"

"They'll think we're high society," Elmer said as he leaned over and put another piece of wood in the stove.

"And the carol does say 'The cattle are lowing,'" Glory offered.

"That's true." Mrs. Hargrove perked up. "It just might work. Think your dad will go for it? He hasn't been in church for years."

Tavis grimaced. "I know. But he'll do it for the town. Work is slow this time of year and the boys and I could do most of the setup."

"It just might work," Mrs. Hargrove repeated as she ripped off her old page in the notebook and started a fresh page. "We'll need ten, no, fifteen bleachers and…"

* * *

Glory half listened throughout the afternoon to the plans for the pageant. Her attention was primarily on the front window of the hardware store, however, or rather, what was happening outside the window. The children did not care about the article in the *Gazette*. They had other thoughts on their minds. Every few minutes she would see a timid wave from a child, and Glory would go to the door. First a pink mitten. Then a blue mitten. Then a gray mitten. All of the children wore warm coats, but she noticed that some of the coat sleeves were too short, as though the coats were several years old and too small. Still, each mittened hand held the same thing: a painstakingly drawn picture of a toy.

Glory made sure each child told her what the toy was called and his or her full name. She was careful to write both on the slip of paper before she went back into the store. She wanted to be sure that each child had their individual present. She knew that any present would be appreciated, but she also knew that the feeling of having a present given especially to you was one that helped children develop self-esteem and the ability to trust.

Matthew knew what Glory was doing. She was making too many quick trips outside for him not to notice. Especially because each time she came back in her cheeks and nose were rosy from the cold. He couldn't decide which he liked better—Glory with the cream-colored skin and freckles or Glory with the roses. She would make a beautiful angel. He was glad she'd been coaxed into staying. He and the twins hadn't had a really happy Christmas since Susie died. He'd barely had the energy to put a tree up this year, and it still wasn't fully decorated. But now this Christmas promised to be one they would never forget. He'd have to get the rest of the Christmas bulbs down from the upstairs closet so the tree could sparkle the way it should.

"You're welcome to listen," Glory said after she'd asked Matthew for the use of his phone again that evening. Her phone card guaranteed she could call from his phone with no charge to him, but she wanted him to know she was making arrangements for the presents. She accepted the fact that Mrs. Hargrove and the two older men didn't believe she could bring the children the presents they wanted, but she had hoped Matthew would believe her. He'd become important to her, and she wanted to know he trusted her.

"I have to set the things out for the twins' lunch tomorrow," Matthew said as he pulled himself up from the sofa. He had no reason to keep sitting there, anyway. Glory had read the twins another Bible story, and they had had their good-night prayers. This time he'd listened from the doorway with a dish towel on his shoulder. He'd been tempted to give up all pretense of not listening and just go in and sit down with his sons. But he hadn't. Glory's voice reading from the Bible lulled him into thinking everything was all right with his soul, and he knew it wasn't. He didn't want a Band-Aid slapped on his relationship with God. He wanted to feel the pain of it until it healed from the inside out.

"Joey said he wants peanut butter," Glory reminded him as she reached for the phone sitting on the coffee table.

"Joey always wants peanut butter," Matthew said as he slipped the crutches under his arms and began to hobble toward the kitchen. "He likes the way it sticks to his mouth."

Matthew limped into the kitchen and then turned and

closed the door between the kitchen and the living room. He wanted to give Glory privacy in his home. He particularly did not want to make her feel as if she had to lie to make him think she was really ordering presents. A gift, after all, came from the heart, and Glory's heart had opened wide to his sons. That was a more important gift than a laser light gun and a Lego machine set.

Glory dialed the number and said hello.

"Glory?" Sylvia's voice came through sounding breathless. "I'm so glad you called."

"Why?" Prickles were running down Glory's spine again. Her friend's voice didn't sound relaxed.

"I've heard some disturbing news." Sylvia paused. "I don't know if it's true—you know how kids are. I wasn't sure if I should say anything yet. I told the police, but I don't know for sure."

"What is it, Sylvia?"

"Two of my kids—they're good kids, but they hang with a bad crowd."

Glory started to breathe more easily. There were always kids in trouble at the youth center where Sylvia worked in Tacoma. Most of the teens were part of tough criminal gangs. "You'll help them go straight— remember the judge will work with you."

"Oh, they didn't do anything—at least, it didn't turn out the way they planned." Sylvia took a deep breath. "They told me there's a hit out on you. Two of the older boys in the gang had been contracted to do it. But then, last night, something happened. My two boys got scared and ended up at the mission. Even went forward for an altar call. I had mentioned your name with the presents you were buying and this morning they came back and told me. Said the hit hadn't gone through, that the guy doing the shooting had missed you and hadn't found you again. No one seems to know who the contact was or if the hit's still on. My boys feel so bad about it they want to go find you and stand in front of you so no bullets can get through.''

A sliver of fear raced down Glory's back.

"Thank God you're in Montana," Sylvia continued in a rush.

"Yes, I should be safe here," Glory repeated in a daze. She slowly twisted the phone card around her finger. "These boys don't know where I am, do they?"

"No. Thank God I didn't mention where you were when I talked about the presents."

"Good."

Sylvia paused. "They did seem genuinely worried. I think they'd protect you if they could."

"Yeah, well, if I stay out of sight I won't need any protection."

Glory kept calm. She went over the list of presents with Sylvia. Glory was used to stress. She knew about shootings and crime. She would be fine. She kept repeating that phrase to herself. But when she hung up the phone she started to shake.

Matthew waited for the lull of voices to stop before he came back into the living room. He knew something was wrong. Glory's face was ashen. Even in the firelight, all warmth had left her face. No smile remained. Her hair still picked up the fire flecks and reflected them back, but all else about her was still.

"It's all right." Matthew hobbled over and sat down on the edge of the sofa. He wanted to reach over and put his arm around her, but she looked too fragile. As though even that movement would snap her control. "No one really expects them."

Glory looked up at him. "What do you mean?"

"The presents," Matthew continued patiently. "No one really expected you to be able to deliver on the presents. It's enough that you wanted to."

Glory started to laugh, even though she knew nothing was funny. Hysteria started this way. She knew that. But she couldn't stop. Matthew thought she couldn't deliver the presents. But the presents were all settled. Her problem was worse than that. She didn't know if she'd ever be able to walk the streets of Seattle again. Someone had been shooting at her. It wasn't a stray bullet. It was meant to hit her. She was the target. *Dear Lord, she was the target!*

Matthew watched Glory's teeth start to chatter, and her laughter calm down to hiccups. Suddenly he didn't care if she pulled away from him. He moved closer and put his arm around her shoulder. She whimpered. He wrapped his arm more fully around her and gathered her to his shoulder. He stroked her head and hummed a lullaby in her ear. He hoped to calm her. But it didn't work. She started to cry in earnest.

"What's wrong?" Matthew had to know. He felt a vise squeezing his heart. Something was wrong.

"They're shooting at me," Glory wailed.

"Who?"

"I don't know."

It was the bullet. Matthew knew the bullet on Wednesday had been too close. "You'll stay in your room. You're not leaving this house unless I'm along. No, you're not leaving even then. You'll just stay here. I can bring you what you need."

The determination in Matthew's voice quieted her. "Forever?"

"If necessary." Matthew nodded grimly. "I'll lock you in."

Glory smiled. She felt much better. "But that's kidnapping."

"Whatever it takes to keep you safe."

Strangely enough, Glory decided, she did feel safe. She'd just learned that there might be a contract out on her life, and yet, she felt safe here in this house. She'd like to pretend that had nothing to do with the man sitting beside her on the sofa worrying about her. But it wasn't true. His fierce protection made her feel as if nothing could harm her, not while he still drew breath.

The Bullet set down his coffee cup.

He shouldn't have stayed, but his phone call last night with Millie had unnerved him. She'd heard Douglas's voice in the background and assumed Douglas was the uncle he visited.

"Yes, I'll invite him to visit," the Bullet had told Millie last night after she kept insisting. "But he doesn't travel much. He won't come. No, not even for Christmas."

If the Bullet had known Millie was making Christmas plans, he would have stalled her. He'd never thought about Christmas coming. Santa stockings and roasting chestnuts were not for a man like him. He usually celebrated Christmas at an all-night bar with a bottle of tequila. That's where a man like him spent Christmas.

Chapter Eight

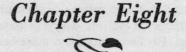

"**Y**ou're going to call?" Matthew was making pancakes for breakfast. He had been up early worrying and had decided to stir up some batter. Glory was in trouble and he needed to find a way to keep her safe. "They must know more at the precinct than they've told you. And they have the photos. They might offer a clue."

"It's not even morning there," Glory said. The small Franklin stove had a fire going in it, but the air inside the house was still cold enough to make foggy breath. She rubbed her hands together. She had pulled on her jeans and a heavy sweater when she heard Matthew moving around the kitchen. They had spent time last night talking about the shooting she'd seen inside Benson's Market. "I don't know for sure if they'll send me copies of the photos—it's not exactly regulation."

"Forget regulation," Matthew demanded as he poured more batter on the griddle and automatically made the batter into a snowman. "Someone's out to get you."

"Only in Seattle."

"That's bad enough." Matthew reached up into the cupboard and found a small canister of raisins. He put eye, nose and button raisins on the snowman.

Glory nodded. Matthew wasn't even aware of what he was doing—making cute pancakes while talking about violence. He did everything a mother would do for his sons. "I'll ask them to send copies of the photos—but I don't know what good they'll do."

"Henry's got a fax at the store. Fax copies of them there," Matthew said as he poured another pancake snowman. He didn't know what good the photos would do, either. He just knew he needed to do something. "And don't talk to anyone but that guy Frank you say you can trust."

"Nobody on the force would sell me out," Glory said, and then thought a minute. She took some silverware from the drawer. The metal was cold to her touch. Maybe Matthew was right. How did she know for sure none of them would tell a hit man where she was if the price was right?

"And you'll work on those drawings? You must have seen something," Matthew said.

Glory had agreed to draw the crime scene again. The captain and she had been over this already. But Matthew sounded a lot like the captain. Both men believed she must be a target because of her trained eyes.

"Someone's worried you're going to remember something." Matthew repeated what he had said last night. "Our job is to find out what that is."

"I've been over it hundreds of times in my mind."

"Have you drawn out the sketches of everything?"

"Just the face of the guy doing the shooting." Glory had thought about that, too. Surely there wouldn't be something in the grocery store itself. Who would leave evidence of a crime in plain sight for dozens of shoppers to see?

"And he's in jail?"

Glory nodded. "And nothing to gain by killing me at this point. I did sketches, but it wasn't necessary. He was arrested at the scene. And there were ten witnesses."

"Now, why would a guy shoot someone in front of ten witnesses?"

"Poor planning," Glory joked as she gathered four cups from the cupboard.

"Or something was happening that required immediate action," Matthew said as he flipped the first snowman pancake. "Something important enough to risk jail time."

"But that's just it—nothing was happening. The butcher was just walking out of the meat department with a package of steak in his hands."

"What kind of steaks?"

Glory looked at Matthew as if he was crazy. "What kind of steaks?"

"Yeah, T-bone, porterhouse, cube…"

"What difference does that make?"

Matthew flipped the other snowman pancake. "Who knows? My guess is it's that kind of little detail that we're looking for, something all of the other ten people have long forgotten. But with your eye, it's still in your head. If you draw it out, who knows? That's what someone is worried about."

"Makes sense." Glory walked toward the kitchen table and set down the cups. Matthew did make sense. If someone was out gunning for her, it was time to empty her mind of all the crime details and put them out front on paper. Maybe then they'd know who—or what—they were up against.

Matthew looked up. He heard the sound of the twins coming down the stairs before Glory did. "Juice in the refrigerator. Apricot syrup, too. Maybe some maple, as well."

Glory nodded and went back to the cupboard to collect plates.

"And butter," Matthew said. "Joey won't eat pancakes without butter."

Once the plates were on the table, Glory went to the refrigerator.

Glory turned when she heard the twins enter the kitchen. They were in slippers and pajamas with sweatshirts pulled over them. Their hair was mussed and their eyes were still sleepy. Joey, in particular, looked as if he was still dreaming.

"Hi, sport," Glory said softly as she put the juice on the table and walked over to Joey, lifting him up. He looked as if he needed a little bit more time to wake up.

Joey snuggled into her shoulder with a sigh.

"Mommy." Joey whispered the word so softly Glory wasn't sure she'd heard it right. But she knew by the look of pain on Matthew's face that he had.

"He's still dreaming," she whispered to Matthew. "He doesn't know what he's saying."

"I know," Matthew said quietly. Some days he could convince himself he could give his sons everything they needed. Today, apparently, was not going to be one of those days.

"It's Glory, honey," she whispered in Joey's ear.

His eyes opened, and he smiled contentedly.

"You're still here. You didn't go back to heaven. I dreamed you were still here."

"I wouldn't go anywhere without saying goodbye."

Joey nodded. "Not even to heaven?"

Glory shook her head. "Not even there."

Joey put his head back on her shoulder and put his thin arms around her neck in a tight hug.

Glory wondered how she was ever going to say goodbye to the twins.

It was midmorning before Glory relaxed her fingers. She was holding her sketch pencil too tight, as though she could force some memory out through her fingers. At first her fingers had been too cold to sketch, but Matthew had taken a pair of women's knit gloves off the shelf and cut the fingers out of them. That kept her hands warm while letting her fingers be free.

"You remember the clock?" Elmer had walked over to where she sat with her sketch pad.

"I remember everything," Glory said as she set her fifth sketch aside. Matthew had fixed up a table for her to work at. By now it was covered with sketches.

"Not quite everything," Elmer said as he looked closely at the sketch she had made of the manager lying on the floor, a bullet through his stomach and the things in his hands scattered. The time card was halfway out of the dead man's pocket. The package of steaks was near his left shoulder.

"What do you mean?"

"That." Elmer pointed at the sketch. "On that package of steaks. That isn't packed right. A T-bone and a cube together. Who'd do that?"

Glory looked at the sketch. She must have made a mistake. Odd, though.

A harsh scraping sound from the storeroom distracted them.

"Matthew." Glory had told Matthew she would help him move any stock he needed to relocate. Elmer had told him the same thing. Even Jacob had appeared eager to pitch in and help. "Stubborn man."

"Found the garland," Matthew announced triumphantly as he hobbled into the main part of the store. A trail of gold-and-white garland followed him and he had a cape of garland wrapped around his shoulders.

"You risked falling to get some garland?"

Matthew grinned. "I didn't know you cared if I fell."

"Of course I care if you fall," Glory said softly. The fool man. "I'm the one that has to pick you up and get you to the clinic."

Matthew's grin disappeared. "Did I ever thank you for that?"

The bell over the door rang. Glory looked up in time to see the deputy sheriff, Carl Wall, walk into the store.

Glory bit back her groan.

"Expected everyone to be out working on the pageant," the deputy said. He looked slowly around the store and his eyes rested on Glory's worktable. He walked over and picked up one of her sketches of the victim after the shooting. "Hmm, not exactly scenery." He looked at Glory.

Glory was leaning against the counter. "I told you I worked for the police."

The deputy grunted. "Maybe you do, at that."

"Want some coffee?" Matthew offered. "You public officials never seem to take time for breaks."

"Some folks say all we do is sit around drinking coffee and eating doughnuts."

"Well, I'm not one of them," Matthew said staunchly. "You have a lot to do making sure there are no undesirables coming into town."

Carl Wall looked puzzled. "I thought you were on the side of the angel."

"The angel—no, no, I don't mean her. I mean any undesirables asking about her."

"Who'd be asking about her?"

"I don't know. Just keep an eye out, all right?"

The deputy shrugged. "Most folks have accepted her. They kind of like someone who might be an angel. Makes them think the Man upstairs cares."

"God can care about Dry Creek without sending an angel," Glory said as she walked back toward her worktable. "Maybe God sent you to Dry Creek instead."

The deputy grunted and rolled his eyes. "Now don't go getting funny on me. I wasn't thinking of me. But at least I'd remember the Price boy."

"Billy Price?" Elmer looked up from the checker game.

"Yeah, I got to thinking. No one would remember him, and he'd like a visit from the angel—maybe a sack of the candy I hear is coming."

"Well, I'll add him to the list."

Glory could hear the silence in Matthew's house. A clock ticked in the kitchen and the water heater gurgled in the distance. She was making her Christmas list and checking it twice. She'd decided to order six extra basketballs and ten extra painting sets plus a couple of additional teddy bears. She wanted to be sure there were enough presents to go around.

With her list in hand, Glory called Sylvia.

The phone rang five times before Sylvia's breathless voice came over the line. "Tacoma-Seattle Youth Center, Sylvia Bannister speaking."

Glory could hear muffled laughter and cheers in the background. "Sounds like someone's happy there."

"We should be. We just got a grant to set up that summer camp you've heard me talk about for two years now. The money's not much, but it's a big start."

"Congratulations! I wish I could be there!"

"The volunteers are going wild. Pat Dawson is even dancing a jig on the table."

"I'm surprised you're not up there with him."

"I had to get down to answer the phone. Besides, I'm too old for that sort of thing."

"Forty! That's not old!"

"Well, I do feel younger since I got the news." Sylvia laughed. "If we can get some of these kids away from the gangs for a summer, I believe we can turn their lives around. Take them someplace where they don't need to worry about being jumped or shot."

"Even with the gangs, you make a difference," Glory reminded her. She herself had volunteered many weekends at the youth center, tutoring or just talking with teenage girls. "I've seen you change the most unlikely ones."

"Ah, the power of prayer. It surprises me at times, too. I always remind myself that I never know what heart God is going to open up next."

"If you have a few extra prayers, you could send them this way." Glory knew of no heart that needed softening more than Matthew's.

"I've been worried about that, too."

"What?" Glory was startled. How had Sylvia known about Matthew?

"I don't want you to worry about that contract, though," Sylvia continued. "The two boys who told me about it are being very responsible today. I think they have made a sincere decision to follow Christ."

"Oh, of course." Glory relaxed. Sylvia was talking about the shooting.

Silence.

"Is there something else bothering you?" Sylvia asked. "Something else I should pray about?"

How did Sylvia always know? Glory wondered. It must be her years of talking with teenagers.

"Just a stubborn man who hasn't forgiven himself and holds it against God."

"Ah, this would be the man you mentioned, the one you're staying with." Sylvia's voice was rich with unspoken speculation. "The minister."

"I'm not staying with him," Glory clarified. "I'm really staying with his five-year-old sons. That's all."

"If you say so."

"I know so."

Sylvia let the subject be changed to the gifts for the children of Dry Creek. Sylvia assured her there were thirty days to pay on the account, and Glory told her she would mail a check tomorrow to cover the presents and the overnight shipping. The total came to twelve hundred dollars.

"I called the shipping place and they said they can only guarantee next-day service to Miles City. They're short-staffed, since it's Christmas, and aren't taking next-day service to places like Dry Creek."

"If they can deliver it to the clinic in Miles City that'll be fine," Glory said. "I thought this might happen, and I called one of the nurses I met there. She said I can pick the boxes up anytime before five." She wanted to go to Miles City, anyway. She had some Christmas shopping to do that she didn't want to do in the toy store.

"You'll need a pickup truck." Tavis from the Big Sheep Mountain Ranch smiled at Glory. He, unlike Jacob and Elmer, was not sitting in a chair. Instead he crouched, cowboy-style, in front of the stove. "I'd be happy to drive you in. I've got a half-ton pickup, a three-quarter ton or a cattle truck. Your choice."

"I can take her." Matthew bristled. He was sitting on his stool by the counter.

"Your old car won't hold a load," Tavis challenged.

"I can take her anyway." Matthew didn't want to spell out the obvious. By now he figured Glory was honest about placing the order. But he knew her credit was no good. He figured she believed the order was coming. He wanted to be the one with her when she found out it wasn't there. She'd need a friend and not a fancy cowboy at her side to help her with her disappointment. Besides, he had some money set aside for a rainy day. He figured they could buy enough little presents in Miles City to make the children of Dry Creek happy.

Glory looked from one man to the other. "I might be able to fit everything in my Jeep."

"Matthew will take you," Mrs. Hargrove calmly announced with a silencing glance at Tavis. "I need Tavis's help with the bleachers."

It was only a trip to town, Glory chided herself that evening as she looked through her suitcase. So far she'd pulled out her gray sweatshirt with Seattle Seahawks written on the back and an ivory turtleneck with a tan vest. Neither one was exactly right. She couldn't remember the last time she'd given this much thought to the question of what to wear. Jeans were an obvious choice because of the cold weather, but she suddenly wished for a sweater with bright colors to go with them. Of course, she had the pink sweater. It was paler than she'd like, but maybe it would do.

She sat on the edge of Matthew's bed, with her suitcase and clothes scattered all around, and shook her head at herself. She was acting as if this was a date. Worse yet, she wanted it to be a date. And that was a fantasy that would be short-lived. She could sit and count the reasons she shouldn't become involved with Matthew. He was a good father; he would want more children. Children she couldn't give him. Even more important, Matthew wasn't following God at this point in his life. She believed he was still a Christian in his heart, but he wasn't willing to let go of his grief and admit it. And then there was his grief. Glory felt her breath catch in her throat at this one. What if Matthew had loved Susie so much he could never love anyone else? Would every other woman seem pale in comparison?

Maybe, she thought as she shook her head again at her clothes, that's why she wanted something bright to wear. She wanted to get Matthew's attention tomorrow. But she'd need more than a bright sweater to do that.

The Bullet watched the inside glass of the telephone booth fog up as he breathed. He was outside a drugstore in Spokane, calling his contact to tell him the search was off. He hadn't picked up the scent of the hit and he was ready to go home.

"You're looking in the wrong place." The clipped

voice came through the phone lines. "She's in Montana. Wonders of modern technology. Do a word search on the AP wire—a name search—and there it is. Glory Beckett in Dry Creek, Montana."

Chapter Nine

Snow, turned grayish-brown by the exhaust of passing cars, lined the isolated highway as Matthew drove down the road. After breakfast he had quickly washed his car, almost freezing his hands in the process. He was a fool to wash anything outside when he was on crutches and the weather gauge read ten below. But he wanted Glory's first impression of his car to be good even if the cleanliness she'd see would be fleeting. Cars might mean something to her. He stole a glance over at her as she sat in the passenger seat.

"The radio doesn't work, but I fixed the cassette player." Matthew fumbled in the storage compartment next to the driver's seat. He couldn't remember what was in there, but he thought he had a Mozart tape. He pulled out three tapes. All three were made by Disney. "I'm afraid I have mostly sing-along music for the twins. But I'll keep looking. I've got one classical and I've been meaning to get some instrumentals, too— maybe a flute tape."

"That's okay. I like the silence."

What does she mean by that, Matthew thought in desperation. Should he be talking more? Should he be talking less? Ever since this morning when he'd decided this trip to town was the closest thing he'd had to a date in years, he'd been tongue-tied. Worse than when he had been a teenager and had been dating. At least back then he'd known when he was on a date and when he wasn't.

"That's one thing we have in Montana. Silence—it goes with the snow."

Montana was known for her open spaces and big blue skies. Both could be seen through the car's windshield. Matthew felt as if they were driving along in a warm cocoon. The car's heater kept the air cozy, and the hum of the engine was soothing.

"In Seattle we have noise and rain."

"You like it there?" Matthew tried to keep the question light, tried to pretend he hadn't wondered if there was any chance she'd move to a small town in Montana if asked.

"I've got my family there."

Matthew held his breath.

"My mother and the captain."

Matthew took a deep breath. So far so good, but he had to know. "Any—you know—boyfriends?"

A butterfly took flight in Glory's stomach. "Not really."

Matthew frowned. What did that mean?

"Well, of course, you date...." Matthew stumbled along.

"Of course." Glory's hands went up to finger her dangling silver earrings. Maybe the jewelry had been a mistake. The zipper of her black ski jacket was open to show her pale pink sweater. Even with denim jeans the silver jewelry might be too dressy for a shopping trip. But it was the only thing in her suitcase that seemed the least bit festive. When she had looked in the mirror this morning, she'd looked colorless, so she'd put on what little makeup she had. Usually red hair clashed with pink, but the pink in her sweater was more pearl than pink. She wore a natural lipstick and barely-pink blush. She'd brushed her hair until it settled around her face in waves. She'd even put a tortoise clip in her hair. She wanted to look good, but now she wondered if she had overdone it. She didn't want to make Matthew feel uncomfortable, as if she had expectations for this trip. Date expectations. Maybe that was why he was asking about boyfriends. Maybe he wanted to be sure she had one and wasn't expecting anything from him. Maybe she should have worn the Seattle Seahawks sweatshirt, after all. There was no mistaking the nondate look of that.

"But is there someone you date regularly?" Matthew persisted with the question. "Someone you are involved with?" Even if she was undercover, she would answer this honestly to tell him there was no chance. Even a government agent would give him that courtesy.

Glory glanced at him. He had his eyes straight ahead, his chin straight forward, his hands squarely on the steering wheel. He was a study in browns. Deep brown leather jacket, open all the way down to show a pressed white shirt. Chestnut-brown hair with blond highlights. Tanned face. Fierce dark eyebrows. It was the small nervous twitch at the edge of his mouth that gave her courage.

"No," Glory said softly. "There's no one special."

"Good." Matthew breathed again. "Good."

The morning suddenly looked brighter to Matthew. The slush at the side of the road didn't look just gray anymore; it looked more like pure silver with the sun shining on it the way it was. And his car might be old, but the seat cushions were made of leather. And the trim looked like wood. He was cruising.

"I was wondering if I could buy you lunch when we're in town." Matthew tapped the steering wheel lightly and turned to smile at Glory. He came from the era when a date meant someone did the inviting, even if it was only for lunch. "There's a steakhouse if you want to play it safe. Or we can go to Billy's—never know what you'll get, but it's good."

"I'd like that—Billy's sounds good." Glory tilted her head so her earrings could sparkle. And she lifted the collar of her sweater and flipped her silver chain outside. The more jewelry the better. She, Glory Beckett, was on a date. Granted, it was a date with the wrong man, but for today she didn't care. She was going to forget he was a grieving widower who'd had a perfect wife. She was going to forget he was not following God because of that wife. She was going to forget she couldn't give him children as that wife had. She was even going to forget that wife had ever existed. She would let her jewelry sparkle like laughter. Just for today she'd forget about his past and their lack of a future. They were definitely on a date.

"We'll have lots of time to shop." Matthew slowed down some. There were likely to be patches of white ice along this strip of road, and he couldn't count on his leg with the sprained knee. Besides, they had plenty of time. "There's a department store—and Buffy's Drug. Buffy's usually carries some toys this time of year, just in case your order doesn't get here in time."

"The boxes should be at Dr. Norris's office already."

"Well, just in case they're held up," Matthew persisted. He didn't want anything to ruin their day. "We can pick up what we need at Buffy's."

"Buffy's won't have a Betsy Tall doll," Glory protested. She'd gone over the children's wish pictures. No small store in Miles City could carry all of the different things the children wanted.

"Maybe not, but they'll have another doll."

"But that's the problem." Glory had seen the hope on the children's faces. "They each have a special request for a present. Something they especially want. Not expensive things, either, just particular things. This Christmas I want them each to have the exact thing they asked for."

"Sometimes we don't get the exact thing we want in life."

"I know, but—" Glory stopped. How could she explain the need children have to be unique in the eyes of God? To be known individually? "They're expecting their angel to make arrangements to see that they get their special gift. It won't be the same if it's just any old gift. It has to be the one."

"They'll be fine." Matthew's face settled into grim lines. "They'll make do."

"Will they?" Glory watched the shutters go down over Matthew's face. She knew they weren't talking about the children. They were talking about Matthew. "Or will they be like you and decide God doesn't care about them?"

A muscle flexed across Matthew's cheek, but he didn't answer.

* * *

Miles City was dressed up for Christmas. Matthew told her the town had grown up around Fort Keogh, an outpost built in 1877 to force the Crow to stay on the nearby reservation.

"We have always been half-decent and half not around here," he continued. "Starting out it was divided—brothels and beer halls to the south, banks and pawnshops to the north."

Glory imagined she could still see the old town in its heyday. The sidewalks were scraped clean of snow and many of the store windows had been decorated with winter scenes and outlined with tiny white lights. Most of the buildings along the main street were solid old buildings, which fit in well with her fantasy. The place, Glory decided, had charm. Some of the stores had Christmas carols playing, and the sounds carried out into the street. Even the other shoppers looked festive in their snow boots and knit scarves.

Matthew drove down the main street and then turned around. "I'm checking the cars."

Glory looked at him.

"Making sure they're all locals," he said.

"Surely you don't think a hit man would be looking for me in Miles City?"

"No, but I'm not taking any chances." Matthew finally pulled into a parking space. "Let's try Buffy's first. I want to get something for the boys."

"Me, too."

Glory wanted to get a gift for the boys that was from her and not from the angel. Some little thing they could have to remember her visit.

The door into Buffy's opened with the ringing of a bell. Buffy's smelled of the perfume and scented soaps she could see in front of the long mirror at the end of the store. Racks of merchandise ran sideways down the length of the store and a checkout counter was located near the front door.

"Can I help you find anything?" An older woman wearing a lilac-flowered dress spoke from behind the counter. The woman smelled of dusting powder. "We've got a special on gloves this week. Men's. Women's. Children's. The lot."

"You must be Buffy?" Glory said, even though she knew the woman couldn't be.

"No, she's my daughter." The woman smiled indulgently and patted the braided bun loosely knotted at the back of her neck. "She's home baking cookies for her two boys for Christmas. Boys need cookies at Christmas."

Cookies and Christmas! Glory had forgotten. She'd decided earlier to buy some chocolate chips before they left Miles City. She wouldn't compete with their mother's oatmeal raisin cookies, but she was sure the twins would love the Beckett family chocolate chip cookies.

"Do you have any children's books?" Glory asked. Buffy must stock good books if she had children of her own. Both Josh and Joey loved having a book read to them. She'd already seen their favorites—*Curious George, The Runaway Rabbit* and a couple of Dr. Seuss books. She knew they loved adventure, and she might even find a book with lions and tigers in it.

The saleswoman nodded to the right. "Over there, behind the lunch boxes."

Matthew watched Glory out of the corner of his eye. He also kept his eye on the door to the store. He'd already studied the three other customers inside Buffy's and decided they were harmless. But he wasn't going to be careless. Not about Glory's safety.

He watched as she looked over the book rack. He knew she was buying presents for his sons, and he'd had a whispered conference with them before he came this morning. Josh had pressed a few nickels into his hand, asking him to buy Glory a golden crown that would light up like the one he'd seen on a Christmas card at school. Matthew suggested a shiny necklace instead. Joey, with his pennies, wanted him to buy her a mirror because he'd seen her use one when she brushed her hair at night. They both advised him that he should buy her a present, too. Matthew knew his sons were worried. They didn't want Glory to leave. He was worried, too. He hadn't known his sons would get so attached to her in just a few days. But then, why shouldn't they? He'd gotten attached himself.

"The other store is just next door." Matthew walked over to Glory. "I don't want to rush you. Why don't I go over there now, and you can come when you're done?" The department store would take longer to check out and he didn't want Glory to know what he was doing.

Glory nodded. She had been wondering how to get Matthew out of the store so she could buy his present. She'd seen a selection of music cassettes near the counter and she'd decided to get him one. It was a gift with the right balance. It showed she didn't expect him to get her anything. It was just a friendly gift.

She waited for Matthew to walk out of the store before she headed for the cassette display. She put two books on the counter. Josh's was about a red dragon. Joey's was about a lost kitten that found his way home.

"I'll take these, and do you have any James Galway tapes?"

"I don't think so." The salesclerk scanned the titles.

"Any instrumentalists?"

"Let me see, we've got *Piano Selections for...*" The salesclerk started to read the title as she pulled the cassette from the display. Black and white piano keys ran the length of the tape cover and there was a red rose lying across them. It looked slow moving, if nothing else.

"I'll take it," Glory said quickly. She thought she saw Matthew's outline in the window. He was doubling back. "Just put it in the bag quick. Christmas present."

The older woman smiled and slipped it into the bag under the two larger books.

"I thought you might want that twenty dollars I owe you," Matthew said quietly as he came inside and held out a twenty-dollar bill.

"What twenty?" Glory looked up from her purse. She opened her wallet. There was her own twenty dollars. "It's not mine."

"Take it anyway," Matthew said, his voice even. "I'm sure I owe it to you for something."

"But—"

"Go ahead and take it, sweetheart," the clerk advised with a shrug of her shoulders. "It isn't every day your husband gives you an extra twenty for Christmas shopping."

"He's not my husband." Glory felt the blush creep up her neck.

Matthew smiled.

"Even more reason to take it, then." The clerk straightened herself and glared at Matthew. "It's the least he can do if he isn't willing to make an honest woman out of you.''

"I'm an honest woman already." Glory lifted her chin indignantly.

"Already married?" The older woman smoothed down the skirt of her flowered dress and shook her head. "In my day—well, you don't want to hear that. It's none of my business whose bed you're sleeping in."

"She's got you there," Matthew whispered. "You *are* sleeping in my bed."

"Well, you're right in there with me." Glory spit out the words and then stumbled when she realized what she'd said. "And if either one of us should care about their reputation it's you—you live here. Besides, you've got the boys."

"My boys couldn't care less about my reputation. They'd love it if I slept with an angel." Matthew chuckled. The one thing he didn't miss about the ministry was worrying about what people thought about him.

"Well." The salesclerk softened as she looked at Matthew. "If he thinks you're an angel…"

"The whole town of Dry Creek thinks I'm an angel."

"Oh, you're the angel at Dry Creek!" The older woman brightened. "Wait'll I tell Buffy. We were reading about you in the 'Southeastern' column."

"I'm not. Look. I've got no wings. No miracles. No divine message."

"Yeah, but you're sweet," the woman said, measuring her with friendly eyes. "And sweetness never hurt anyone. Right?" The clerk looked at Matthew.

Matthew nodded. The clerk was absolutely right.

That's why people were drawn to Glory. She was a kind, sweet woman. She didn't need to be an angel.

"Let's eat lunch and then we'll hit the department store." Matthew put his hand under Glory's elbow. They were on the sidewalk outside Buffy's. He looked both ways for suspicious-looking cars and didn't see any. Mostly there were farm pickups parked on the street, since it was winter. "Slippery out here."

"Let's stop by Dr. Norris's first. The clinic might close early, since it's so close to Christmas."

"Okay." Matthew felt helpless. His worry shifted. He could protect Glory from suspicious-looking cars, but he didn't know how to protect her from disappointment. "You're sure you don't want to eat first?"

"Come on. Let's get the boxes."

Forty-five. Forty-six. Glory was sitting across the restaurant table from Matthew and counting to one hundred. She'd taken her ski jacket off and draped it over the back of her chair.

Glory barely noticed the knotty pine paneling in the room or the ferns that hung from the ceiling. Everything was clean, but old. The air smelled of cooking meat and she faintly heard the rattle of silverware coming from the kitchen as well as the murmured talk of the other customers sitting at nearby tables.

Glory hadn't realized it until now—Matthew didn't believe her. He fussed all over her in his worry about a hit man, but when it came to believing in her integrity, he didn't. She knew he hadn't believed her at first. But she'd thought that somewhere during the past days he would have decided she wasn't crazy. The boxes were coming. Sylvia had called to tell her the order had been processed. Just because the nurse at the clinic said the boxes hadn't come with the shipment today didn't mean they wouldn't come tomorrow. The nurse had promised she'd bring them with her when she came out to see the pageant tomorrow. The nurse—a stranger, really—seemed to believe her. Matthew didn't.

"We can go back to Buffy's." Matthew wasn't looking her in the eyes. Instead, his gaze kept focused on the wall behind her. "I can buy some things. You know, backup presents. Some puzzles. Some books. Maybe some coloring books."

Glory shook her head. "These kids have asked for specific things. The boxes will be here." The right presents simply needed to come. She'd call Sylvia when she got home.

Glory was at a loss. She didn't know how to manufacture faith or trust in Matthew. He didn't believe her, and there wasn't anything she could do about it. No one ever forced another one to have faith. Faith and trust came from the heart. Maybe that's why it was so upsetting to her that Matthew did not trust her. She had thought they were friends. And friends should stand beside each other.

"So what is it—crazy or lying?" Glory finally asked.

Matthew was startled. He stopped staring over her shoulder and looked her in the eye. "What?"

"Me and the boxes. Do you figure I am crazy or lying?"

"Well, n-neither…" Matthew stammered.

Glory noticed with satisfaction that he looked uncomfortable. "It's got to be one or the other. Which is it? Am I lying about the boxes coming or am I crazy to say they are coming?"

Silence. "I know you *want* the boxes to come." His

blue-green eyes looked bone weary and his shoulders slumped

Glory nodded sadly. So that was as far as he could get. "Overly optimistic, huh?"

Matthew nodded. His eyes moved to a spot on the table. Glory wondered what was so fascinating about a red-checked plastic tablecloth with silverware wrapped in a paper napkin.

"Hi, folks." A bearded man set down two menus in front of them. "Welcome to Billy's, home of the best food west of the Dakotas."

Matthew looked up at the waiter in pure relief. "What've you got?"

"The special today is meat loaf with mushroom sauce and garlic mashed potatoes." The man smiled fondly. He wore blue jeans, a red-checked logger's shirt, work boots and—over it all and spotless—a white BBQ apron. "Wife's in the kitchen today and she likes to make things fancy. When I'm cooking, it's plain meat loaf and plain potatoes. No chives. No parsley. No garlic."

"Which is better?" Glory liked the way the man's eyes lit up when he talked about his wife. He couldn't be over forty, but he looked as if he'd worked long and hard in this life. The only softness on his face was the love that showed when he talked about his wife.

"Hers are," the man leaned down and whispered. "But don't tell her I said so. I like to keep the rivalry going. Keeps the marriage interesting."

"In that case, I'll have the meat loaf." She'd have to remember this man and his wife for her next talk with Linda. Apparently even meat loaf recipes could be part of what kept a couple happy. "See how your wife makes it."

"You know, my wife is really something." The man had a scar on his cheek and a faint trace of whiskers on his face, but he looked like an old-fashioned knight. "When I started this place, no one believed I could stick with it. I'd been a drifter—cattle hand mostly—until I met her three years ago. But when they said I couldn't do it, she stood by me. We weren't even married then, so she didn't have to take my side. She believed in me when no one else did. I'll never forget that."

"Good for her," Glory said softly. She envied the couple their devotion. "She must be special."

"She is." The man cleared his throat. His neck grew flushed and he had a suspicious moistness in his eyes. "Didn't mean to go on like that."

"I'm glad you did." Glory handed back her menu. "It'll make the meat loaf more memorable."

"You want extra mushroom sauce with that? Her sauce is sure good."

"I'd like that."

"And you? What'll you have?" The man looked at Matthew.

"I don't suppose you have any crow on the menu, do you?" Matthew asked sheepishly.

"Well, no…" The man looked momentarily puzzled and then he grinned. "Too close to home, huh?"

Matthew nodded.

Glory watched the shadows lift from Matthew's face. His weariness shifted, and it was as if a load was lifted off him. He looked directly at Glory. "I know I should trust you. Please forgive me."

"Should?"

"I want to do better. I just don't trust easy."

Glory nodded. She saw the sincerity in his eyes. "I

guess wanting to trust someone is a step in the right direction.''

''And the answer is neither crazy or lying,'' Matthew said firmly as he handed his menu back to the man.

Glory grinned.

''And I'll have the meat loaf, too.'' Matthew looked up at the man. ''With extra sauce.''

''I'll be back in a jiffy,'' the man said, then carried their menus to the back counter and took their order slip into the kitchen.

It was one o'clock, and they had just eaten the last bite of meat loaf. Matthew had to admit he'd been loitering. He checked the door for suspicious-looking people periodically, but the people who came into Billy's were humble. Besides, Mrs. Hargrove was watching the twins, and he wanted this date to last as long as it could. He loved to watch Glory's eyes when she laughed. He'd told her some of the twins' favorite jokes just to get her started. Josh had a whole series of chicken-crossing-the-road jokes that were pure corn. Her blue-gray eyes crinkled with gold when she laughed. Her bronze hair sparkled in the sunlight coming in the side window. She threw her head back and the delicate curve of her neck made him think of a swan.

''You're beautiful.'' The words came out before Matthew thought about whether he should say them.

Glory stopped laughing and blushed.

He cleared his throat and added, ''Very beautiful.'' He'd never seen anything prettier than Glory blushing. She didn't blush red like some people—she just pinked. She was a pearl. He smiled. ''You truly do look like an angel.''

''Oh—'' Glory looked flustered. Then she glanced

down at her watch. "Speaking of angels, I better get back and make sure the costume fits."

Matthew nodded. All dates did come to an end. Then he brightened up. The date didn't end until he pulled in to the driveway. They still had the drive home left.

The afternoon sun reflected off the snow as Matthew drove his car back to Dry Creek. The back seat was filled with groceries and lumpy bags. The heater made the inside of the car a little stuffy.

"Mind if I turn it down?"

Glory nodded. She'd been thinking about Matthew's reluctance to trust her or anyone else, up to and including God. He couldn't have been born that distrustful. Her experience with young children was that trust came easily. "Did you grow up around here?"

"Here and a million other places."

"Father in the service?"

"Maybe." Glory noticed Matthew's fingers tighten on the wheel of the car until his knuckles were white.

"Maybe?"

"My father left us when I was six. We never heard from him regularly. But shortly after he left one of his old friends called one day—drunk—asking for Sergeant Curtis. Mom thought maybe Dad had enlisted. He'd always wanted to be in the military. Least, according to her."

"I'm sorry." Glory wanted to reach over and put her hand over Matthew's fingers, but she wasn't sure he'd welcome her touch. He looked brittle.

"Don't be." Matthew took his eyes off the road briefly to look over at her. "He wasn't much of a father when he was around."

"Your poor mother. Where is she now?"

"Died when I was eighteen. I'd just barely graduated from high school. It was like she was waiting to finish her job with me so she could leave."

"Oh, dear, no wonder you have a hard time trusting God."

Matthew grimaced and looked back at her. His eyes were deep with pain. "What makes you think it's God I don't trust?"

"Why, who else?"

"It's myself I don't trust." Matthew spit the words out. He tried to stop them, but they seemed to come of their own power. "It's me I don't trust. It's me that messes up. It's me that can't get it right."

"And was it you that let Susie die?" Glory felt as if they were lancing a boil. Was this the poison that Matthew kept inside his heart?

"Yes," Matthew whispered. "It was me that let her die. Me that let my mother die. Me that let my father leave. It was all me."

"No, oh, no." Glory reached over to touch Matthew's hand. "It wasn't you at all."

Matthew grimaced and then turned coldly polite. "Then who was it? God?"

"No. No." Glory was at a loss. How could she convince Matthew he did not carry the fate of the whole world on his shoulders? That the choice was not just between him and God. Life threw curves. She'd had her own battles with guilt over her father's accident, but it was nothing like the burden Matthew carried.

Dear Lord, help Matthew. Help me help Matthew. Show me how to help him.

Glory wished Socrates were sitting in this car next to Matthew instead of her. Or Solomon. Even Dear

Abby would do. Glory felt so inadequate. She'd tried to talk to Matthew about his feelings three times already as they drove back to Dry Creek, but each time he'd put her off with a joke or a shrug. The snow-covered tops of the Big Sheep Mountains in the distance were more likely to thaw out and talk to her than Matthew was.

"If you don't want to talk to me about it, that's fine." Glory gathered her ski jacket closer to her. It was still only midafternoon, but the outside cold seemed more of a threat than it had earlier. "Not talking isn't good. It's not healthy. But it's fine."

"I just don't want to talk about it now," Matthew said patiently. Some charming date he'd turned out to be. She probably thought he was a basket case. In his mind they were supposed to be talking about amusing things, light things—date things. At least, that was the way it was back when he was dating. Things couldn't have changed that much. "You never have told me about your artwork. What your favorite medium is, who your favorite artist is, your favorite art museum..."

"Refusing to talk about these things won't make them go away," Glory persisted. They'd turned the heater off to let the car cool down somewhat and Glory's ears were beginning to be chilly. She rubbed her left ear.

"Talking about them won't make them go away, either." Matthew shrugged as he slowed down so that a car behind him could pass. He switched the heater back on. "And I thought you were going to let me know when you felt chilly. I have this leather jacket on—I'd be warm in a snowdrift. But you've only got that light ski jacket."

"My jacket's warm enough. Nothing wrong with it."

Matthew sighed. He couldn't seem to say anything right. "Of course there's nothing wrong with it. You look beautiful in it. Black's a good color for you. And that shade of pink of your sweater is good, too."

Out of the corner of his eye, Matthew could see Glory smile. Now, this was the way a date was supposed to be. "I noticed you've done your hair different, too. Sort of softlike. It's good. And your earrings. I've watched them all day. They put me in mind of dolphins, with the graceful shape they have to them."

"Okay, you win," Glory said. "We won't talk about your issues now, but we will later."

Matthew nodded. He hoped he and Glory would have lots of laters to talk about all of their issues. If he was lucky, he could keep her talking to him all winter. Maybe by then she'd be charmed by eastern Montana and decide to stay. He chided himself. He shouldn't think long-term with Glory. He knew he wasn't good enough for her. He wasn't the Christian man she deserved to marry. But even if they didn't marry, he'd like to have her in his life somewhere. *Who am I fooling? Could I bear to have her in my life and not have her belong to me as my wife?*

"Mail it for me, will you?" The Bullet was back at Douglas's. He pulled two twenties from his pocket and handed them to Douglas along with an addressed box that he'd had wrapped at the store. "Overnight it. It's Millie's Christmas present and I can't wait for the post office to open."

"You're not going to be there for Christmas? Not with Millie?"

"No."

Chapter Ten

The afternoon sun was starting its slide down by the time Matthew pulled the car into Dry Creek. He'd primed Glory with a question or two, and she'd spent the rest of the drive back telling him about her desire to paint faces. He told her about the Custer County Art Center back in Miles City. He knew Glory loved art, and he wanted her to know art had a place around Dry Creek. They were, in fact, close to Charles M. Russell country, and they had his museum in Great Falls. Not that far to drive if she stayed a while.

Matthew loved to watch Glory. Her whole face lit up when she talked about art. She was a woman who noticed color and shadow and— Matthew looked down the street of Dry Creek. Over half of the houses needed painting. The whole town definitely needed tending. He hadn't noticed that it was run-down when he moved here. But now, driving up with Glory in his car, he wondered if a city woman, an artistic city woman, could ever live in a place like this. And it wasn't just the lack of a coat of paint. He could get a brush out

himself and do most of the houses if needed. There
were so many other things. Dry Creek wasn't Seattle.
Why, there wouldn't be movies in town if it wasn't for
the rack of family videos they carried for rent at the
hardware store. And there wasn't a hair salon, unless
you counted the back room at Marcy Enger's. She'd
never had any formal training, but the people around
agreed she had a knack for cutting hair. An art center
and an art museum wouldn't make up for all that. Not
to a woman who liked flavored coffee.

"Look at that!" Glory said as she pointed to the old
café.

Matthew groaned. And the old café—it was an eye-
sore. He didn't need that called to his attention. "Sorry
about that. Businesses don't always make it in Dry
Creek."

"Well, this one just might," Glory said as she
pointed again. "Look at that sign."

Matthew looked again. He was so used to seeing the
old café, he hadn't really looked before. He'd missed
the banner. And the clean windows. And the open door.

"Christmas Jazz and Italian Pasta—$5.00." Mat-
thew read the words of the foot-high banner that had
been strung across the door. "What in the world is
that?"

The trim around the big window had been painted a
bright red, and someone was pasting a frosted star inside the window's left corner. The person's head was
bent, but Glory thought the hair and angle of the neck
looked familiar. She was right. Matthew hadn't even
parked his car before the woman in the window looked
up and waved.

Linda called to them before they even got the car
parked. "Come and see."

The first thing Glory noticed when she stepped into the old café was that Linda's black lipstick was gone. The young woman's face was bare of any makeup—which was a good thing, since that left room for the traces of dust that trailed over her cheek. But, while there was dirt on Linda, there didn't look as if there was a speck of dirt hiding anywhere else in the large room. Wooden tables had been righted and scrubbed. The floor had been freshly mopped. The pine smell of disinfectant came from the kitchen.

"Jazz, honey," Linda called into the kitchen. "The rev and the angel are here."

Matthew winced. Glory laughed.

Duane came out of the kitchen. He didn't look like the Jazz Man now. Instead of a black leather jacket he wore an old flannel shirt that had holes in the sleeves and grease spots on the front. He was even more thoroughly dirty than Linda. He waved his arm in the direction of the back room. "Been getting the heater set up back there. Can't open up without heat."

"Open up? You're going to open up?"

"Just for Christmas Eve, at least so far," Linda said. Her eyes shone with excitement. "And word is spreading. We have a ton of cousins that are helping. The Alfsons and the Bymasters had to go home for supper, but they'll be back. So will the Lucas kids. It was Jazz's idea, really." Linda stopped to look at her boyfriend adoringly. "He got to thinking that all those people coming to the pageant might like to have a spaghetti dinner."

"Actually, Mrs. Hargrove gave me the nudge. Told me God answered prayers. It's just that sometimes He answered with our hard work. Then she gave me the keys and suggested Linda and I take a step of faith, as she called it. I wasn't so sure at first, but then I figured if the reverend can cook so can I. And then Linda said that music makes any meal better.'' Duane pointed to a raised area at the side of the room. "The band'll set up there.''

"What a great idea!" Glory said, and turned to Matthew. "We could help them get ready, can't we?"

"I don't see why not. At least, until I have to get the twins.''

Matthew disappeared into the back to help the Jazz Man with the furnace and Glory rolled up her sleeves to help Linda explore the cabinets under the counter next to the kitchen. Glory could smell that the cabinets had been cleaned. Everything that could be done in a short period of time had been done.

Linda pulled on one of the cabinet doors. She had to tug to open it. "Those two ladies who used to own this place had good taste, all right—and they didn't mind spending some money. This café was some kind of a hobby with them. I think they were planning to bring tea and civilization to the wild West.''

"They seem to have left it soon enough.''

"Dry Creek didn't match their dreams." Linda held out a large apron for Glory. "Here, wrap this around you. You don't want to get dirty like I did.''

"Not match their dreams? Why not?" Glory said indignantly as she slipped the apron over her neck and tied the strings around her. "Everything I've seen is charming, quaint, full of real people and their lives.''

Linda laughed as she opened a bottom cupboard door. "Not everyone wants real.''

Glory leaned down with Linda to look into the cupboard. Inside the cupboard were stacks of old-fashioned restaurant dinner plates, the white plates with a thin green band around the rim. "Well, well, look at this. There must be a hundred plates there." Glory quickly counted the stacks of plates. She'd estimate there might be 120.

"This'll be great!" Linda lifted out a small stack of the plates. "We thought we'd have to spring for paper plates—but this, this has more style."

Glory pulled open a drawer and found it full of stainless steel spoons.

"And forks!" Linda pulled open another drawer.

"They must not have even packed when they left," Glory said as she reached up and opened a top cupboard. There in thick plastic bags were linen tablecloths and napkins.

Dust filtered down as Glory and Linda pulled the bags off the shelf. Neither one of them saw the glass pitcher leaning against the bags. When Glory pulled out the last bag, the glass pitcher rolled off the shelf, fell to the floor and shattered.

Surprised, both Linda and Glory screamed.

"No!" Matthew's roar could be heard before he burst from the kitchen and into the dining area. He didn't stop in the doorway of the room to look around. Instead, wielding a piece of pipe, he simply threw himself in front of Glory and gently but quickly pushed her to the floor. He stood, half-crouched, over her.

Only then did he look around. "Where is he?"

Matthew's face had gone pale, and he looked fierce. He had a streak of black soot on his cheek and his hair had a film of white ash covering it. His eyes were pink from some irritant in the kitchen. He even wore a dish towel slung around his hips like a holster. He looked more like a back-alley bum than a hero. But all Glory saw was a warrior ready to do battle to defend his friend.

Glory was humbled. She'd never had anyone leap to her defense. She lay on the linoleum catching her breath. "It was a pitcher."

"A water pitcher?" Matthew was puzzled until Glory gestured to her left. His face went even whiter when he saw the pieces of glass. "Well—why—thank God I didn't push you in that direction. I could have hurt you myself."

"But you didn't," Glory quickly offered. She felt nothing but smooth linoleum beneath her arms and legs. "You thought it was a bullet, and you rushed to my defense."

Glory had forgotten she and Matthew were not alone.

"A bullet?" Linda whispered. Her voice cracked. "A real bullet? Here?"

Glory pushed herself up until she was sitting. The Jazz Man was standing in the doorway from the kitchen, and Linda was still standing beside the counter with the bag of table linens in her hand.

"There's no need to worry." Glory stood and brushed her jeans off even though she knew there was no dirt left on the floor. "It's nothing."

"But why would you think there'd be a bullet?" Linda persisted. Her eyes had grown round, and she looked even younger than the first day Glory had met her.

"You some kind of crook or something?" the Jazz Man questioned Glory. He measured her and still appeared unconvinced. "The police after you?"

"No, the crooks are after her." Matthew laid his piece of pipe down on the counter and took two steps over to Glory.

Matthew willed his panic to still itself. His pulse was pounding. His hands had been too scared to sweat until now. He knew he wasn't the man for Glory. Not really. But none of that mattered to him when he thought the bullets were flying. He felt a primitive need to protect her, as an animal needs to protect his mate. It was un-thinking and unquestioned. If Glory needed protection, he needed to protect her.

And that wasn't all. Matthew stepped closer to Glory and tucked her into his arms. He could smell her spice perfume and feel stray strands of her hair as they brushed his chin. But for all that, he held her loosely. It was her, not him, that he was most aware of. He didn't kiss her. Didn't dream of doing more than hold her. For now, holding her within the circle of his arms was enough. Just to simply stand together with his arms wrapped around her. Matthew slowed his breathing un-til his pace matched hers, and they breathed as one.

The Jazz Man cleared his throat, but neither Matthew nor Glory responded. They just stood together. Finally Linda tugged at the Jazz Man's sleeve, and they both walked into the kitchen.

Glory didn't even notice they had gone. She was wrapped in a safe, safe cocoon. She felt as if she was underwater. As if everything that was noisy or de-manding was distant. Nothing could reach her. Nothing could touch her. She had never felt as safe as she did now.

"We need to check back with the department," Mat-thew finally said. He uncurled himself from around her. "They might know more about this hit."

"Yeah," Glory agreed as she fought her sense of loss. Reality was intruding, demanding her attention. She missed the sense of being detached with Matthew.

If all that ever happened with a scare like this was that Matthew hugged her because he was worried about her, she wouldn't mind a bullet drill every half hour.

"I see," Glory said fifteen minutes later as she stood beside the counter in the hardware store and talked to her friend Frank back at the department. The fire from the potbellied stove warmed the inside of the hardware store. The air smelled faintly of this morning's coffee and fresh popcorn. The hardware store was much too homey to be a backdrop for the hesitant words she heard over the telephone from Frank's mouth.

"What'd he say?" Matthew asked, tight-lipped, when she hung up the phone.

"Sylvia called him." Glory kept her voice even. She wondered if this was how a person in shock felt. The sense that she was not inside her own body. "Those two boys she told me about—the ones that said there was a hit out on me—didn't show at the center today. Not even for basketball. Another kid said they had flown out on business last night. Frank checked the airport. They bought tickets for Billings, Montana."

Matthew felt the breath leave his body. It just whooshed away. *Dear God, we are in trouble. Help us.* He didn't even notice he had uttered his first prayer in two years.

"Can they ID them? Has the flight landed in Billings yet? Maybe we could contact the authorities there."

Glory smiled. Matthew thought like a cop. "Yes, Sylvia gave pictures to the Seattle police. Frank will fax them to us with the ones of the crime scene, said he'd fax them all right away. And yes, they contacted the Billings authorities. And yes, the boys were on the plane. But they were too late. The plane had landed, and they'd picked up their luggage forty minutes before Sylvia knew they were gone. They'd already left the airport terminal.''

"So they're here."

Glory nodded. She felt like a guppy in a fishbowl. No matter which way she turned she was too visible. Where would she be safe now?

"Car rental agencies? Did they check with car rental agencies?"

"The Billings police have the whole airport under surveillance. But Sylvia didn't think they would rent a car. They don't have a credit card, don't even have legitimate driver's licenses." Sylvia had added that they probably had fake licenses, since they'd gotten on the airplane, but Matthew didn't need to know that.

Matthew raised an eyebrow. "How old are these kids?"

"One's fourteen. The other's fifteen. They probably look older."

"Great. We're doing battle with babies," Matthew muttered as he ran his hand through his hair.

"These babies have been in a gang for the past five or six years." Glory bit her lip. She needed to think. "They can probably kill someone with a knife quicker than they can cut up an apple—and with less mess."

Matthew smiled wearily and started to pace. Even on his crutches, he seemed to need to move. "I know. I'm just not used to how tough children are these days. Makes me worry about the twins."

"The twins have you. They'll be okay."

Matthew nodded, then suddenly turned. "Kids like that—how'd they get the money for airplane tickets?"

"I don't know." Glory hadn't wanted to tell him this. The tickets were a problem.

"Did they pay cash?"

Glory nodded. She bit her lip again. She desperately needed to think.

Matthew stopped pacing and sat down in a straight-backed chair beside the counter. "Somebody gave them the money, then?"

Glory nodded. She didn't need to say what was obvious. The boys were on a job. How else could they afford to fly to Montana?

Matthew ran his hands through his hair again. He stood up as though he couldn't bear to sit and, once he was up, sat down again as though he couldn't bear to stand, either.

"Where are those drawings you've made?" Matthew demanded. "If we can figure out why someone wants to shoot you, they won't have just one target. They'll have to kill us both."

"What! That'd be crazy!"

"We could let Frank in on the theory, too," Matthew continued. "Once the authorities know why you're a target, you won't be a target."

Glory nodded. It made sense. Besides, work sounded good. If nothing else, it would stop the slow scream she felt working its way up from her belly. She'd never been hunted before. And to have the hunters be two of Sylvia's kids... Something was wrong with the world.

The drawings she'd made yesterday were still on the table near the front window of the store. She'd drawn the murdered butcher from several different angles and at several different times, ranging from when he'd just been shot to a final picture of the chalk outline just after the police came and were ready to take the body away.

"You have a photographic memory?" Matthew

asked as he looked at the set of drawings for the fifth time.

Glory nodded. ''For pictures, when I see something I remember it.''

''Do you think it through or just close your eyes and remember?''

''Mostly, close my eyes and remember. Why?''

''Then maybe somebody switched that package of meat on you,'' Matthew suggested. He pointed at the only two drawings that included the fallen package of meat. Each drawing had the meat in the corner where it had flown out of the butcher's hand when he was shot. At first glance, the packages looked alike. But then Glory saw the differences. The sticker was on the right for one package and on the left for the other. There were three small steaks in one package and two medium-size ones in the other.

''I must have remembered it wrong.''

''Have you ever remembered something wrong before—a picture you were drawing?''

Glory thought of the hundreds of photos she'd drawn as a student and as a sketch artist. She'd gone from bowls of fruit to crowd scenes. In school she'd learned to be quick with details and at the police station she'd learned to be accurate. Even now she could close her eyes and see the scenes from the murder scene. ''No, I've never gotten it wrong before. At least, not that I know of, and I would have known.''

Matthew nodded as though that's what he'd expected. ''Then we have our first clue.''

''But why in the world would anyone switch the packages of meat?''

''And who would do it?''

''And when,'' Glory added. Matthew was right.

They just might have their first clue. "They had to do it while we were sitting there waiting for the police to arrive."

"Was the gunman still loose?"

"No, he was tied up with some guy's belt. A customer tied him to the end of a display case. The gunman didn't even try to escape. He just lay there on the floor and waited."

"So whoever changed the meat was just hanging around, then."

"I suppose, but there was hardly anyone near us. The store manager had some of that 'Caution—Wet Surface' tape on his counter and he taped us in."

"Us?"

"Myself, the gunman and two other customers. But the other customers were holding the gunman down. Even when he was tied up, they didn't leave his side."

"Was the meat package close enough to the tape that a customer outside the taped area could switch it?"

"Not unless he had arms the size of King Kong's."

"Then that leaves the manager."

"The manager?"

Matthew nodded. "Wasn't it Sherlock Holmes who said once you've eliminated the impossible, whatever remains, however improbable, is the truth?"

"I suppose the manager could have done it. He was walking around swinging that tape here and there. He had big pockets in his butcher's apron, too."

"Now all we need to do is figure out why."

"That's the hard one."

"We don't have time for hard." Matthew picked up the telephone. "What did you say was the name of that market?"

"You're going to call Benson's Market?"

"How else am I going to talk to this manager?"

It took Matthew five minutes to be connected to the manager at Benson's Market. It took him only two minutes and four questions to have the man swearing at him and threatening to turn state's evidence and tell the feds.

"Who'd he think you were?"

Matthew shrugged. "I told him I was Matthew. He must have heard there was a Matthew somewhere."

"Or he's so eager to squeal, he doesn't care who knows what."

Matthew nodded. "He told me there wasn't supposed to be any hassle. That the meat deal was supposed to be low risk. The money isn't that much, not when there's the murder, and he swears he didn't know about the murder. And then someone's calling asking pointed questions sounding like they know something…"

"Not that you know anything."

Matthew grinned. "He didn't know that."

"We'll have Frank call him and lean on him, too."

Matthew nodded. "I'm beginning to think the road between here and Seattle is probably sprinkled with stolen meat."

"The rustling!" Glory put the two together.

"What better way to make a profit on stolen cattle than to have them butchered and sold in independent stores?"

"But why change the package of meat?"

"Something about the codes. The manager was actually pocketing a good sum of money by buying the stolen meat. When the butcher started talking about the computer red-flagging super sales based on the price the meat was logged into the system, the manager pan-

icked. The manager was shadowing the real prices behind the invented prices to keep track of his windfall
and something was going wrong.''

Pieces of the puzzle clicked together in Glory's
mind. ''And the butcher figured this out. That's why
they killed him.'' They'd solved the mystery. That's
what had been itching at her mind. The fact that her
visual pictures were different when she recalled the
scene. Someone must have found out about her memory. She was noted in the police department for never
forgetting a crime picture.

''I'm safe. Now that the pictures are out, there's no
reason to kill me.''

''All we need to do is find those boys and convince
them of that.''

Glory nodded. That was the problem, all right. Find-
ing those boys before they found her.

Matthew spent the afternoon making and waiting for
phone calls to Seattle. He talked to Frank. He tried to
talk to Sylvia, but he finally found out that she had left
shortly after warning Glory about the boys and was
flying into Montana herself.

''Billings airport is going to be busy.''

''Billings can't possibly be busier than this place,''
Glory grumbled. Mrs. Hargrove came into the store carrying a bent shepherd's staff.

''What's this I hear about bullets flying and hit men
coming to town?'' Mrs. Hargrove demanded as she
walked toward the counter. She was wearing a black
wool coat over a green gingham dress.

''I know now's not a good time, with the pageant
and all.'' Glory said. ''I didn't plan this.''

''Well, of course you didn't, dear. And don't worry
about the pageant. A few bullets won't stop us.''

"Speaking of the pageant, I might not be able to be your angel."

"Well, surely you don't think they'd try anything at the pageant." Mrs. Hargrove was shocked. "That's a holy moment!"

"That didn't stop Herod in the original pageant." Matthew was worried. With everyone in costume, two teenagers could sneak up before he could pick them out. A bathrobe and a loose turban was all the disguise they'd need. He wasn't sure he'd be able to pick them out fast enough to protect Glory.

"Well, if need be I'll fly from those rafters myself," Mrs. Hargrove said starchily. "I won't fit into the costume, but I can wear a big white apron and some of my husband's winter long johns."

Glory blinked. Had she heard right? Long johns and... *"Fly from the rafters?"*

Mrs. Hargrove gulped. "I guess we haven't told you yet. Tavis had this great idea." Her face beamed. "A flying angel. Now, won't that make the pageant special?"

Glory blinked again. "A flying angel? Me?"

"Well, it won't all be flying. First you'll start out standing on the rafters, singing a carol."

"Singing? Me? I haven't even practiced." Glory didn't know what was more alarming, the singing or the flying.

"Don't worry about it, dear. I'm sure whatever you sing will be just fine."

By nine o'clock that night Glory had practiced "Silent Night" exactly three times. Each time Matthew and the twins sang it beautifully. She wasn't so sure herself.

"Hang this one on that low branch," Glory directed from her place on the chair. She, Matthew and the twins were finishing decorating the five-foot pine tree at Matthew's house. She held out a golden ornament to Matthew.

"And don't bunch all the red ones together."

"Are you really going to fly?" Joey asked for the fourth time that evening.

"It's more like a swing." Glory had gotten very specific descriptions from Mrs. Hargrove and Tavis. The ropes were heavy and the rafters strong enough to hoist machinery. The angel's long robe would hide the seat of the swing, and the ropes, Tavis had assured her, would be scarcely visible in the darkened barn.

"Nobody's going to fly or swing anywhere unless we find those two boys," Matthew said sternly. After closing the hardware store, he'd looked both ways down the street before he'd rushed Glory to the car. They'd stopped at the café so Matthew could show the faxed photos to Duane and Linda and ask them to keep an eye out for the boys.

"Don't stop them," Matthew had directed the two. "You've got the number. Call the police. Those two are armed and dangerous."

"I'll show them dangerous." Duane scowled and pushed up the sleeves on the flannel shirt he was wearing.

"No heroics," Matthew ordered. "We just need an ID. I've already put Carl Wall on alert. We just call him—he'll come running. Let the other kids know."

Duane nodded. "I'll pass the word around. If they come, we'll pick them out."

"Thanks."

When Matthew had got Glory and the twins inside

the house, he'd rummaged through a kitchen drawer until he'd found the keys to his house. For the first time since he'd moved to Dry Creek, he'd locked both doors. The windows were all frosted shut, but he'd checked the latches on them anyway. Then he'd pulled the shades down. Halfway through locking up, he'd started to pray—actually, it wasn't praying exactly. It was more like cursing at God for allowing Glory to be in danger. But as the words spent themselves, his anger had dried up and left him feeling empty. Glory would not appreciate him cursing at God on her behalf. Still, his anger was there anyway, ready to defend her against anyone, even God himself.

The Bullet was in the airport in Billings, Montana. He wasn't two feet inside the place before he started spotting the cops. A dozen of them, at least. He never checked his luggage, so he went to the first car rental booth he found.

The clerk seemed nervous and excited, but not about the Bullet.

The Bullet smiled. "Busy day?"

"The police have been here for hours looking for two boys," the clerk leaned over and whispered confidentially.

"Runaways?" the Bullet asked, careful to keep his voice only mildly interested.

The clerk pulled his credit card toward her and shook her head . "Much worse than runaways. The woman at the snack counter dates one of those officers, and he told her these kids are contract killers. Think of that! Hit men! In Billings!"

The Bullet clucked sympathetically. His blood went

cold but he didn't let it show. There couldn't be two contracts so close to Christmas in this part of Montana. No, these kids were trouble. His trouble. They needed to be taken out of the game.

Chapter Eleven

December 24. Glory repeated the date to herself while she lay in bed the next morning, feeling lazy. It had snowed last night, and a thick layer of frost covered the window to her room. She hadn't had a white Christmas for years. It made her feel as if she was wrapped inside a Norman Rockwell sketch. Surely, contracts and hit men had no place in her life. Especially not on the day of the pageant. Not the day before the birth of Christ was celebrated.

Glory turned over and looked at the luminous hands on the alarm clock sitting on the bedside table. Almost six. Matthew would be up. She could hear him stirring around already, his crutch making an irregular thump on the floor in the kitchen. She breathed deeply. And she could smell the coffee. A gourmet orange flavor if she wasn't mistaken.

The floor was cold enough to make her dance from foot to foot when she stepped out of bed and looked in her suitcase for a pair of socks. There she found some gray woollies. Perfect. Glory sat back on the bed and

pulled the socks over her tingling toes. She had a busy
day today. She needed to check with the nurse in Miles
City to make sure her boxes had arrived. She'd spoken
last night with Mrs. Hargrove about the bags of candy
the angel was to distribute. She decided she'd count on
the twins to spread the word that the children's Christmas gifts would be given out after the pageant was over
and the children had all taken off their costumes.

Glory pulled out a hunter-green turtleneck to wear
with her jeans. Ideally, she should have red, but she
hadn't packed anything with Christmas in mind. Green
would have to do. Maybe she could snag a sprig of
holly somewhere to pin on her collar. Lacking that, she
might tie a string of Christmas ribbon around her neck.
Matthew had assured her he had wrapping paper for
Christmas. He must have ribbon, too. She glanced over
at the presents she'd purchased yesterday. They were
still in the bag; she'd need to wrap them this afternoon.
Maybe while she made cookies.

Glory had promised the twins they would sit together
and read the Christmas story before they got ready for
the pageant. She wanted both boys to have a cookie in
their hands while she read to them. Christmas, after all,
was the birth of hope. Every child deserved to have
Christmas memories of abundance.

Once Glory was dressed and ready to go downstairs,
she picked up her Bible. She always had her morning
devotions before breakfast. She'd read a psalm and then
pray. Since she'd been in Dry Creek, she'd had these
devotions alone in Matthew's bedroom. But today was
the day before Christmas. A miracle could happen. She
was going to march downstairs and ask Matthew to
have devotions with her.

* * *

Miracles didn't always happen on Christmas Eve day, Glory thought. Matthew had made a blueberry coffee cake and gourmet coffee for her, but he wouldn't have devotions with her.

"It wouldn't be right," he mumbled vaguely as he opened a can of frozen orange juice.

Wouldn't be right, Glory fumed. "And why not?"

"Sometimes devotions are just a habit. That would be all it would be for me. Just words."

"Well, sometimes lack of faith is just a habit, too." Glory didn't add that bullheaded stubbornness could be a habit, too. And refusing to take another risk once you've been burned could be a habit, too.

"I suppose," Matthew said mildly as he gave her the plate of coffee cake to put on the table. "But I have other things to worry about today instead of habits."

Glory wasn't finished with him. "Well, then I guess I'll just go off by myself and have a few minutes of Bible reading and prayer..." She paused to be sure she had his attention. "Maybe on the front porch."

Matthew almost dropped the pot of coffee. "You can't sit on the front porch! There are hit men out there."

Glory shrugged and started to walk away. "I've got other things to worry about today besides hit men."

Matthew growled and set the pot of coffee back on its stand. "This is blackmail, you know." He walked over to the table and sat down.

"I know." Glory grinned and sat down at the table, too.

Matthew decided it wasn't so bad. He loved watching Glory's lips move while she read, and it was cozy here in the kitchen. The sun was beginning to flirt with

the idea of rising, making the light outside soft. He
never got over the morning light in Montana. It was as
if the day just snapped into focus.

Matthew smiled. Glory had given him a reprieve so
he could bring them both a cup of steaming coffee, and
he sipped his now. He could get accustomed to flavored
coffee. He even half listened to the words Glory was
reading—Psalm 61. A psalm full of faith from its
"Hear my cry" to its "vows day after day." He'd
preached a sermon on that psalm once—a rather com-
pelling one. He'd used the old-fashioned illustration of
a tapestry that was beautiful on the top even though a
person looking at the back might not see the pattern.
He hadn't realized at the time that a single snag could
pull the whole tapestry apart. The threads were so connected. He'd never seen the backside of faith, the side
he was on now. He wished he had the words to tell
Glory about the confusion in his heart. Sometimes he
thought the problem wasn't that he had too little faith
now, but that he'd once had too much faith. If he had
not expected so much of God, he wouldn't have fallen
flat on his face when God let him down. But he hadn't
thought it was too much to ask for Susie to live. Not
from his God. He'd gripped God with all his might and
refused to let go, never once thinking that God might
let go of him.

"'Lead thou me to the rock that is higher than I.'"
Glory reread the words aloud. "'For thou art my ref-
uge, a strong tower against the enemy. Let me dwell in
thy tent for ever! Oh, to be safe under the shelter of
thy wings!'"

Nothing but the sound of the oven timer ticking
could be heard when Glory finished. Glory stole a
glance at Matthew. His face was stoic. Only the white

knuckles on his hand gripping the coffee cup gave away his feelings.

Glory opened her mouth to speak, but Matthew stirred instead.

"Yeah, well," Matthew muttered as he drained the last of his coffee.

"Isn't it inspiring?" Glory ignored Matthew's indifference and continued. "It's one of my favorite psalms."

"I'm glad it means so much to you."

Glory held her breath. She usually didn't push. She knew no one was ever forced into faith. But she had to try. "It could mean as much to you."

Matthew grimaced. "It did once."

"It could again." Glory looked directly at Matthew. She thought she'd see annoyance in his eyes, but she saw only sadness. "Just ask Him to help you."

Matthew didn't answer for a long minute. Then he took a final gulp of coffee and rose from his chair. "I need to finish getting breakfast ready for the twins."

"With me it was guilt," Glory said, talking to Matthew's back as he reached into the cupboard for the cereal boxes.

"Hmm?"

"Guilt. That's what stopped me from accepting God's love. I didn't see how I could take in His love when I was alive and my father was dead. I was driving the car. I should have died. Not him. I didn't deserve God's love."

"Oh, no." Matthew turned around and balanced on his one crutch. "You must never think that. Accidents happen. It wasn't your fault. God wouldn't hold that against you."

"What does it matter to you? You don't accept His love, why should I?"

Matthew frowned. "You're not me, that's why."

"You're not the only one who can be a martyr."

"I'm not a martyr—"

The phone rang, interrupting Matthew.

"I can get it." Glory stood.

"Sit down," Matthew commanded as he began to hobble across the kitchen. "And watch the windows. No one's supposed to know you're here."

Glory snorted. "The whole town of Dry Creek knows I'm here."

"It's not the people of Dry Creek I'm worried about," Matthew said from the living room as he grabbed the telephone. "It's who else that might be snooping around."

"Hello." Matthew twisted the telephone cord as he sat down on the sofa.

Glory went to the door to the living room and listened. In Seattle, a 6:00 a.m. phone call was unusual and likely to be bad news, but here six o'clock was almost prime time.

"It's your friend Sylvia." Matthew held the phone out to her.

"From the airport?" Glory walked to the sofa and sat down next to Matthew.

The telephone connection was filled with static. "Sylvia?"

"Glory, thank God it's you. Are you all right?"

Glory gripped the phone. Sylvia sounded a million miles away. "I'm fine. Where are you? Can I come get you?"

"No." There was noise in the background. It sounded like the grinding of metal objects. Sylvia herself sounded breathless and shaken. "I can get a ride into Dry Creek."

"Where are you? You're not thinking of hitching a ride, are you? It's not safe."

"No, Mr. Elkton is going to give me a ride."

Glory strained to hear Sylvia's voice. Something was definitely not right. Usually cheer spilled out of Sylvia's lips. Even when she was worried, Sylvia always sounded confident. But her voice now reminded Glory of a little girl, a little orphaned girl with no friends.

"Are you all right?" Glory pressed. "Mr. Elkton, who's that?" Glory searched her mind. The name was familiar. Then she saw Matthew mouth some words. "You don't mean Tavis Elkton's father? The owner of the Big Sheep Mountain Ranch?"

"Yes," Sylvia said at the same time as Matthew nodded.

"But how did you meet him?"

"I took a wrong exit off the interstate. Someone moved the exit sign to Dry Creek. Instead of leading to Dry Creek the sign led to a dirt road on Mr. Elkton's property. I took the exit and ended up with my car in the ditch."

"You weren't hurt?"

"No, I'm fine," Sylvia said. "Mr. Elkton found me."

"Well, thank God for that. Who would do a fool thing like move the exit sign?"

"That's what Garth—I mean Mr. Elkton—would like to know."

Glory listened. She had heard Sylvia talk about pregnant teenagers, arrested teenagers, addicted teenagers, but she'd never heard this particular tone in her voice before. Then it dawned on her. Glory grinned. Sylvia was flustered. That's what she was hearing through the telephone lines.

"I haven't met Mr. Elkton," Glory said calmly. "About how old is he?"

"Old? I don't know. Maybe in his forties."

"Hmm, a man of forty is in his prime here in Montana. Lots of outdoor exercise. Sunshine. Nature. I suppose he's attractive."

Glory looked at Matthew sitting on the sofa. He was eyeing her as if she'd lost her senses.

"He probably thinks so," Sylvia fumed.

"It's awfully nice of him to drive you into Dry Creek."

"He said he needed to drive in anyway. Something about getting some nails from the hardware store."

"Nails from the hardware store," Glory repeated for Matthew's benefit. "Mr. Elkton needs nails." Glory smiled as Matthew raised his eyebrows. It was as she thought. "Well, then, I'll see you when you get here."

"You're not going outside, are you?" Sylvia asked, sounding worried. "They didn't pick up K.J. and John at the airport. They're around here somewhere. You should just stay put."

"There's no point in hiding. They could shoot me inside as well as outside. Besides, it's probably safer at the hardware store than here. It's inside, too, and I stay away from the windows."

"Well, be sure to have the police check the place out before you go in. And tell them to give you an escort across the street."

"That'll be the day," Glory muttered. She could just see Carl Wall escorting her anywhere

"I'll get to Dry Creek as soon as I can. If they're hiding, they might come out if they see me."

"It'll be good to see you. And to meet Mr. Elkton. Just have him bring you to the hardware store."

"I'll be there soon. See you then."

"Yeah, see you then." Glory hung up the telephone.

Glory couldn't stop smiling. It was definitely Christmas.

"You look like the cat that swallowed the cream," Matthew observed.

"I think Sylvia's got a boyfriend."

"Garth Elkton?" Matthew asked dubiously. "I doubt that. He's a confirmed bachelor these days if I've seen one. His last marriage soured him on women. Not that he might not have an affair. But marriage? No."

Glory shrugged. "Well, Sylvia isn't the kind of woman a man has an affair with, so maybe you're right."

"But he is coming in for nails," Matthew muttered as he shook his head. "The last thing the Big Sheep Ranch needs is more nails."

Matthew thought Sylvia's idea of an armed escort was a good one. "Carl Wall doesn't have anything better to do. Besides, he likes to stop at the store for coffee."

Glory was sitting on the sofa with the twins, looking at the Christmas tree. The boys sat huddled in quilts, one on each side of her. They were still drowsy with sleep. Glory smoothed back Josh's hair. "Call him if you want to, but let's not talk about it now."

"They know about it anyway," Matthew said quietly with a pointed look at the twins. "I'm sure the whole town knows. News like this doesn't keep quiet."

"But we still don't have to talk about it before breakfast."

"No." Matthew smiled. "We don't."

"We have enough to talk about, anyway," Glory said as she squeezed each twin. "This afternoon we make cookies and then we celebrate just a little before the pageant."

"I need a new scarf for my costume," Joey said. "To tie me in with. Judy Eslick got gum on my old one."

"Well, we'll see to that before cookies. Maybe we can get the gum out. And I'll want to hear your lines for the pageant."

"I say, 'Look yonder,'" Josh announced.

"And I point at the angel," Joey added. "That's you."

Matthew cleared his throat and sat down on the sofa next to the twins. "I know how much you're looking forward to having Glory be the angel, but she might not be able to, not tonight."

The twins nodded. "That's what Mrs. Hargrove said."

"But I can watch you," Glory offered.

Matthew frowned. "I don't know if that's a good idea."

"Well, the whole town is going to be there," Glory said. "It's probably safer there than anywhere else."

Glory was surprised that Carl Wall agreed to escort her and Matthew over to the hardware store. She gathered from his comments that she was now one of his pigeons and, as such, would be defended from outsiders like every other citizen of Dry Creek.

"I've cleared the street," the deputy said as he stood on Matthew's porch. "We best move while everything's empty."

"But it's only seven-thirty," Glory protested. Mrs. Hargrove had stopped by to pick up the twins already. "Matthew doesn't open the hardware store until eight."

"I can open early," Matthew said as he balanced on one crutch so he could put on his leather jacket.

"That's right. You don't want to go by your usual schedules," the deputy warned them. "Do the unexpected. Change your routine. That way no one can set an ambush."

"Makes sense." Glory put her arms into an old army jacket the deputy had brought with him. It was his version of a disguise.

"And put your hair under this." The deputy held out a gray scarf and then a baseball cap. "Then put this on."

"Sorry for the trouble I caused you earlier," Glory said.

"Ah, that was just a little misunderstanding. No hard feelings, I hope." The deputy had done an about-face with her. Glory suspected he might have run a check on her and found out that she did work for the Seattle Police Department.

Glory smiled. "No. No hard feelings."

"Matthew?" the deputy asked.

"All's forgotten and forgiven." Matthew held the door open for Glory, then, before she could go through it, put a hand out to delay her and went through the door himself instead. "Need to change the order. Keep it unexpected."

"But if—" Glory gulped. If someone was planning to shoot her while she was going through a door, she wouldn't want them to shoot Matthew instead. For the first time, the bullets seemed all too real. It wasn't just her life that was in danger; it was the lives of those she cared about, too.

The few steps to the deputy's patrol car were cold and slippery. A fine sheen of frost was still on the ground from the night's low temperatures. Glory almost slipped twice hurrying down the sidewalk to the patrol car. Matthew struggled to keep up with her on his crutches, but she deliberately kept ahead of him. If she was a target, she didn't want him near her.

"Keep low in the seat," Carl said when Glory slid into the back seat of the car. He already had the heater going and the ice scraped off all the windows. Except for the sound of the car's engine, the day was silent. No traffic. No children outside walking anywhere. Not even any dogs barking.

It was only three blocks to the hardware store, but the deputy kept his eyes darting about the whole time. He studied the porch of each house that lined the street, starting with Mr. Gossett's. Nothing was unusual.

The deputy pulled up as close to the hardware store as possible, even though he had to park in a crust of old snow that had been shoveled up next to the store. Car exhaust had turned the top of the snow gray.

Glory had her hand on the door handle when Matthew reached over from the seat beside her to stop her.

"Not now," Matthew commanded, and jerked his head toward the store. "We got company inside."

"What?" The deputy rolled down his window and lifted his nose in the air as if he could smell something. "Smoke."

"There's a fire going in the stove."

Glory looked up. The sky was a washed-out morning blue, but she still saw the thin trail of vapor. It was so small it was almost invisible. "I don't suppose Elmer or Jacob would have gone inside and built a fire?"

Matthew shook his head.

The deputy reached for the radio in his car. "I'm calling for backup."

"Backup won't do us any good if they're inside watching us. It'll take the guys from Miles City twenty minutes to get here." Matthew ran his hands through his hair and looked over at Glory. "And stay down on the seat, for pity's sake."

"I won't stay down unless we all stay down."

"What?"

"I know about decoys," Glory said stubbornly. She refused to be the only one who wasn't a target. "Making them think they have a target just to draw a reaction."

Matthew grinned. "Now you're thinking."

Glory gasped. "I meant I don't want anyone to be a decoy. You're not to take any chances." Glory looked at the deputy, who was speaking into the radio. "Either of you!"

"But what about him?" Matthew pointed to his crutch that was lying sideways on the floor of the back seat. "We could put the deputy's hat on my crutch and wave it in front of the window. Those windows are so frosted up all anyone will see is a shadow."

"It's worth a try." The deputy hung up the radio. "Especially since everyone's out on a call already. I'd guess it'll be forty-five minutes before anyone gets here to help us."

Matthew pulled a handkerchief out of his pocket and wrapped it around the handle of his crutch to make the shape of a face. The deputy took off his cap and handed it back to Matthew.

"I'll walk it along," the deputy said to Matthew. "You stay with Glory."

"No, you stay with her." Matthew touched the door handle.

"But…" the deputy started.

"You have the gun," Matthew answered simply. "Even if you left it with me, I'm not sure what my aim would be. If something happens, I want the gun with you."

"You can't do this," Glory protested. No one had ever risked their life before for her, and now Matthew seemed to be doing it all morning. "You could be hurt." *Or worse.*

The windows on the car were still iced, even though the heater in the patrol car was spitting out coughs of heat. Glory herself was shivering. But Matthew's forehead had a thin sheen of sweat covering it.

"Don't worry." Matthew tied his jacket around the crutch, too. His crutch now looked like a skinny scarecrow.

"Of course I'll worry," Glory fretted.

"Well, pray instead, then," Matthew offered mildly as he unlatched the door.

"Pray," Glory squeaked. She tried, but the words spun in her throat. Matthew stepped out of the car. His boots crunched on the snow. She wanted to close her eyes. But she couldn't. *Dear Lord*— the words finally came —*Oh, dear Lord. Help this man, this exasperating man, the one I don't want to see hurt, the one I care about.…*

The car windows were beginning to fog over, so Glory saw Matthew as if he was in a grainy out-of-focus film. He crouched low, keeping his crutch held high. With every step he took Glory expected an explosion of gunfire. But the silence held. Finally Matthew was in front of the side window to the store. His jacket waved in front of the window. Whoever was inside wouldn't resist a target like that.

Glory felt she didn't breathe for the next two minutes. It seemed like hours, but she knew it was only two minutes because she watched the minutes change on the digital clock in the patrol car. One minute. Two minutes.

"I better go in the front door," the deputy finally said, pushing open his car door. "Maybe someone just forgot to put the fire out yesterday."

Glory began to breathe again. That must be it. So much had been happening yesterday that everyone's nerves were stretched. Matthew had just forgotten to see that the fire was completely out. Maybe Jacob or Mrs. Hargrove had put in a large chunk of wood at the day's end and it had lain smoldering all night. That must be it.

The car door handle was cool to Glory's touch. "I'll go tell Matthew."

Matthew had already turned toward them, and gave a relieved thumbs-up sign.

Glory pushed the store door open first. Matthew had twisted the key in the lock. The deputy took his hand off the butt of his gun to put his cap back on his own head. All three of them were standing in the doorway unraveling Matthew's crutch decoy.

Glory looked into the dim store first. It was too early for the morning sun to come in through the display window, and the inside was poorly lit. Matthew had left three salt blocks and a small box of bolts close to the counter for Timothy Stemm to pick up this morning. Glory reached for the switch to the overhead lights.

The overhead lights came on.

"What the—?" Glory blinked. It looked as if there was a big bundle of blankets tied to the large center post. Gray blankets. Khaki blankets. Then she saw a foot.

Matthew slammed the door shut and looked at Glory. "Back into the car."

"But—"

"This time he's right," the deputy said as he drew his gun.

Glory stepped back to the side of the store. "That's as far away as I can go."

Matthew frowned, but the deputy was already slowly opening the door.

"Deputy Sheriff Wall here. Don't try anything. We're coming in."

"We ain't done nothing." The muffled wail came from inside the store.

When Glory got to the door, Matthew was holding two thin teenage boys by the scruff of their necks as if they were puppies. When she got closer, she saw that their hands were tied behind their backs and they were both anchored with another rope to the center post.

"You've got it all wrong," one of the boys protested. "We're the good guys. We was here to stop the hit man. He's the one that tied us up."

"Contract killers aren't known for using rope to do their business," the deputy said wryly as he patted the blankets in a weapons search.

"Or building fires to keep their victims warm," Matthew added. He'd sat down on the floor next to the boys so he could keep them still while the deputy searched.

"But he did!" the boy with a Seahawks cap insisted.

"We was trying to help. We tried to keep him away. Even moved the road sign off the interstate so he'd get lost."

"You know it's illegal to tamper with road signs?" Matthew scolded.

One of the boys shrugged. Glory figured they had done worse than move a road sign or two in their short lives.

"No wonder Sylvia got lost," Matthew half muttered.

"Sylvia?" The jaws of both boys dropped. They were clearly worried more about her than they were about the law. "*Sylvia's* here!"

"You'll have some explaining to do." Glory looked at her watch. "In about one hour, I'd say."

"What's Sylvia doing here?"

"She came to keep you out of trouble," Glory scolded.

"Ahh, man."

"No guns," the deputy reported after a thorough search of the blankets.

Glory watched the boys exchange worried looks. It was clear they didn't want to disappoint Sylvia. Glory wondered how long they had been gang members. They each had a small gold earring in each ear, but that was more fashion than rebellion these days. The one with a Seahawks cap had a recent haircut and a bruise on his chin. The other boy had a tattoo that ran the length of his arm. Both wore white T-shirts and jeans.

"Where are your coats?" Matthew asked.

Glory noticed for the first time that both boys had goose bumps on their arms and the tips of their ears were red.

"Don't need none," one of the boys declared defiantly. "It's not cold."

Matthew looked at the two boys a moment and then nodded. "I'll see what we have in back. I think we have a jacket or two. That'll keep you until we rebuild the fire."

The deputy shook his head as he laid one of the wool blankets over each boy's shoulders. "You boys would have frozen out there last night without even a coat. This is Montana. You need to thank whoever brought you here."

The boy with the tattoo scowled. "Ain't going to thank no killer."

"Wonder who it was who put them here." The deputy looked up as Matthew hobbled back into the main room of the store. Matthew had his crutch under one arm and two worn jackets under the other.

Matthew tossed the jackets to the deputy. "I figure the whole county saw that picture I gave to Duane and Linda. Most likely one or two of the hands at the Big Sheep Mountain Ranch caught them asking questions. They wouldn't have wanted to wait for morning to come—chores awaiting—so they left them here for us to find this morning."

The deputy nodded. "Makes sense."

Glory was glad something made sense. She hadn't caught her breath all morning. Something was chewing its way into her consciousness, but she couldn't grasp it. Maybe it was because she was still reeling from the way Matthew had risked taking a bullet from these two boys and then noticed so quickly that they needed coats. If she hadn't already decided Matthew was a natural minister, she would have known it after this morning. Matthew was someone who was off course with his life. He'd given up his calling because his wife had died.

That must be it, Glory decided with relief. She was only worried about Matthew. Worried that he wasn't doing what he wanted with his life. Worried that he was so wrapped up in remembered love that he couldn't live.

That must be it, Glory tried to convince herself. She was only worried for Matthew. She let her breath escape—and that's when it hit her.

She remembered the moment. The stab of knowing. She'd sat in the back seat of the patrol car, watching Matthew wave his crutch around to tempt a bullet out of the boys inside the store, and fear had emptied her mind. And then her mind had filled in a flash with one thought and one thought only. She'd sat there motionless and realized that if a bullet hit Matthew it would hit her, too. Square in the middle of her heart. She'd seen the truth and then she'd pushed it away until now. Cautiously she let the thought come back. She worried over her revelation, afraid to even say the words to herself. But she couldn't stop them. It was true.

She was in love with Matthew.

Yes, she, Glory Beckett, was in love.

She knew it was foolish to love him. She knew he did not love her now and probably would not love her in the future. She knew they would never marry. They would probably not even see each other after Christmas. But she knew when she left Dry Creek she'd leave her heart behind. This wasn't at all how she'd planned to fall in love.

The Bullet pulled the brim on the Stetson down lower. He wondered if the farmer would notice that his hat and overalls had been stolen out of his pickup last night.

It had snowed last night—frigid, stingy flakes with more wind than moisture—and the porch where the Bullet chose to hide was cold.

The sun had barely risen when the Bullet heard the patrol car drive up to the house where he knew Glory was staying. He didn't even raise his head to look over the porch railing at her. No, it was too soon in the game. A patient cat waited for the mice to weary themselves before he stretched out his claws.

Chapter Twelve

Glory watched Sylvia question the two boys. Sylvia was petite, only four-eleven in the short stacked heels she wore. But Sylvia didn't need height. She was second-generation Italian and waved her arms around fearlessly while she spoke. Her gold rings flashed and her long fingernails pointed. She towered over the teenagers, who still huddled by the stove. Sylvia alternated between sympathy and scolding. The love she had for the teens was so obvious she had them talking in minutes. They told her everything.

"But what about the plane tickets?" Matthew was sitting on a stool behind the counter watching Sylvia's drama.

"I told you, man. I earned that money," insisted K.J., the teenager with the tattoo. "Busted my butt all last summer sweeping up in my uncle's restaurant."

"You told me before you worked for him for nothing," Sylvia challenged. Her blue eyes snapped and her lips drew together reprovingly.

K.J. grimaced. "Yeah, well..."

Sylvia looked at the two teenagers for a moment. Her face relaxed.

Glory saw that Sylvia was tired. Faint lines gathered around her usually laughing eyes. Her black hair, shiny and full, was bunched up and tied back with a scarf. *A scarf?* Glory looked more closely. It wasn't a scarf. The material tying Sylvia's hair back was a red bandanna, the kind the ranchers here used. And unless Glory was mistaken, the thick knot holding the bandanna in place could only have been tied by the expert fingers of a rancher.

Glory slid her gaze over to the only rancher in the store. Garth Elkton. He didn't look any too fresh, either, now that she looked at him closely. He needed a shave and his scowl seemed to fasten on Sylvia with some regularity.

"What's your uncle's name?" Matthew asked K.J. "I'm sure the police can find out if you worked for him."

"Ah, don't call the police," K.J. whined. "My uncle'll freak. Besides, you shouldn't keep worrying about us when there's a killer out there."

"A killer?" The deputy paused. "Describe him."

"Well, he's sort of average looking."

"What color's his hair?"

"Brown. No, black." The boy looked miserable. "Just hair. No particular color."

"Can't you describe him any more than that?"

K.J. frowned. "He's hard to remember. The kind of guy that hangs out in the shadows at school. You'd hardly know he was around except for the gun."

"I thought so," the deputy said smugly. "You never saw anybody."

"Hey, I ain't lying. We're innocent. All we did was move the road sign."

"Son, you're lucky you're dealing with Sylvia and not me." Garth Elkton spoke for the first time. His voice was low and gravelly. "I'd turn you over my knee and show you the consequence of moving road signs. This is snow country. People could die if they take the wrong turn in a blizzard. Someone could have died last night because of you."

"Nobody did, did they?" K.J. asked in alarm.

"Hey, we didn't mean to kill nobody," protested John, the other boy. "We've been trying to do good to show—"

John bit back his words to a mumble.

"To show what?" Sylvia persisted.

"That we meant it." John looked down at the floor and whispered, "The other day in church, we meant it."

Glory looked at their faces. They looked honest. Besides, it was almost Christmas, and they were so young. She turned to Sylvia. "Maybe it has all been one of those misunderstandings."

"Maybe." Sylvia looked thoughtful.

"I guess no harm's been done," Glory offered.

"You don't want to press charges, then?" the deputy asked.

Glory looked at Matthew. He answered, "If they leave today with no funny business, we'll let it go."

"I already called the airport in Billings and got two tickets back to Seattle for this afternoon. If no one minds, I'll put them on the plane myself," the deputy said eagerly. He clearly wanted the boys out of there.

Sylvia nodded. "I'll go with them."

"Can't. I had to pressure the agents to get these two

tickets. There's a waiting list a mile long. Seems everyone wants to go someplace the day before Christmas.''

Sylvia bit her lip. ''I see. Well, I guess I'll need to stay, then.''

''Good.'' Garth Elkton rocked back on his boot heels. He'd already removed his Stetson and laid it on the store counter. His sheepskin coat was open, showing off a green flannel shirt. He looked down and smiled politely at Sylvia. ''You can go to dinner with me, then.''

Sylvia looked up at him as if he'd just grown two heads. ''Us? Dinner?''

The polite smile ended. A muscle tensed in the rancher's cheek. ''It's a custom.''

''I—I can't,'' Sylvia stammered, frantically looking around until she latched on to Glory. ''I have to—to help Glory with the pageant.''

''We can eat before the pageant.'' The rancher's eyes grew flint hard.

Sylvia flushed, and she looked at the floor. ''Before the pageant I, ah, I need to help Glory get dressed up in her angel costume.''

The rancher looked around coldly. ''Matthew here can help her. It's only wings and a halo.''

''It might only be wings and a halo to you, but Glory here cares how she looks in that costume,'' Sylvia protested as she walked over and put her arm around Glory.

''I do?'' Glory squeaked. Sylvia pinched her. Glory corrected herself. ''I mean, yes, of course, I do care.''

The rancher looked exasperated. ''Look, we eat and talk or we just talk. Take your pick. We've got business to finish. And we might as well eat while we do it. If you want to stay in Dry Creek, we'll eat the spaghetti dinner those kids are fixing up. After all their hard work, they deserve some support.''

"Kids?" Sylvia looked up.

Glory smiled. Whether the rancher knew it or not, he had hooked Sylvia. Nothing got to her like kids.

"They're going to have music," Glory offered mildly. "You have to eat anyway."

"I suppose we could eat a short meal together."

"We'll call it a snack." The rancher smiled.

Sylvia took her eyes off the rancher and returned them to the boys. "I'm going to call Pat Dawson and have him meet your plane. I'm also going to call the police. And don't even think of ditching this flight along the way. If I hear you're not in Seattle by tonight I'll have the police in fifty states looking for you."

"Yes, ma'am," both boys said.

"Well, we best get going into Billings," the deputy said. "I want to make it back and see this pageant myself. Especially now that the angel is going to be in it."

Matthew pondered. "I guess there's no reason why she can't be the angel now."

Glory grunted. She could think of a reason or two not to be the angel. But she doubted anyone would listen. "In that case, I better see about my halo."

The midday sun shone in the display window of the hardware store. Jacob and Elmer were sitting beside the wood-burning stove with their legs stretched out in front of them. Matthew was moving around in the back storage room. He'd already brought out the gold garland and cut off a length for a halo. He was back there now looking for glitter to sprinkle on the cardboard wings they'd brought over from the church.

Glory was putting the last of the oils on the portrait of the twins' mother. She added a smudge of light gray paint to the woman's cheek. Glory patted it to make it look like a dusting of flour. She was going to give the painting to the twins to be opened after the pageant. That reminded her she would need to go back to the house soon and make cookies for the twins.

The bell above the door rang, and Glory looked up to see Linda come in. The young woman was all dressed up for the holidays. She'd dyed one streak of hair Christmas red and another hunter green. A jingling bell earring dangled from each ear and she had a sprig of holly behind one ear. She wore red leotards and a white sweater.

"Figure I'll get more tips if I look Christmassy," Linda whispered as she came over to where Glory painted. "Least, that's what my friend Sara Enger said. She even took a picture of me with Gus in his Santa suit."

"Gus?"

Linda shrugged. "This old cowboy that's been helping us. Used to work for one of the ranchers up north that sold out. Jazz told him he could bunk down in the kitchen for a while if he helped us tonight by being Santa. He don't talk much, but he sure can look jolly."

"How's the sauce coming?" Glory asked. Matthew had already reported that there were several gallons of spaghetti sauce simmering away at the old café. Young people and apparently some older ones had been coming and going from the place all day. The smell of Italian herbs was settling over Dry Creek, and when a person walked down the street they could hear the faint sounds of a band practicing inside the café.

"We're almost ready for everyone. You and Matthew are coming, aren't you?"

"Wouldn't miss it," Glory assured her.

"Hey, you should wear your costume for dinner." Linda snapped her gum.

"This angel would need a bib as big as a sheet if I had to eat with my wings on."

"Yeah, I suppose it wouldn't work too well with the wings."

The door to the hardware store opened again, and Sylvia came in.

"Cold out there." Sylvia blew on her hands to warm them.

"It's not too bad, really." Glory felt like a Montana native. "Not cold enough to crack the vinyl on car seats or to freeze your nose hairs or to—"

"I get the picture," Sylvia interrupted.

Glory grinned. "I thought maybe a certain rancher would keep you warm—give you his jacket, that kind of thing."

Sylvia snorted. "The only thing Garth Elkton is going to give me is high blood pressure. That man is impossible."

"If you say so," Glory assured her friend with another grin.

Just then Matthew hobbled out from the back storeroom. Glory's grin faded. It was all she could do to keep her mouth from dropping open. His chestnut hair was rumpled and shot through with gold. In fact, he was golden all over from his forehead to his big toe. His face was sprinkled with gold. His clothes were sprinkled with gold. It appeared Matthew had found the glitter.

"Speaking of keeping warm," Sylvia leaned over

and muttered to Glory. "You never did tell me how you ended up catching a man like him."

"Catching? Matthew?" Glory's voice squeaked. She continued in a whisper. "I didn't catch anyone. Matthew is just a friend. He's not caught at all."

"If you say so." Sylvia righted herself and patted her hair. "I better get back to the barn. Mrs. Hargrove needs help with some pine cones she's arranging."

"She still at it?" Elmer groaned and stood up. He slapped Jacob on the knee. "Guess we better go give her a hand."

Matthew shook his head. Glitter spun off him. "Give me a minute to get this stuff off me and I'll go give everyone a hand, too. I'll just put a note on the door so anyone who wants to buy something knows where to find me."

They all stood in the door to the barn. It was high noon and the air was cold enough so that they all looked like smokers when they breathed. Each word brought a puff of gray-white air. The barn itself was rough-hewn. Unvarnished pine boards lined the walls and the thirty-foot-high ceiling. A hayloft hung down from the front of the barn and Glory could see the angel's swing that the ranch hands had built. Two thick ropes hung from a hoist and met at the swing's bottom with a wide plank to stand on. The swing looked like every child's fantasy. Glory was beginning to anticipate soaring over the heads of everyone as she swung from side to side in the barn.

"You'll have to wear some ruffled petticoats," Sylvia offered. "They'd swish and sway when you swing. It'll look very feminine. Southern belle-like."

"Petticoats?" Matthew frowned. Suddenly he wasn't

so sure about Glory and this swing. There were too many single men out at the Big Sheep Mountain Ranch. They'd love to get a glimpse of Glory's petticoats. "Long johns," Matthew said decisively. "You'll wear a pair of my long johns. I won't have anyone ogling your legs."

"Long johns?" Glory frowned. "I don't think an angel would wear long johns."

"In Montana they do. We've got cold winters here," Matthew insisted.

"It is cold, isn't it?" Mrs. Hargrove said as she walked over to them. She rubbed her hands even though they were in knit mittens. "We've been trying to think of a way to warm up this barn for tonight."

"Henry has some secondhand camp stoves," Matthew suggested. "They'd at least take the edge off the cold."

"I'll buy them from you," Tavis offered.

"I'm sure Henry won't mind if we use them on loan. They're already used."

"I'd like to buy them anyway. I've been thinking we might use this barn for other things, too. Plays, maybe concerts."

"We could have rock concerts," Linda gushed. "Wait'll I tell the Jazz Man. We could set up right here!"

"Not a bad idea," Mrs. Hargrove agreed, and turned to Tavis. "But what will your dad say? I'm surprised he even agreed to the pageant."

"Me, too." Tavis grinned. "That's why I thought I'd ask about the rest—he's not himself lately. Aunt Francis has him rattled. She's cleaning everything in sight. Even threw away his favorite coffee mug because it was stained. He probably doesn't even know what he's agreeing to, but he's a man of his word. Once he's said yes, he won't back down. Besides, we've built all these bleachers and we don't need the barn anyway. Only use it for trucking, and that was before we built the good road to the main corrals.''

Glory looked around her. The barn had been transformed. Six rows of sturdy bleachers lined both sides of the barn. The floor of the barn had been hosed down and polished until it shone. At the front of the barn, a fake building front stood with the words *Bethlehem Inn* painted across it. Nearby an open stable was fashioned with bales of hay strewn around. A metallic gold star hung down from the hayloft above the manger. As she looked more closely, she noticed that the gold star was on a pulley so that it could travel on a wire from one end of the barn to the other.

''Amazing,'' Glory complimented Tavis and Mrs. Hargrove.

The older woman beamed. ''Tavis and the other ranch hands did most of it.''

Tavis shrugged. ''Just some sawing and hammering.''

''It's perfect.'' Sylvia added her praise.

Mrs. Hargrove nodded proudly. ''We've got it all set to go. The only thing we're missing is a minister to say a prayer before we begin.'' Mrs. Hargrove looked at Matthew. ''It could be an already printed prayer. Maybe from a book or something.''

''Then anybody can say it.'' Matthew leaned on his crutch.

''Not everybody has the voice,'' Mrs. Hargrove explained wistfully. ''There's something about the voice of a minister. It would add the right touch.'' She added quickly, "Don't say no yet. Think about it. If you don't do it, Elmer will stand in."

"I'll think about it," Matthew agreed as he turned around to leave.

Glory watched Matthew walk slowly out of the barn. The floor was smooth and he had to place his crutches with care. She wished she knew what he was thinking.

"He won't do it." Glory spoke aloud.

"I'm thinking he will," Mrs. Hargrove contradicted confidently. "He's been walled in long enough. It's time for him to take back his faith."

"I'm not even sure he's planning to read the Christmas story to the twins," Glory said, worrying aloud. "If he won't do that, he surely won't pray."

"Wait and see," Mrs. Hargrove advised. "That man may surprise you."

The smell of chocolate chip cookies carried all through the house. Glory had added a few more ornaments to the tree so that it shone and sparkled from every angle. The nurse from Dr. Norris's clinic had called and told her the boxes had arrived and she would bring them with her to the pageant. Knowing that the children's presents were taken care of, Glory carefully wrapped her own gifts and placed them beneath the tree. The books for the twins were easy to tie up in red tissue paper. She had more trouble with Matthew's gift. She hadn't looked closely enough at the cassette when she bought it. It was *Piano Selections for Lovers. Lovers!* Since she didn't have anything else for him, she'd put it in her purse. If he gave her a present, she'd give it to him.

The big present for the twins was still upstairs in Matthew's room—the picture she had painted of their

mother. Glory imagined the look on the twins' faces
when they saw their mother for the first time. She wondered if they would ever realize that half of the love
that shone out at them from the picture belonged to her,
Glory. In the last brush strokes of the painting, Glory
had begun to cry herself. She felt the love of the twins'
mother as surely as though the woman were standing
in the room with her. And Glory felt her own love pour
out of her heart onto the canvas.

"Are you all right?" Matthew pushed open the front
door and hobbled into the house. Snowflakes covered
his hair and the shoulders of his wool jacket. He wasn't
using his crutches properly. He'd obviously been using
his own feet and carrying the crutches.

"Yeah, why wouldn't I be?"

Matthew frowned. "I told you to keep the door
locked."

"Oh, there's no need now," Glory said. "The boys
are on a plane back to Seattle."

"Still, we can't be too careful." Matthew turned
around and twisted the lock.

"Well, nobody around here is going to hurt me,"
Glory protested. "At least, not with a bullet. I'm more
likely to fall off that angel swing than anything."

"We're going to tie you in. I've already thought of
that and fixed it so you can't fall. And I thought of a
way to tie your skirts down while we're at it."

"A straitlaced angel?"

"Angels are supposed to be straitlaced. Besides—"
Matthew caught himself and stopped.

"Besides what?"

Matthew smiled slightly. "Besides, you're so beautiful nobody's going to care about sneaking a look at
your legs. They'll just be looking at your face."

Glory blushed. "You're just saying that so I'll weaken and give you one of the cookies I made for the twins."

"I thought I smelled chocolate."

It was almost five o'clock, but it was already dark outside. The winter sky was sprinkled with stars. Matthew had added a large log to the fireplace in the living room and made spiced cider for everyone. Glory had plugged in the lights to the Christmas tree, and the twins had taken their baths early in honor of the evening.

The twins sat on the sofa with a cookie in each hand, waiting impatiently for Matthew to finish pouring the cups of cider.

"Before we open the presents we need to read the Christmas story." Glory twisted two new bulbs onto the strand of lights. All of the lights shone now.

"We could read it real fast," Josh suggested as he took another bite of cookie.

"Not too fast. You'll want to know about the presents they gave to the little baby Jesus before we open ours," Glory said, trying to make the story relevant to the boys.

"What'd He get? Lego?" Josh asked.

"Not exactly. He got gold, myrrh and frankincense."

"We know about frankin—whatever," Josh explained. "We got a book about him at preschool."

"Him?" Glory was bewildered.

"Yeah. Frankin—frankin—sense." Josh laid his cookies down and stood up from the sofa. "He walks like this." Josh held his arms out stiffly and clumped along.

"Oh, Frankenstein." Glory deciphered his meaning. "But that's not—"

"I'll bet he's a Terminator," Joey said excitedly. "And God sent him to be a bodyguard for the baby Jesus."

"That's a cool gift." Josh sat back down on the sofa. "And I bet this Frank guy has a laser gun that zaps people." Josh held out a pretend gun and took aim at the fireplace. "Rat-tat-tat-tat!"

"Nobody is zapping anyone around here," Matthew said firmly as he set down four mugs of cider on the coffee table. "And no guns."

"I was pointing at the fireplace," Josh explained. "That's okay. It's not people."

"Frankincense wasn't a person or a machine," Glory said as she moved one of Josh's cookies and sat down beside the twins.

"Oh." Josh picked up the cookie and thought a moment. "Was it a car?"

"They didn't have cars when Jesus was born."

"No cars!" Joey squirmed closer to Glory. "What was it, then?"

"It's a...well, a...perfume."

"Like in soap?" Josh asked skeptically.

Glory nodded. "Something like that."

"Who'd give a baby soap for Christmas?" Josh was getting indignant.

"Had Jesus been a bad boy?" Joey asked in awe.

"Well, no, not at all. Jesus was only a baby. A very good baby."

Josh snorted. "Good boys don't get soap in their stocking."

Glory looked at the two boys and then looked at

Matthew. ''It wasn't like that at all,'' she protested weakly.

''Maybe I better read the story from the Bible,'' Matthew said, and grinned at Glory. ''We can't have them thinking Jesus was a bad boy or that He needed a Terminator to protect Him. Of course—'' Matthew eyed his two sons thoughtfully ''—He did have that trouble with the bad guys coming to get Him.''

''Bad guys?''

Matthew hobbled over to the bookshelf and pulled the family Bible down. He held it in his hands briefly before he turned around and came back to the sofa. ''It all started two thousand years ago halfway around the world in a town called Bethlehem.''

''Is that farther away than Billings?'' Joey asked.

''It's a lot farther away than Billings,'' Matthew assured his sons, and then looked at Glory. ''Remind me to get a globe for these boys. They have no idea.''

Glory smiled. She thought it was rather sweet for five-year-old boys to think the whole world was in their backyard.

Glory leaned back. She couldn't believe it. Matthew was reading the Bible to his sons as if he did it every day.

She watched his face in the firelight. She smiled as he made donkey noises to make his sons giggle when he told of Mary and Joseph's trip to Bethlehem. The two boys looked up at their father with rapt attention.

Glory felt the happiness squeeze into her heart. She'd never thought she'd love someone like Matthew. Someone strong and good and kind. Someone who took in a stranger like her just because his sons thought she was an angel. *How many ways do I love you, Matthew Curtis?* she asked herself. *How many ways?*

"No," she heard Matthew say to Josh. "The wise men couldn't just call the cops. Besides, they weren't lost. They were following the star."

The Bullet patted his very red stomach and hitched up his very black belt. He circulated through the little café and gave out candy canes to everyone. He even posed for pictures with some of the diners. He hoped all of the jolliness would pay off.

The Bullet had spent the day planning. The more he thought about when to shoot the woman, the closer he came to realizing he couldn't do it. He just wasn't up to pulling another trigger. He'd be a marked man, of course. But he was so tired of killing people.

He was going to march outside to the pay phone and call Millie. He'd spend Christmas with her and then head down to Mexico. She might even come with him.

The air was brittle, and the Bullet needed to take his gloves off to punch the numbers on the telephone. He'd expected Millie to pick up on the first ring. But the phone rang right through to the message.

He heard Millie's breathless voice. "Forrest, if that's you, your uncle stopped by. We're out to dinner." A giggle. "He said to tell you he's taking real good care of me."

The Bullet's mouth went dry. This client that knew Forrest's name would know he used an old uncle as a screen for his trips. Since the Bullet had no uncle, that left only one conclusion. The client had Millie. The Bullet let the knowledge slice through him.

Chapter Thirteen

The early-evening light filtered into the church. Glory could hear the women outside in the church kitchen as they put the coffee on to brew. Through the open door she saw the kitchen counter piled high with cookies. Lemon bars. Gingersnaps. Sugar cookies. Plus trays and trays of date bars. Glory wished she was out there chatting with the ranchers' wives she'd just met—Margaret Ann and Doris June. But instead she was the angel, so she was inside the costume room listening to Matthew's quiet breathing as he helped her adjust her wings. The bare overhead light was bright and, once Matthew had pushed some choir robes out of the way, she could see herself in the old full-length mirror.

Glory wrinkled her nose at her reflection as she circled her head with garland. She'd loosely pulled her hair up on top of her head to help keep the garland in place. Tiny flecks of gold fluttered down on her nose. Not that it mattered. She was already covered with specks of glitter from when Matthew had hooked her wings onto the harness she wore under her white angel gown. The wings had been recently dipped in glitter.

Glory blew a strand of hair off her forehead, knowing she had to be careful what she touched. Mrs. Hargrove had unearthed a pair of long white gloves so that Glory could point with a white finger when she said, "Behold…"

"Not many angels look like they're ready to swear," Matthew observed mildly as he bent the flap on Glory's left wing to attach it more firmly. "Well, I expect the Archangel did a time or two—all that wrath and destruction."

"They all would look that way if they had to fly around in wings like this." Glory cautiously flexed a shoulder. She had a tiny little itch under the harness.

Matthew chuckled. "I doubt they could even get off the ground with those wings."

"Now you tell me."

"They'll do fine in the swing, though." Matthew cleared his throat. He thought he was doing pretty well with the chitchat. No one would know his hands trembled from adjusting Glory's wings. She wasn't an angel; she was a goddess. Her flaming red hair, more copper than gold, was gathered on top of her head. But it was so fine, wisps of hair circled her head. She scarcely needed a halo. Her hair floating around her sparkled as much as the glitter. Matthew leaned just a little closer to her hair and breathed deeply.

"Peaches?"

"My shampoo," Glory answered. She had forgotten her lipstick and rouge, but she had remembered her favorite matching shampoo and lotion.

Matthew nodded. "I'd better pin your garland on

better. Wouldn't want the halo to slip when you're out there.''

Matthew stood behind Glory, positioning her halo and noticing once again the graceful line of her neck. Swanlike didn't begin to cover it. Glory looked so much like an angelic bride as she stood there that Matthew couldn't help himself. He leaned closer and pressed his lips very lightly to the back of her neck. His kiss was more of a breath than an act.

"My hair's falling down." Glory tried to reach her arm up to her neck. That's all she needed. "I just felt it fall."

"You're fine."

"Yeah, men always say that, even when we have broccoli in our teeth."

"You don't have broccoli in your teeth."

"I know. It's my hair."

Matthew decided he was a rat all the way. He put his hands up to Glory's hair and did what wasn't necessary. He pretended to smooth it back up. Her hair was silky soft. He smoothed it again. "There." His voice was little more than a whisper. "Your hair's fine."

"Thank you."

"It's time we got you to the barn." Matthew's voice was thick. He knew they still had a half hour before the performance started, but he also knew that he'd better get Glory over to the barn and away from this small room before he gave in to the urge to kiss more than her neck. Not even that growing stack of cookies on the counter would distract the church women if they happened to look over into the small room and see him kissing the Christmas angel the way he wanted to right now.

* * *

Glory stood in the door of the barn. Matthew had walked over with her, refusing to use his crutch so that he could hold a blanket around her shoulders even though it was almost impossible to do so with her wings jutting out behind them. The night was cold and starless. Fluffy snowflakes were beginning to fall. When they got to the door of the barn, Glory had had to enter sideways so that her wings would not be bent.

"I don't know what I'd do without you," Glory said to Matthew as he bent to unhook the hem of her white gown that had caught on a nail by the door.

"I'll get a hammer and come back and smooth that over," Matthew muttered as he stood. "Yours won't be the only hem it catches."

Matthew was right. Glory looked around. There was an abundance of long, flowing robes. She'd never seen such a colorful array of little boys in bathrobes, most of them dragging along the barn floor. Some had pastel-striped robes; some had white cotton robes; some had plain colored robes. All of them had a striped dish towel wrapped around their heads with a band of red material holding it in place. Several boys had a wooden staff in their hands. Two of the boys even had leashes. Leashes? Glory looked again. If there were leashes, there must be— Yes, there they were. The animals.

"Come see," Josh called excitedly to Matthew and Glory. "We've got sheep!"

"I'll believe this when I see it," Matthew whispered to Glory as they walked over to where a group of boys stood.

"Don't knock it. The sheep are as real as the angel." Glory had never realized that a dog wrapped in a fluffy white towel could look so much like a sheep in the shadows.

"Hey, Glory," a woman called to her from the front of the bleachers.

Glory turned and recognized Debra Hanson, the nurse from Dr. Norris's office, who had promised to bring the boxes of toys Glory had ordered.

"I got them, honey," Debra said in a stage whisper as Glory walked closer. Debra snapped her gum and spoke with a Southern accent. She wore a red scarf wrapped around her head like a turban and a long black coat. Christmas bell earrings shimmered as she spoke. "Where do you want me to put them?"

Glory looked around. She'd like to surprise the children. "Behind the stable."

"I'll tell the boys." Debra turned and smiled at a couple of the hands from the Big Sheep Mountain Ranch. She raised her hand to wave and used one of her red-tipped fingers to summon the men over to her. They came eagerly.

Glory decided her boxes were in good hands, so she could mingle. Since this was a barn, there was no backstage area. The six-foot-high, ten-foot-wide stable was the only structure. The actors were in plain sight doing last-minute errands. One little choir angel had a nosebleed, and one of the older shepherds took him outside to get some snow to put on his nose. One of the boys was teasing Mary about the makeup someone had put on her. Mrs. Hargrove was muttering to herself.

Glory decided Mrs. Hargrove was the one who needed rescuing the most. "Everything looks ready," Glory said reassuringly when she came near the older woman. Glory had noticed the musicians from the café setting up their small sound system at the side of the stable.

Mrs. Hargrove had abandoned her usual gingham dresses and wore a green wool suit with a hat. She was rubbing her hands so fiercely Glory feared for the woman's skin.

"It'll go all right," Glory added. "The pageant will be just fine."

"Well, not with *him* here," Mrs. Hargrove seethed. "It's practically blasphemy!"

"Who?"

"Him." Mrs. Hargrove jerked her head in the direction of the Santa Claus who had entertained diners at the café earlier.

"Oh, he's all right," Glory said. Linda had told her the man was an old cowboy who was down on his luck. He certainly looked down on his luck with his fake white beard and red stocking hat. His shoulders slumped as if he carried the weight of the world. Even at that, though, he was handing out candy canes. "He's just cheering folks up."

"Folks don't need cheering up! This is Christmas." Mrs. Hargrove pursed her lips.

Just then the girl who was playing Mary tugged on Mrs. Hargrove's arm.

"Yes, dear?" the older woman said as she leaned over.

Mrs. Hargrove's voice softened when she talked to the girl and Glory could see why. Lori was all pink and blue in her costume. She looked sugar sweet, except for her eyes.

"Johnny Ellis stole the dish towels!" The girl's eyes snapped with anger.

"Dish towels?" Mrs. Hargrove seemed disoriented.

"The swaddlin' clothes!" the girl wailed, and burst into tears. "For my baby!"

Mrs. Hargrove soothed the girl and then straightened herself for battle. "Just wait until I get my hands on Johnny Ellis."

The girl stopped crying and perked up significantly when Mrs. Hargrove left.

Matthew came over and stood slightly behind Glory. She would have known he was there by the smell of his aftershave even if she hadn't heard the quiet thumping of his crutches. She'd noticed the pleasing scent at dinner and wondered if he was meeting someone special at the pageant. Not that it was any of her business, she reminded herself.

"Boys can be so annoying, can't they, Lori?" Matthew said sympathetically.

Glory was inclined to agree, but she didn't expect the girl to nod her head so vigorously.

"Thinks he's so smart—ordering me around saying he's my husband," Lori said.

"Well, he won't be your husband for long," Glory consoled her. "After the pageant he goes back to being plain Johnny Ellis." Glory couldn't resist a little consciousness-raising. "Besides, just because he's your husband doesn't mean he gets to order you around."

"Yeah." The girl brightened. "I could order him, too."

"That's not what I meant," Glory said, but it was too late. Lori had gone off to find Johnny Ellis.

Glory looked at Matthew. He was a constant surprise to her. Just when she thought his head was filled with hammering loose nails she found out that he'd had time to watch over the little children.

She fought the impulse to adjust Matthew's tie. It

didn't need adjusting, not really. But he wouldn't know that and it would give her a good cover as she leaned closer to smell his aftershave.

Fortunately, she was saved from her own foolishness by Mrs. Hargrove, who fluttered by gathering up children like a mother hen circling her chicks. "It'll be time to start soon. I'm having the children go to the back of the barn, by the far bleachers, so we can file in when we start the Scripture reading."

"I better get up in the hayloft, then." Glory picked up her long skirts.

"Let me go with you," Matthew said. "Make sure your skirt doesn't get caught on those narrow stairs."

"Oh, I asked Tavis to help her." Mrs. Hargrove looked down at a clipboard that she had picked up from somewhere. "Someone needs to go up with her and help her with the swing. You're on crutches."

"I'll help her," Matthew muttered as he positioned the crutches under his shoulders. A look of stubborn determination settled on his face. "I'm the one that knows how to add the extra train to the outfit so that people won't be looking at the angel's legs. Besides, I don't trust Tavis alone with the angel around all that hay."

"Well." Mrs. Hargrove studied Matthew with a bright, pleased look in her eyes. Then she took the pen off the clipboard and made a couple of check marks on her list.

There was a rail instead of a wall on the inside of the stairs leading to the overhead hayloft, and it was just as well. Glory could never have squeezed between two walls with her seven-foot wingspan.

"Ever wonder why angels just appear?" Glory muttered as she twisted her shoulders so her wings wouldn't be dented. "They can't get around in these things, so they have to—puff—appear out of nowhere. Puffing is a lot easier than flying."

Matthew looked down at her. He had half hobbled, half crawled to the top of the stairs and stood waiting for her. He leaned his crutches against the wall of the hayloft and reached down a hand to Glory. "Here, let me help you."

The smell of dry hay greeted Glory when she stood on the floor of the hayloft. The decorators for the pageant had not come up here. It was still ready for cattle. Several bales of hay were broken and strewn around. A pitchfork stood upright, embedded in one bale. Straw and wisps of hay lay all over the rough wood floor.

The hayloft was dim. The bright light from downstairs filtered through the end of the hayloft and gave everything a warm cast. Glory looked around. While she and Matthew could see the people down below, no one from down there could see the two of them. It was a perfect place for— Glory pushed the thought aside. She knew this ex-minister would never kiss an angel. Best not to even think about it.

Ten minutes later Glory was sitting on a bale of hay watching Matthew. Men! He had spent the entire past ten minutes going over every inch of the swing that she was going to use. "You're making me nervous. Besides, Tavis has already checked everything."

Matthew scowled up at her from where he was crouched by the ropes.

"It's even got a safety rope. See?" Glory pointed to her backup rope.

Glory sighed. Mention of the safety rope only gave Matthew another thing to check out.

People were filling up the bleachers down below

them. Glory saw just the tops of everyone, but she could tell people had dressed up for the occasion. She saw black Stetson hats and gray Stetson hats. The men who didn't have Stetson hats wore hunter-green caps. And the women's hair—from gray to towheaded—was shiny and curled.

The only one who stood out was Santa in his bright red cap. He'd stopped giving out candy canes and sat at the end of one of the far bleachers. The old man must be tired. Glory could think of no other reason why he seemed to be staring up at the hayloft where she was.

Just then a crackle of static sounded through the barn.

"It's—" Elmer's voice came out over the loudspeaker "—time."

The rustle of the audience stilled. Elmer stood beside the manger. Someone turned off a few of the lights.

Elmer cleared his throat. "I want to thank all you friends and neighbors for coming to celebrate the birth of our Lord. The children of Dry Creek have worked hard to prepare for this pageant, and so have the adults." Elmer paused. "We may as well get to it." He bent his head over a Bible and began to read. "'And it came to pass in those days, that there went out a decree from Caesar Augustus, that all the world should be taxed....'"

Glory smiled. Elmer's grandfatherly voice was perfect for the reading.

The band's sound system must have been more than a microphone, because the sound of a symphony filled the barn as Joseph started to walk the length of the barn leading a young heifer that was carrying a very pregnant Mary. The girl's long robe fell against the heifer's side and the heifer kept swishing its tail trying to get rid of the annoyance.

"'And Joseph also went up from Galilee, out of the city of Nazareth, into Judea, unto the city of David, which is called Bethlehem.'"

The heifer stopped in front of the wooden storefront that said Bethlehem Inn. A boy wearing a white butcher's apron came out of a door in the storefront. He was carrying a chicken under one arm and a No Vacancy sign under the other. The chicken was squawking indignantly at being carried, and when the boy went to hang the No Vacancy sign on the larger sign, the chicken escaped and flew to a perch on the very top of the stable. The boy stood watching the chicken with his mouth open.

There was silence. Mrs. Hargrove cleared her throat loudly. There was more silence.

Finally Mary spoke from her position on top of the heifer. "Does that—" she pointed to the sign the boy still held "—mean there's no room in the inn?"

"No..." The boy regained his lines. He repeated loudly, "No room in the inn."

Mary nodded, satisfied. "I thought so. We'll stay in the stable." And then she slid to the floor, took the heifer's rope and said with an unmistakable tone of command, "Joseph, you bring the bags. And don't forget the baby things."

Slack jawed with surprise, Joseph watched her leave and then hurried to catch up.

A choir of children's voices started singing "Away in the Manger."

In the hayloft Matthew had finally stopped checking equipment and sat down on the hay bale across from Glory. Glory smiled up at him and moved some of the yards of material so Matthew could move closer. "Mrs. Hargrove must have decided to use animals after all."

"Goes with the barn theme," Matthew whispered.

The carol ended and Elmer's voice continued with his reading. "'And so it was, that, while they were there, the days were accomplished that she should be delivered....'"

"We'd better get you in that swing," Matthew whispered. "The angel's coming up pretty soon."

Glory nodded, stood, and then it happened. A hiccup.

"I—can't—" Glory hiccuped again. She looked at Matthew. "I've got—the—" She hiccuped again.

Some miracles happen, Matthew decided. Others are snatched out of the possibilities of the moment, like this one. He did what he'd wanted to do ever since they climbed into the loft. He dipped his head and kissed Glory.

Matthew felt surprise ripple through Glory, so he deepened the kiss. His own surprise slugged him in the belly a second later. Who would know it would be like this? Her lips tasted like molten honey. Hot and sweet. He decided he might as well hang for the real thing as for a polite peck, so he deepened it even further. He could be dead and kissing a real angel for all he knew—or cared.

Glory stopped breathing. She half thought she might have stopped living. Everything stopped except Matthew's kiss.

Matthew pulled his lips away.

"You—k-kissed—" Glory stuttered. "Me."

"Yes." Matthew tried to stop the lightness inside him. If he wasn't careful, he'd be able to float alongside Glory even without a swing.

"The hiccups. They stopped." Glory put her hand

to her cheek. She needed to stop staring. He'd think she'd never been kissed before. And she had. Not like that, of course, but she had. Only, why had he kissed her now? Of course. The hiccups. That must be it. "Is that an old remedy?"

"Remedy?"

"For the hiccups. A grandmother's remedy? Like a slap on the back?"

Matthew winced. Granted, he'd thought the hiccups were a good cover for a kiss before he began the kiss, but now... Surely she knew it meant more now. And even at that, his kisses surely weren't grandmotherly.

The microphone below crackled as Elmer read. Glory stepped onto the swing. She hooked on the material that Matthew had rigged to trail beneath her. She hoped Matthew was satisfied. No one could see her feet, let alone her legs, with all that material. She watched as Matthew fastened the safety ropes.

"'And there were in the same country shepherds abiding in the field, keeping watch over their flock by night.'" Elmer's voice continued.

The boys in bathrobes and their "sheep" walked to the center of the barn and sat down. Two of the boys even lay down.

"'And, lo,'" Elmer read. "'An angel of the lord came upon them...'"

"I'm off," Glory whispered to Matthew before she took a deep breath.

Matthew helped her push off. The swing slid off its mooring and she was free. She felt the rush of air as she swooped over the shepherds below. Maybe, she thought, it wouldn't be so bad being an angel, after all. She'd talked Mrs. Hargrove into letting the children sing instead of the angel, so she concentrated on flying.

Glory's ecstasy was short-lived. The chicken, perched on top of the stable, had not been there earlier in Glory's practice run. And when Glory had practiced, she hadn't had a long white train of angel gown following her in flight. It was Matthew's modesty veil. When the chicken saw the thick cloud of material coming straight at it, it panicked and took flight again. Unfortunately, by taking flight, the chicken only rose up higher until it was swept along in the train of angel gown as Glory swung low over the stable.

"Oh, oh," Glory whispered to herself, and then added for the benefit of the passenger she carried beneath her, "Good chickie, good chickie. Just stay calm."

The chicken didn't stay calm. It screeched indignantly as it clung with its claws and beak to the train of angel gown.

Glory reached the arc of her swing just as the dogs decided they'd rather be dogs than sheep. They started to howl at Glory as if she was the moon. She comforted herself with the thought that maybe they were baying at the chicken.

Elmer kept reading. "'And the glory of the Lord shone round about them: and they were sore afraid.'"

Glory was sore afraid herself. The weight of the chicken began to pull even harder on the gown she wore, and she heard a slow tearing sound. She'd be lucky if the bird didn't pull the gown right off her and leave her swinging in the white long johns Matthew had insisted she wear. She could just see the headlines in the *Billings Gazette:* Chicken Strips Angel At Church Pageant. She'd probably make the tabloids with that one.

Not even looking up, Elmer kept reading. "'And the angel said unto them...'"

Glory took a deep breath. She pointed out with her white-gloved finger and shouted loudly, "'Fear not, for behold, I bring you good tidings of great joy.'"

Amazingly, Glory's words calmed the chicken. Unless— *I wonder if the poor bird finally had too much and went into shock?*

With the chicken silent, the dogs quit howling and lay down like the sheep they were meant to be. Even the shepherds looked reverent as they watched the angel swing back toward the hayloft.

Elmer took up the angel's pronouncement for her. "'For unto you is born this day in the city of David a Savior, which is Christ the Lord.'"

Glory swung back and straight into Matthew's arms. Unfortunately, she'd built up so much speed she knocked them both to the floor of the hayloft.

"Oh." Glory blinked.

Elmer's voice continued. "'And suddenly there was with the angel a multitude of the heavenly host praising God and saying...'"

The children's choir began to sing "Glory to God."

"Oh." Glory blinked again. She was lying on top of Matthew and she couldn't seem to move. She could hear Matthew breathing beneath her. Fact is, she could feel him breathing as his chest rose and fell. He hadn't screamed, so her wings must not have jabbed him. He was all right. It was her. She couldn't move. It must be the excitement of the swing, she consoled herself. After all, look what the swing had done to that chicken—

"The chicken!" Glory exclaimed, remembering.

Matthew felt Glory lift herself up. He wanted to pull

her back and try another home remedy. As far as he was concerned, he could lie right there until he died. He was singing the Hallelujah chorus and it had nothing to do with Christmas. But she was right, there was the chicken to consider.

"It looks all right," Glory whispered as she studied the chicken. They had unhooked the train to Glory's gown and unfolded the material until they freed the bird. The chicken fluffed itself up and then started hopping around looking for something to eat.

"Why don't you unhook my wings, too?" Glory asked. She was already kneeling. "I want to get them off before I do major damage."

The wise men were ready to make their entrance by the time Glory and Matthew got back to the pageant. The shepherds were surrounding the manger and the children's choir was standing in front of the inn. The dogs had decided the excitement was over for the day and were lying half-asleep at their masters' feet.

Elmer's voice continued his reading, "'When they saw the star, they rejoiced with exceeding great joy.'"

Matthew stood up to slowly pull the metal star on the pulley toward the stable. It was rigged like an old-fashioned laundry line. In fact, as Glory looked at the brackets more closely, she saw that it *was* an old-fashioned laundry line.

Solemnly the wise men followed the star until it reached the stable.

"We brought you some presents," one of the wise men announced proudly as he pulled out three prettily wrapped packages. The wise men turned to Mary. "We got receipts so you can return them if you want."

Mary nodded her thanks.

The children's choir and the shepherds began to sing "Silent Night." The pageant was drawing to a close.

Christmas truly was a time of goodwill, Glory thought as she shook the hand of another well-wisher. Everyone along the Yellowstone River was out and thanking her for being their angel. Why, there was almost a crowd in this barn, Glory decided as she looked over the people. She recognized a few of them. Linda, of course, and a couple of the hands from the Big Sheep Mountain Ranch. And then there was Sylvia and the rancher, talking animatedly in the corner of the barn. Glory decided now wasn't the time to go and say hello to her friend.

Mrs. Hargrove invited everyone over to the church for refreshments, and people began adjusting scarves for the walk over to the other building. Matthew stood talking with Deputy Wall.

Glory decided it was time to slip behind the stable and get her presents ready for the children. She'd seen Josh look her way several times, so she knew he was hopeful. Glory walked over to him and bent down to whisper in his ear, "Tell everyone the angel's giving out presents behind the stable in five minutes."

Josh's eyes lit up and he nodded.

The Bullet had let the people of Dry Creek have their pageant. But now he watched the angel make her way to the rear of the barn.

The light was dim behind the stable, but the space was completely out of sight of the other people. And there was the angel, kneeling down and sorting through one of several huge boxes of toys.

The Bullet unbuttoned his red shirt and drew out his gun.

He'd hoped the angel would not even look up, but she did. Her eyes widened as he put his arm out and aimed the gun.

Then the Bullet heard a sound behind him.

"Santa?" a small voice asked. The Bullet turned his head slightly and saw the twin boys staring at him.

Chapter Fourteen

Glory felt all the blood drain from her head when she saw the gun. She thought she'd faint. When she saw the twins, she knew she didn't have the luxury of fainting.

"Oh, boys," she called out, hoping her voice was bright and normal. "You caught us. Santa was trying out some of the toys."

Please, Lord, Glory prayed. *Have the man go along with me. Let him have a heart. If I need to die, don't take the twins, too.*

"He's not supposed to point guns at people," Josh said righteously.

"That's right," Glory agreed. "But Santa and I need a few more minutes. Go back to your dad now. And keep the other kids away, too."

Glory kept her eyes on the killer. She begged him silently to let the twins go. "No one knows what Santa looks like," she reminded him. "Not with a beard and the suit."

"Yeah, get out of here, kids," the killer finally said.

Josh turned to go, but Glory watched the indecision on Joey's face.

"Run along, Joey." Glory tried not to let her voice plead as loudly as her heart. "Go to your dad."

"I want us to go home, now," Joey said softly. "We don't need more presents."

Glory wished she were a better actress. "Please, just do what I ask, sweetheart."

Joey waited a minute before finally turning to go. Glory watched him reluctantly step around the corner of the stable.

"Thank you," Glory whispered softly as she looked up at the killer.

Santa nodded as he reaimed his gun.

Glory closed her eyes.

"You going to pray, too?" the man asked incredulously.

Glory opened her eyes. "If I may." She wouldn't tell him she'd closed her eyes not to pray but so she wouldn't have to watch him pull the trigger. "Sort of my last request."

"Hit men don't do last requests. That's the feds." But he lowered his gun.

"Dear Lord," Glory whispered aloud. She wanted the hit man to know she was still praying. "I've had a good life. So much to be thankful for. My mother. The captain. Sylvia. The twins—and their father—"

"Hurry it up, lady. This isn't the Oscars," the killer interrupted. "I haven't got all day to wait while you thank the little people. Wrap it up."

"The Oscars?" Glory forced herself to laugh. "Very clever. Did you see them?"

Santa glowered at her. "No."

"Oh." Glory folded her hands together just as the

twins did when they prayed. She couldn't think of what to pray when it looked as if she would see God in a few seconds anyway. Then she thought of the comforting prayer and closed her eyes to begin. "Now I lay me down to sleep. I pray the Lord my soul to keep. If I should—"

Glory heard the loud sound of a gun cocking. Odd, she thought Santa had already pulled the hammer back. Then she heard the voice.

"Hold it right there, Santa!"

Glory opened her eyes. Deputy Wall was standing with his gun aimed at Santa's belly. The only problem was that Santa still had his gun aimed at Glory. Both men seemed to realize the difficulties of that arrangement as quickly as she did.

"You shoot her, I'll get you," Deputy Wall threatened as he steadied his aim.

Santa shrugged without lowering his gun. "She'll still be dead."

"They'll put you away for murder if you kill her," the deputy promised.

"They'll put me away for murder if I give up, too," Santa countered.

Glory decided now was as good a time as any to faint. She willed herself to faint. She held her breath. In the end, she had to half fake her slide down to the barn floor.

She'd no sooner started her slide than a shot was fired. Glory's last conscious thought was that Santa swore like a sailor.

Matthew blamed himself all the way to the stable. Why had he let Mrs. Hargrove lead him off with some story about the wise men so that Josh took longer to find him? Josh had gotten only the words *Santa* and *gun* out of his mouth before Matthew was frantically looking around the barn. Where was Glory?

"I told the deputy, too," Josh was saying proudly. "He knows you shouldn't point guns at people."

Matthew saw the deputy slip behind the stable.

"Stay here, son," Matthew called down as he started toward the stable. His crutches were only slowing him down, so he tossed them away and started to lope along.

"Glory!" Matthew whispered when he rounded the corner and saw what was behind the stable wall. The air smelled like burned gunpowder. And Glory lay there so still.

"You shot her!" Matthew started to lunge toward Santa.

Deputy Wall dropped his gun and grabbed Matthew. Deputy Wall was 250 pounds of muscle, but he didn't stop Matthew easily. "I've wrestled bulls tamer than you." The deputy spit the words out after he'd steadied Matthew. "That man has a gun, for Pete's sake. Keep still."

"Don't worry. I didn't even hit her," Santa said disgustedly. He turned so the gun was now aimed at the two men. "She slid right out of my range. The bullet hit the wall."

Matthew took a deep breath. He looked at Glory carefully. In all of that white, blood would show up readily and so would the scorched mark a bullet would make in passing. There was no sign of either and she appeared to be breathing normally. Besides, there was a bullet hole in the back of the stable.

"You don't need to kill her, anyway." Matthew began to pray. *Help me, God.* "Glory already told the police about the tie-in with the rustling. The manager at the grocery store is going to turn state's evidence.''

Santa grunted. ''None of my concern. Not my side of the business.''

It must have been twenty degrees in the barn, and Matthew's hands were sweating. *Lord, I need you. I won't ask for anything else. Just keep Glory alive.*

''If you want to shoot someone, shoot me instead,'' Matthew offered.

Matthew heard the surprised protest from Deputy Wall, but he didn't turn to look at the officer. Matthew kept his eyes trained on Santa.

''Nobody's paying me to shoot you,'' Santa snorted indignantly. ''I don't just go around shooting people. I'm a professional.''

''I see.'' Matthew did some quick arithmetic in his head. ''If you're a professional, how much would it cost to unshoot someone?''

Santa just laughed. ''Money won't do me any good if I don't shoot her.''

''Ah, they'd come and get you?'' Matthew asked to keep the killer talking. The longer Santa kept talking the longer Matthew had to think of something.

''That isn't the half of it,'' Santa muttered into his fake beard. ''It's who else they'd get that worries me.''

Matthew knew from his ministerial counseling that sometimes it was these half-muttered, throwaway lines that no one expected anyone else to listen to that were the most important in understanding a person's troubles.

''A child?'' Matthew probed.

Santa shook his head and mumbled, ''Girlfriend.''

''Girlfriend?'' the deputy wailed. ''How can you get a girl when I can't?''

"Charm," Santa said without looking at the deputy.

"Aah, a girlfriend." Matthew nodded as if he understood. He kept his eyes focused on Santa's brown eyes. *Lord, Lord, be with me.*

"They've already got Millie," Santa continued, as if the worry couldn't stay trapped inside him any longer. "If I don't shoot this Beckett woman, they'll shoot my Millie."

"Aah." Matthew nodded this time because he did understand. "So we're just two men trying to protect our women."

Santa eyed Matthew skeptically. "Yeah, I suppose so."

Matthew started to breathe again. He'd made the first rung in negotiations. He'd found a common ground from which they could work. "Now all we need to do is figure out a way to keep both of them alive."

"Like what?" Santa asked.

Matthew began to pray even more earnestly. The bait was being nibbled. "Well, what happens if you couldn't kill Glory?"

"What do you mean 'couldn't' kill her?"

"What if there was a storm and Montana was cut off from the rest of the country for a month? No one in or out?"

"Well…" Santa began to think. "I suppose in unusual circumstances they wouldn't hold me to the contract. But they read the papers. They'd know about a storm."

"What about if you were arrested before you got to Glory? Like on a speeding ticket?"

"Well, I suppose if I was arrested and put in jail they couldn't complain too much," Santa agreed, and then pointed out, "But I haven't got a speeding ticket."

"The deputy here could give you one," Matthew offered.

"You want me to give him a *ticket?* A cold-blooded killer? A *speeding ticket?*"

"What do you think, Santa? We could give you a speeding ticket and fingerprint you and then find out about some past crimes."

Santa was thinking. "I work clean. You wouldn't find much. Besides, what if they found out it didn't happen that way? These guys have moles everywhere."

"They don't have any moles in Dry Creek, Montana," Deputy Wall said proudly.

"Well, that's probably true," Santa said as he lowered his gun. "Might not be a better place anywhere to cut a deal."

Matthew left the two men and went over to kneel beside Glory. He picked up her arm to feel her pulse. Her heart was certainly beating strongly.

"Now, about that ticket, what speed were you driving when you came into Dry Creek?" Deputy Wall said as he took Santa's gun.

"Hey, I thought there's no speed limit in Montana."

"There is in towns. We're posted for forty-five. We'll say you were doing eighty." The deputy unclasped his handcuffs and snapped them around Santa's hands.

"She okay?" asked Deputy Wall, turning toward Matthew.

"Seems fine. Just give her a minute."

"Aah…" Santa squirmed as the deputy started to leave. "Mind if we go out the back way? There's a lot of kids out there who don't need to see Santa in handcuffs."

"I'll settle him in my car," the deputy said as he passed Matthew. "Then I'll be back for Glory."

"Back for Glory?"

"She can't stay here now," Deputy Wall patiently explained. "There's a contract out. He—" he nodded at Santa "—he might not be the only one. We'll need to take Glory into protective custody. For her own good."

Glory wondered how long she could feign unconsciousness before someone called a doctor. She supposed she needed to open her eyes, but her world was already here. She knew Matthew held her. She smelled the aftershave and heard the soft murmur of his prayers. She would lie in his arms forever if it kept Matthew praying.

But she supposed it wasn't fair.

"Glory—" The voice that finally pulled her out of her daze was Mrs. Hargrove's. The older woman's voice was determined enough to call back the dead. Glory didn't feel as if she should resist it for something as minor as a slipping spell. Glory refused to accept that she might have fainted, just for a minute. She preferred to think she'd purposely slipped into a daze.

"Are you all right, dear?" Mrs. Hargrove was pressing something wet against Glory's forehead.

Glory opened her eyes. She supposed it was time.

"You'll need to come with me," Deputy Wall ordered Glory. "I've radioed ahead. They'll have a couple of cells ready."

"You can't put her in jail. Not on Christmas Eve." Mrs. Hargrove was horrified.

"I'm not putting her in jail," the deputy explained impatiently. "Protective custody."

"It's for the best," Glory assured the older woman.

Glory looked up at the circle of concerned people looking down at her. All of these people would be in danger if she stayed in Dry Creek before everything was settled. If one contract killer could get through, another one might not be far behind. And bullets didn't always just hit the one for whom they were intended.

"I'll go with her to jail," Matthew offered decisively. "That is, if you'll take the twins home with you tonight, Mrs. Hargrove?"

Mrs. Hargrove nodded. "They're so excited they'll probably fall right to sleep on my sofa."

Matthew didn't correct her, although he was pretty sure the reverse would be true. The boys would be up all night talking about the gunman.

"And hand out the presents," Glory added.

For the first time everyone looked at the boxes.

"That's them?" Matthew asked, and then corrected himself. "I mean, of course that's them. Glad to see they got delivered in time."

"W-well, I'll be…" Mrs. Hargrove stammered. "I'll be."

"The names are already on them," Glory said. "Sylvia saw to that in the ordering."

"Well, the children will be very pleased," Mrs. Hargrove finally managed.

Deputy Wall cleared his throat. "We better be going."

"I can't go like this." Glory looked down at herself. "Let me stop and put on some jeans."

"If you're quick about it," the deputy agreed as Glory started to stand.

The jail clanked. Metal scraped every time anyone moved. And it smelled like a closed-up basement. But,

Glory thought to herself, it was safe. And Matthew was here, sitting on the cot on the other side of the cell. They were both safe. No one could shoot a bullet through those thick cement walls, and no one would even try to get in the door past the four deputies called out for special duty tonight.

"Sorry you're missing Christmas Eve with your family," Glory called out to one of the young deputies as he walked past their opened cell.

"It's okay." The deputy ducked his head. "We've never had a hit man in these cells."

"You know, he didn't seem bad for a hit man," Glory mused as she wrapped herself in the blankets she and Matthew had picked up from his house.

From the outside office the strains of the hymn "O Holy Night" reached them in the cells.

"Somebody thought to bring a CD player," Matthew noted.

"And spiced cider." The sweet apple smell began to cut through the basement smell in their cell.

Just then Sylvia stepped through the door from the deputy's office. She was wearing a red Santa's hat and carrying a big box tied up with a silver bow. Behind her came the rancher Garth Elkton, carrying a CD player and a large cup of cider.

"Merry Christmas," Sylvia shouted, and suddenly it was.

An hour later Glory folded up the metallic paper. Sylvia and the rancher had set up a coffeepot of spiced cider outside. There was unmistakable tension between the two of them, but they'd done their job of delivering Christmas cheer very well. They'd even brought a large plate of cookies, compliments of the ladies at the church. There was more than enough for all the deputies and inmates. Of course, the only inmates were Glory, Matthew and the Bullet, as he called himself. Glory shuddered at the name.

Sylvia had sat with Glory while she opened the silver box. It contained a dozen jars of homemade jam from the booth the women of Dry Creek had set up outside the barn tonight. Chokecherry jam. Rhubarb jam. It couldn't be a more perfect gift. Every time Glory opened a jar she'd think of the people of Dry Creek. She looked across the cell at Matthew. There was one person she couldn't bear to remember only with jam.

"The twins will be sleeping now," she said.

Matthew grunted. He'd been waiting for a romantic moment and it wasn't easy to find one in a cramped cement cell in the middle of winter. When they'd stopped by his house for Glory to change to jeans and a sweatshirt, he'd picked up the gift he'd bought for her. He was waiting for the right time to give it to her, but maybe that moment wouldn't come tonight. He might as well do it now. At least they were alone— something that rarely happened, as one or the other of the deputies was always walking back to chat.

"I have a present for you." Matthew reached into the pocket of his black leather jacket and pulled out a small box wrapped in white tissue paper. "It's not much, but—"

Glory's face lit up. "I got a present for you, too, but it's at your house."

"You've already given me the best Christmas gift." Matthew handed her the box. "Being an angel in this pageant was important to my boys."

Glory opened the little box and pulled out a silver

necklace charm in the shape of an angel. "It's beautiful."

"I'll always remember what you've done for me and my boys," Matthew began. He was a man accustomed to words, so he had no excuse for not being able to just spit out the words that would tell Glory what he was feeling. But those words were hard. He wished he were a better man. He knew Glory deserved someone better. Someone whose faith had not been shipwrecked. He wasn't going to ask her to settle for less than she deserved and he wasn't going to ask her to wait for him to become the man she deserved. He just wanted her to know he wished it were different.

Before Matthew could speak again, a burly barrel of a man stomped through the door.

"Captain!" Glory whispered in surprise. "What are you doing here?"

It took the captain only an hour to get Glory and Matthew out of the cell. "There's feds all over Dry Creek by now. Frank talked to that grocery-store manager and we found out the hit had been ordered by the men selling the stolen meat. They were afraid you'd put the pieces together and talk to that store manager. He cracked just like they suspected. They located you through the AP wire—that silly angel story." The captain shook his head. "You were lucky. That hit man—" The captain shook his head again. "When they ran his fingerprints, they didn't find anything. But then they checked with an informant and half the bureau headed to Dry Creek. Funny, you folks catching him here on a speeding ticket."

Glory shrugged. The best story of her police career,

and she'd never be able to tell it around the water-cooler.

Glory took her time repacking her suitcase. She was upstairs at Matthew's house and the early-morning sun was just beginning to warm up the sky. The captain had insisted she return with him, and he was right. Until the business of the contract on her was settled, she didn't want to jeopardize Matthew or the boys. So, instead of thinking of excuses to stay another day, she folded her socks and laid them in the suitcase one pair at a time.

Even inside the house, Glory could feel the activity in Dry Creek. The captain was outside now talking with the federal agents who were combing through Dry Creek looking for clues. They were mildly puzzled that a pro like the Bullet would trip up on a traffic ticket, but they were so relieved to have him in custody they didn't press their questions.

Finally, Glory snapped the lid shut on her suitcase. It was time.

Glory started down the stairs for the last time, smiling slightly when she came to the step where Matthew had fallen. That one step had changed her whole life. They should put a plaque there, she mused.

Matthew was sitting on the sofa waiting for her. Glory had half expected him to be outside checking with the feds to make sure they kept her safe, but he appeared willing to let them do their jobs now that they were here in such numbers.

With each step down Glory took, she tried to think of something suitable to say to Matthew. But her mind was as empty as her heart was full. None of the words seemed right.

It wasn't until Glory reached the last step on the stairs that she realized what Matthew was doing. He was staring at the portrait of his late wife, Susie. Glory had put all of the twins' presents down under the tree so that they'd see them when they came over later this morning. She hadn't wrapped the portrait, so they could see their mother the first thing. She hadn't counted on Matthew sitting on the sofa silently weeping in front of the woman's picture.

All of the hopeful words that Glory had been trying to form died unspoken. What could she say to a man who was still so in love with his late wife that he sat there weeping?

"Take care of the twins." Glory managed the words. She focused on Matthew's back. "I'll stop at Mrs. Hargrove's to tell them goodbye."

"Goodbye?" The word seemed dragged from Matthew.

He turned to look at her. Glory meant to look away, but she couldn't. The pain and despair in Matthew's eyes struck deep inside her. His cheeks were wet with new tears and his eyes were red with unshed ones. He must still love his wife very much.

"You're not going?"

"I'll call," Glory said as she stumbled to the door. It was time for her to leave.

"But—?" Matthew protested, and then mumbled in defeat, "Maybe it is best for now. You'll call?"

Glory nodded as she opened the door. She didn't trust her voice to speak.

The Bullet waited impatiently for morning. He had one call coming, and he didn't want to waste it on the answering machine.

The Bullet punched in the numbers and held his breath. One ring. Two rings—

"Hello, Millie's place." A man's voice answered.

The Bullet almost hung up, but he needed to know. "Is Millie there?"

"Forrest, is that you?" The man's voice warmed. "It's me. Douglas from Spokane."

"Douglas?"

"Yeah, I got Millie's number off the shipping label you left and called to wish her a Merry Christmas. We got to talking and she invited me out to spend the holiday with the two of you. Only you never showed. You all right?"

"Not exactly." Relief poured through the Bullet. Douglas would take care of Millie. He'd ask him to take her back to Spokane. No one would find her there.

Chapter Fifteen

Almost two months later, Glory was sitting at her drawing board in the Seattle police station. She was spending as much time as possible at work. The captain had insisted she stay with him and her mother until the federal agents arrested the distributors in the cattle-rustling ring. Glory had given in to the captain rather than argue. Besides, she hadn't wanted to be alone. For weeks she kept expecting to hear the twins giggle, and then she'd look up from her sketching or her reading and realize she'd probably never see them again—or their father.

Being with her family helped her feel better, but she couldn't stay with them forever. The feds had arrested the distributors last week, and she had moved back into her own apartment. The distributors had squealed loud and clear, but they didn't know enough to help the feds find the actual rustlers. Still, Glory was safe.

She had thought that when she moved back into her apartment she'd feel more like her old self, but she didn't. Her life stretched forward with nothing but gray in it.

Glory laid down the black pencil she held in her hand and sighed. The face of crime never changed. All of the perpetrators were beginning to look alike. Actually, in her moments of acute honesty, she realized they all had a tendency to look like Matthew. It didn't help that today was Valentine's Day and that was the deadline she'd set for him. When she first returned to Seattle, she'd had a message on her answering machine telling her he'd call later when he had things worked out. Later was stretching into never as far as she could tell. If he hadn't called her by today, she decided that someplace deep and cold she'd bury her hopes of being with him. Like the North Pole. Or maybe Siberia.

"Anyone home?" Sylvia stood in the door of Glory's small office with her hands behind her back and a secretive smile spreading across her face.

"Come in." Glory welcomed her friend, grateful for the distraction. "What brings you here on a work day?"

"Roses," Sylvia replied as she stepped into the office. "Or should I say one rose?"

Sylvia held a vase with a yellow rose. "For you— from some of the kids."

"John and K.J.?"

Sylvia nodded as she set the vase on the corner of Glory's table. "They still feel bad about that contract business."

Glory chuckled. "Tell them thanks for the rose and for not fulfilling the contract."

Sylvia nodded as she settled into a chair. "Don't suppose you heard from anyone else on Valentine's Day? Say someone from Dry Creek?"

Glory snorted. "Of course not. It would appear the phone lines don't work between here and Dry Creek, even though Garth Elkton seems to do fine."

Sylvia blushed. "Garth only called once—and that was to ask about the kids. And you," Sylvia continued. "He asked about you. Said something about Matthew being depressed. Speaking of whom, I thought Matthew asked you to call?"

"But that was months ago. He should call. I wouldn't know what to say."

"Well, maybe he doesn't, either."

"He could send a postcard."

Sylvia winced. "Ever try to put your heart on a postcard?"

"Even that man—the Bullet—sent me a postcard from prison. To apologize. And let me know he's in a Bible study there. He managed to write."

"Well, don't be too hard on Matthew. After all—" Sylvia stood up and flung her arms wide "—he came all the way to Seattle to see you."

Glory shook her ears. She wasn't hearing right. "What?"

"He came all the way to Seattle to see you," Sylvia repeated with satisfaction in her voice. "Garth brought him."

"Oh." The pieces clicked into place now. "Garth brought him?"

Sylvia nodded. "Garth thought the two of you needed to talk."

"You don't suppose it's the other way around, do you? That Garth wanted to talk to you and Matthew is his excuse?"

"Don't be silly. Garth didn't even know where to find me. He had to hunt on foot for the center. Almost got into trouble until John rescued him. By the way, Matthew's taking you out to dinner tonight.''

"I'm busy."

"I already told him you were free." Sylvia winked. "Give the guy a break. It's Valentine's Day. And he's taking you to dinner at the top of the space needle."

"He won't be able to do that," Glory protested in relief. "People had to make reservations weeks ago for Valentine's night there."

Sylvia smiled. "I know. Matthew says he made them weeks ago." She turned to leave and then said over her shoulder, "Wear your black dress—with the pearls."

"It's too short."

"No, it's not."

The dress was too short. Glory frowned at herself in the mirror. Especially to be with Matthew. She didn't want him to think she was trying to get his attention. If he wasn't interested in her in blue jeans, he wouldn't be interested in her in a black dress that showed more leg than it should.

The doorbell of her apartment rang. That must be him. She'd told Sylvia she'd meet Matthew at the foot of the needle. But Matthew was a stubborn man. He'd told Sylvia he had hired a limo to take them to dinner, and she would be picked up at six-thirty.

Glory almost walked away from the door instead of toward it. She wasn't looking forward to tonight. She expected Matthew did want to talk to her, to explain how sorry he was that he was unable to be more to her than a distant friend because of his feelings for his late wife. But Glory would just as soon skip the speech.

The doorbell rang again.

When Glory answered the door, Matthew stood there

in a black tux holding a dozen red roses. She'd never realized how good he would look in a tux. His chestnut hair was brushed back in soft waves. His freshly shaven chin was set in a determined smile. His blue-green eyes looked hopeful.

It was too much. Glory almost shut the door in his face.

Matthew watched the emotions chase themselves across Glory's face. He'd held his breath until she opened the door, fearful she wouldn't come, and when he saw her he almost couldn't get his breath anyway. Glory was dazzling. Her golden-bronze hair was pulled up in the Grecian-goddess style he well remembered. She could be Venus with arms. Her eyes went from molten to icy in the space of a heartbeat. Quicksilver. That was Glory. She wore a black dress that was too sophisticated and sexy for him. He wondered if he'd even get the nerve to talk to her when she looked so polished. And then he saw it. Around her neck she wore a little silver angel charm on a chain.

Glory saw the direction Matthew's eyes were taking and stifled the impulse to hide the charm with her hand. She'd forgotten to take it off. She was so used to wearing it under everything she wore and not having it show that she'd forgotten about it. She hadn't realized the low-cut black dress would reveal that much about her.

Matthew smiled. "I'm glad you're wearing my angel."

Glory gritted her teeth and nodded. "I like silver."

Sitting in the restaurant at the top of the space needle was like sitting on top of the world. The tables were arranged in a circle on the inside rim of the revolving restaurant. Each table had a big window to view the city below. At night, the lights below sparkled clear to the ocean.

"How are the boys?" Glory asked politely as she folded the linen napkin on her lap.

"Fine. Thanks for calling them at Mrs. Hargrove's. They get so excited."

Glory nodded. "I'm fond of them."

"They like you, too," Matthew replied.

"They have really good bread here," Glory said as she took another piece of fresh sourdough from the basket.

Matthew despaired. Were they going to small-talk the night away?

"My boys aren't the only ones who like you." Matthew took a deep breath and plunged. There, he'd started it.

Glory looked at him skeptically.

Maybe, Matthew thought, he needed to be more specific. "I like you, too."

Glory smiled woodenly. "Thank you."

Silence stretched between them.

"When you went away, I felt like Job," Matthew finally said. Glory looked at him quizzically. He had her attention. "The day Job said, 'He hath taken me by my neck, and shaken me to pieces.' That was me with God. He needed to get my attention and turn me around before I could be any good to Him or anyone else. Fortunately, He did...."

Matthew had his hand lying on the table and Glory reached over to cover it with her own. "I'm so glad," she said.

"I've never prayed so much in my life. Not even in seminary. Now I know what it means to wrestle with God. You lose and win all at the same time."

Glory looked into Matthew's eyes. If she hadn't been so distracted by her own emotions earlier, she would have noticed the peace she now saw there.

"I went up to Havre for a couple of weeks and stayed with an old minister friend of mine," Matthew continued. "I never listened before when he said other ministers have gone through what I did." Matthew smiled. "I thought I was the only one who'd ever been deeply disappointed. He told me I needed to learn I wasn't in control of the world. God is. As believers, we can pray to Him, but our job isn't to carry the world on our shoulders. Our job is to trust."

"You're going back to the ministry, aren't you?" Glory asked softly. Joy rose within her.

Matthew nodded. "In Dry Creek for now. I don't want to move the twins again, and this way I can keep working at the hardware store, too."

"Mrs. Hargrove got her wish, after all."

"Mrs. Hargrove is so pleased with me she's even watching the twins for me while I'm here."

Glory smiled. "So this is what you wanted to tell me. Sort of like the steps in Alcoholics Anonymous where you go and speak to the people you've met and tell them you've changed."

Glory gave a sigh of relief. She didn't know what she'd expected of the evening, but it wasn't this. She was happy about Matthew, though, and glad she'd come to dinner.

"No," Matthew said in alarm. "That's not it. I mean—that's part of it. But I can't stop with that."

"Oh. I haven't done something, have I? Something I need to apologize for?"

"What could you have done?" Matthew asked in astonishment.

"Then it must be you. Did you do something you need to apologize to me for?"

Matthew finally realized what she was talking about—the AA practice of asking for forgiveness. "No! This has nothing to do with AA." Matthew was starting to sweat now and it was February in Seattle. "I guess the subtle way isn't working. I'm trying to work up to asking you to marry me."

"Marry you?" Glory was dumbfounded.

Matthew grimaced. He hadn't meant to blurt it out quite that way. "Well, now that I'm back in the ministry and..."

Glory's heart went from hot to cold. "That's why you want to marry me," she said flatly. "Because you're in the ministry and every minister needs a wife."

Just then the waiter appeared with their dinners. "Blackened chicken for the lady and grilled mahimahi for the gentleman. Will there be anything else?" The waiter beamed.

Glory found her teeth were beginning to ache from the effort to keep her jaw from clenching. "If you'll excuse me for a moment, I need to go, ah, powder my nose."

Glory stood and walked to the ladies' rest room.

Matthew stared after her in dismay. How had everything gone so wrong? He knew he wasn't a Don Juan, but he hadn't expected to chase a woman away from her dinner with his proposal.

Glory stood in front of the full-length mirror in the rest room and counted to ten. She supposed she shouldn't be so angry. At least Matthew had been honest about what he wanted. He hadn't pretended to have a feeling that he was apparently reserving for the memory of his late wife. Glory sighed. It was so hard to compete with a dead woman. But still, the marriage offer did come from Matthew.

Matthew watched Glory walk back to the table. She held her head high with pride, and he scrambled around in his mind for words to apologize with....

"All right," Glory said quite calmly as she picked up her fork. "I'll marry you."

"What?" Matthew's roar was so loud the other people in the restaurant looked at him. He didn't care.

Apparently Glory did care. "Eat your fish. It'll get cold."

Matthew was speechless.

"Well, you did ask me," Glory reminded him after a moment of silence.

"But—" Matthew looked at her. "You don't seem very happy about the idea. I don't want you to marry me out of pity." Matthew had a sudden insight. "It's the boys, isn't it? You're marrying me for the sake of the twins. You think they need a mother."

Glory's heart broke. She'd forgotten. She couldn't marry Matthew. "I can't be a mother."

"But you like the twins."

"I love the twins. But I can't have children myself. I'm sorry, I should have told you before I accepted your proposal. I, of course, withdraw my acceptance." Glory speared another bite with her fork. "Delicious chicken."

"Hang the chicken," Matthew said. The muscle along his cheek started to twitch. "Look at me. We're not going to get married for the boys or for the ministry."

Glory laid down her fork, but she couldn't look at

him. Not square in the eye. She didn't want him to see the tears that waited for a moment's privacy to fall.

"You may not be able to marry me because you love me," Matthew said softly. "But please, at least, marry me because I love you."

"You?" Glory lifted her eyes. "You do?"

"Of course. That's what I've been trying to tell you."

"Well, it wasn't very clear."

Matthew held her eyes steady with his. She'd never seen him look so serious. "Then let me make it clear. I love you, Glory Beckett. I love you so much it takes my breath away. It has, in fact, taken my breath away a time or two. I can't even begin to count the ways in which I love you. You own my heart."

"But what about the children I can't have?"

"We have the twins. If we want more children, we can adopt."

"And what about Susie?" Glory couldn't help asking. "On Christmas Day I saw you looking at her picture and crying."

Matthew smiled. "I was crying for all the anger toward God I've carried inside me because of Susie. Seeing that gun pointed at you that night—with me being unable to save you—brought everything back. Feeling so helpless. But it was you I was crying for. Susie doesn't make me cry anymore."

"Really?"

Matthew nodded. "Really."

They looked into each other's eyes for a minute. The restaurant was filled with candlelight and the sound of soft music.

"You're sure?" Glory asked again.

Matthew nodded. "I'm sure."

Glory studied him some more. "Really?"

Matthew grinned. "Finish your chicken so I can take you someplace and convince you I'm seriously in love with you."

Glory smiled and rose from the table. "I'm not really that hungry, after all."

"Me neither."

The waiter insisted on boxing up their dinners to go. He didn't seem surprised about their decision to leave early. He said it happened quite often on Valentine's Day.

The limousine chauffeur didn't find it odd that they returned after just twenty minutes, either. He merely suggested a drive around to look at the lights of Seattle. Matthew told him to make it a very long drive—maybe over to Puget Sound—and Glory couldn't have agreed more. After all, Matthew had promised to tell her, in detail, why he really, really loved her. And she was going to do the same.

*   *   *   *   *

Dear Reader,

Thank you for visiting Dry Creek with me. Although Dry Creek is a fictitious place, it is inspired by dozens of small communities in rural Montana. In many of these areas there is a church that adds strength to the whole community. I was privileged to grow up in one of these churches, the Fort Shaw Community Church in Fort Shaw, Montana. If you have a chance, stop in and visit the good people there. (Sunday services at 11:00, but you'll want to go for Sunday school, too, at 9:45.) You will find a group of people who are faithful to God and each other.

When God asks us to "gather together in His name," I believe He does so more for our good than for His. Old-fashioned fellowship—with friendships and commitments that have spanned years and even decades—strengthens our faith and enriches us deeply. Troubles shared are troubles made lighter with prayer and comfort. Joys shared are joys made brighter with common rejoicing—especially during the Christmas season when we all have reason to celebrate.

So, if you're currently part of a church family, cherish those ties. If you are not, my hope and prayer for you is that you find one soon so that you can rejoice in the Christmas season with them.

Janet Tronstad